INTO
SHADOW

T. D. SHIELDS

First edition printed 2015
Second edition printed by Aelurus Publishing, March 2017

Cover design by Molly Phipps

ISBN 13: 978-0-9956325-7-8

www.aeluruspublishing.com

DEDICATION

Thank you to my family, and especially my husband, for all your encouragement and help with this project! I could have never done it without you.

CHAPTER ONE

I sat at my dressing table, touching up my makeup with a deft hand while focusing most of my attention on the slender, gray-haired woman perched on a chair to my left.

"You'll need to leave the awards ceremony no later than eleven in order to make it to The St. Lucien hotel by lunch. That's a lunch meeting in the hotel's Tea Room with Madelaine Carlson and Clarissa Wender to discuss a theme and begin planning for this year's Congressional Scholarship fundraising gala. Wrap that up by two because you're visiting the West Goodland Primary School at two-thirty. If you're done there by four, you'll have enough time to return to the White House and change for dinner.

"You'll be acting as hostess for your father tonight. This is intended as a casual meal. Think dining with your father and some business associates rather than dining with the President and the governors of the Union of American States, Canadian Federation, and Mexican Federation."

"Right," I joked. "Just a casual barbecue with dad's golfing buddies then. I assume we'll be grilling burgers on the South Lawn?"

"Very funny, Poppy." Louisa's lips pursed more tightly than usual as she responded. She never thought my jokes were funny.

"Dinner will be in the East Dining Room. The menu and dinner service have already been arranged. Please plan to arrive before six p.m. Your father will escort the governors to the East Library, as they are coming directly from afternoon councils. He would like you to play the piano for approximately thirty minutes.

"This will allow time for the gentlemen to transition from political discussion to more casual conversation. You can then lead them to the dining room and take charge of the dinner conversation."

"Cha," I sighed. Taking charge of the dinner conversation meant steering talk away from any potentially interesting subjects. Heaven forbid anyone should address a controversial topic over broiled salmon. I realized that Louisa was staring at me with her lips pressed into a prim line of disapproval. What had I done to annoy her this time?

Oh right, I'd dared to use slang. "Cha" was one of many words that others could use in casual conversation, but which Louisa felt was "inappropriate for a woman in my position." I rolled my eyes but rephrased my response with practiced obedience.

"Yes, Louisa. Are there any additional guests with the governors?"

"Only some aides and secretaries for this trip. They'll be dining separately."

"Marvi." I used the slang term for marvelous deliberately, just to tweak Louisa's sour dignity. "I'll be off then."

I leaned closer to the mirror to check my hair before I left. I was admittedly vain when it came to my hair and considered it my best feature. It was a rich, deep red that could actually verge a little on orange unless I used a discreet color wash to tame the shade. Rippling to the small of my back in perfect waves, it had just enough body to frame my face and was never frizzy. I loved my hair.

Assured that my hair looked good, I stood and fluffed my skirts to shake out any wrinkles formed by sitting at the makeup table. Several of today's events were sure to be recorded for the evening news-hologram, so I was dressed up, as always. But I'd chosen a pale yellow, tunic-style gown that landed just above my knees and minimal jewelry to keep the ensemble as casual as I could get away with. I stretched and twisted in a few directions as a last check to be sure the dress wasn't binding. While I was certainly a little pampered and spoiled, I had also been trained to be able to take care of myself and others in an emergency. That training was ingrained enough that I always chose clothing that was comfortable and allowed me free movement.

"I still believe that the blue chiffon I had selected would be a better choice for today. It's more dignified," Louisa said.

As usual, she did not understand or approve of the reasons behind my clothing choices. She was more concerned with fashion and appearances than my ability to fight in a given outfit. Since I always traveled with guards, Louisa felt I could leave security concerns to them and concentrate on looking good. I disagreed, and so I wore the yellow tunic instead of the blue chiffon. Louisa curled her lip in slight disapproval as she gave me a last once-over and reached out to twitch the chains of my long silver necklace into a more pleasing line.

I sighed, and briefly wished I had worn the blue dress just to make Louisa happy. The chiffon certainly was more dignified. And it was also more suitable for a woman Louisa's age than for a nineteen-year-old girl. Still, Louisa had bought it for me herself, and I didn't want her to think I didn't appreciate that gesture. In spite of her perpetually sour attitude, I knew

Louisa was always doing her best to ensure that I was a proper representative for my father. I decided to compromise enough to make her happy.

"I thought the blue chiffon would be better for this evening. Since I have the school visit today, I didn't want to take the chance that such a nice dress would get dirty or torn or anything."

Louisa looked primly horrified by such a possibility, and then gratified that I was taking such care with her gift. Now that I'd planted the idea that my clothing might be ruined by messy schoolchildren, she was happy to send me off in my casual yellow dress instead of the fussy blue gown.

Leaving Louisa with a quick squeeze of her bony hand in thanks, I headed down the stairs to meet the large group of people escorting me today. I would be surrounded by a dozen Secret Service officers and a few members of the White House press corps. Along with my White House escort, a small crowd of paparazzi and a citizen or two looking for an autograph or photo op often followed me. It was difficult to go anywhere unaccompanied when you were the president's daughter and First Lady of the North American Alliance.

CHAPTER TWO

The day sped by in a bit of a blur. Since I spent almost every day attending ceremonies, luncheons, and various other events on behalf of my father, I didn't have to pay a lot of attention. I just had to smile, nod, and shake hands…over and over again.

As I stepped through the huge double doors of The St. Lucien following my lunch meeting, I paused for a moment to enjoy one of my favorite views of the city. The government sector of Goodland was crowded with buildings sheathed in bright, white stone, and the afternoon sun bounced off the gleaming walls with cheerful intensity.

Even the long, wide streets were a pale gray stone that reflected the intense light. The trees, flowers, and flawless blue sky were such a vivid contrast to the shining white buildings and streets that the whole scene resembled something from a movie. And from this viewpoint, there was a view straight up the main boulevard that highlighted the graceful lines of the White House at the eastern end of the street. If I turned in the opposite direction, I knew I would see the impressive dome of the Capitol building and the dignified pillars of the Supreme Court dominating the western end.

Of course, these weren't the original government buildings. Those historic buildings had been destroyed by the flooding that had inundated Washington, D.C. and most of the other cities on the East Coast as a result of melting polar ice caps back in the late 2100s. The East Coast had then been further decimated by intense bombing during the Third World War until all that remained were crumbled ruins covered by shallow seas. The area was a favorite spot for recreational diving and snorkeling now.

During the war, the country had been governed from a series of hidden locations throughout the North American Alliance. But when the war finally came to an end in 2241, it was time to create a permanent national capital again. Goodland, Kansas was the eventual choice for the new seat of government due to its location near the center of the newly formed alliance and the hopeful tone evoked by the city's name. Goodland—what political spin artist could resist the chance to work with a perfect name like that? And, probably most important, Goodland was in an area that had been largely untouched by the war or the widespread flooding resulting from the melting of the arctic ice sheets.

Old news reports had occasionally referred to the center of the United States as "fly-over states," meaning that many politicians at the time didn't feel that those areas were important enough to visit and would just "fly over" them on their way to the more politically significant East Coast and West Coast cities.

But that status worked to their advantage during the war, as attacks were so focused on eliminating population centers that they also flew right over the inland areas on their way to more prominent targets. While many large cities, especially those on each coast, were partially or entirely destroyed, Goodland and other small interior cities survived.

To relocate the government, a veritable army of architects, city planners, and construction crews had descended on the quiet town of Goodland and transformed it into a major metropolis. It was a beautiful city now with soaring towers of steel and glass, wide, well-planned streets, an extensive and convenient transportation system, and an abundance of landscaped public parks and gardens.

They had re-created the iconic government buildings as a symbol of the continuity of government in spite of adversity. Almost twenty years after the government section of the city was built, the buildings stood as strong emblems of law and order. This beautiful city had been my home since I was seven years old, and I loved it fiercely.

My view of the street and the White House was interrupted by a large umbrella that a Secret Service agent had opened and extended over my head. I sighed a little and resisted the urge to shove the umbrella away. While most people outside at this time of day carried umbrellas or wore hats as a shade from the strong UV rays, I preferred to soak up the dazzling sunlight when I had the chance.

Accepting that my small moment of relaxation had come to an end, I allowed the Secret Service agent to take my arm and guide me to the limo waiting on mag-lev tracks in front of the hotel.

All city streets had multiple mag-lev rails embedded in the concrete. Since fossil-fueled vehicles were no longer allowed, the rails were for mag-lev vehicles like the limo. These vehicles had an undercarriage coated in strong solar-powered electromagnets that pushed back against the magnetized rails to allow the vehicle to levitate a short distance above the rail. Additional magnets created a push-pull effect to propel the vehicle along the track.

Mag-lev buses and trains were everywhere in Goodland. The public transport system was so comprehensive that almost no one needed personal vehicles anymore. The mag-lev limos used by White House residents and guests were almost always the only small passenger vehicles on the road, though I could see a few mag-lev bikes slipping through the streams of traffic.

I slid into the limo and kicked off my shoes before the door even closed behind me. Alone in the limo, having sent all my companions to ride in other vehicles, I allowed myself a few long, lazy stretches. I could have used a nap but had to content myself with fifteen minutes of solitude as we slid along the mag-lev tracks on the way to the school appearance.

When I was younger, I'd found this lifestyle incredibly glamorous and exciting. But at nineteen, I'd already been the Acting First Lady for seven years, ever since my father had decided that a civilized government should have a First Lady and appointed me to the role.

Though the public didn't know what to think of a twelve-year-old First Lady at first, my father and I had always taken the job very seriously. With Louisa's dour assistance, I had learned to hostess state dinners, mingle with foreign and domestic dignitaries, and truly fill the role of a First Lady.

I mostly enjoyed my position, and I felt like I was doing some good. I supported various worthy causes, especially anything relating to helping children, a particular passion of mine. I helped things run smoothly at the White House as my father's hostess, which some might see as trivial, but I knew that the meetings and events at the White House contributed to the peace and wellbeing of the country. If I occasionally tired of my duties and wondered what it would be like to be a normal teenager, I usually regained my enthusiasm with some rest. Maybe it wasn't a normal life, but it was my life and I was happy with it.

I didn't have to motivate myself for the next item on my schedule though. I loved it when I had the chance to visit a school and meet some of the nation's children. Due to security concerns, I had taken my own education courses either online or with tutors who came to the White House, so I'd never actually attended school. Because it was so different from my own learning experiences, it always felt like a treat to make a school visit.

The Secret Service detail whisked me quickly from the limo to the classroom, but I had time to glimpse the colorful playset where children could run, climb, and slide. I'd never had the chance to play on one myself, but they looked like fun. I wondered what the evening news-holos would have to say if I suddenly broke free of my security detail to go swinging across the monkey bars.

A smile at the ridiculous image still curved my lips as I entered the classroom. The smile grew wider when I saw the group of primary school students chosen for this session. They waited for me on a colorful rug in the center of the room. Several of them were practically vibrating with excitement as we walked into the room.

Without waiting for introductions or instructions from the adults, I took a seat on the low, cushioned stool that sat on the rug. The students were seated in a semi-circle around me, crowding as close as they could reasonably get. I didn't mind the little touches and pats or even the occasional child hugging my legs. I enjoyed their innocent smiles and enthusiasm so much.

Leaning forward to catch their attention, I asked the children, "I hear that you are the best history and government students in the school. Is that true?"

They heads bobbed up and down with enthusiasm, and they talked over each other in an attempt to tell me what great history students they were. I listened to everyone as best I could with a smile on my face and then gently interrupted. Otherwise, I think the children would have been happy to chatter at me all afternoon.

"Who can tell me what holiday we're celebrating next week?"

Hands shot up around the room, and I randomly selected a child to answer. Her name tag read, "Linett, age 11."

"Go ahead, Linett," I encouraged.

"Next week is Establishment Day. That's the day that the North American Alliance was formed from the countries of Canada, the United States, and Mexico."

"Very good," I praised her, and she beamed at me. "Next week marks twenty-five years since the North American Alliance was established. I bet one of you can tell me the reasons that the Alliance was formed..."

More eager volunteers waved at me, and this time I selected a little boy whose tag said he was "Tobee, age 10." Thrilled to be chosen, he took a deep breath before he began to speak. Someone smothered a laugh and another teacher murmured, "Here we go."

A moment later, Tobee began spitting out facts so fast I could barely understand his words. "The country of Russia started taking over other countries because they wanted more power, and lots of countries tried to work together to fight against Russia. And then China started taking over other countries, too, because they needed more land for all their people after

16

the rising sea levels took away a lot of their country and they thought everyone was so busy fighting with Russia that they wouldn't pay attention to China.

"Russia and China were really big and powerful, so all the smaller countries started joining together to defend themselves. And then after a while, there were only ten countries in the world."

A teacher jumped in to dam the flow of words by prompting the kids to sing a little tune created to help them learn the names of the countries of the world, obviously something they had practiced together in school.

"China, the European Union, Korea-Japan, the Latin American Federation, New Persia, the North American Alliance, Oceania, Pan-Arabia, Russia, and the United African Republics. These are the countries of the world."

"Very good!" I praised them. "You've been paying attention to your lessons and I really liked the song."

Tobee flashed a proud grin, and I smiled back before continuing.

"You all know that my father is the President of the NAA. And my job is to help him with his job. Our biggest goal is to preserve world peace. Now that the Third World War is finally over, I think everyone just wants things to stay calm and peaceful, right?"

There was a lot of enthusiastic nodding, and the children started showing off their knowledge again, spouting random facts in my direction to impress me with their intelligence. I listened with a cheerful expression, assuring each child that I was thoroughly engaged.

"Your father has been President for ten years already."

"The war lasted thirty years, and that's prob'ly the longest a war ever lasted."

"And then after the war, the new government built a whole new capital city 'cause the old one got bombed and stuff."

"Yeah! Lots and lots of cities got bombed, and now nobody can even live there anymore."

"Not just 'cause of the bombs though. Some of the cities got flooded 'cause of the oceans getting higher and some places people can't live 'cause the weather changed too much. That's why we have lots of different cities now."

"Especially in Mexico and Canada! They got flooded lots and lots and have too many places that are too cold or too hot now, so that's why most people live in what used to be the USA."

"My dad says that if I want to, I could maybe be President when I'm grown up. But I think I would rather be a 'splorer and explore the ruined cities. They look marvi."

Finally, I had to draw our conversation to a close. I received hugs from all the children as I was leaving and entered the limo with a happy glow I'd been missing earlier. I sighed with contentment as the limo whisked me back to the White House to get ready for dinner with my father and the governors.

CHAPTER THREE

The dining room looked beautiful, dinner preparations were almost complete, and I went to my suite to change into an evening dress. Louisa had laid out the blue chiffon gown we'd agreed upon earlier. It really wasn't so bad, I told myself. The soft chiffon layers floating from a demure, square neckline and tiny cap sleeves were a little out of style, but still pretty.

I pulled on the dress and inspected my reflection in the mirror. The fit was a bit unflattering. The layers of fluttering fabric did nothing for my hourglass figure, skimming over my curves and making me look like a stocky box.

Hours of working out in the gym with my father as we discussed politics and upcoming events ensured that I was in great shape. It was a little annoying that the dress made me look like I'd never seen the inside of a fitness room.

However, I loved the way the subtle sparkle in the navy fabric took the color from somber to sophisticated. And the boxy style of the dress meant that the fit was loose enough to allow easy movement, so that was a plus.

Of course, it didn't have any pockets. Evening attire never did, which was a frequent source of frustration for me. I really did need to keep my tablet with me, but I didn't want to carry an evening bag just to visit another part of the house.

After a moment's thought, I tucked the tablet into my cleavage. It was only a palm-size unit, so it was nicely concealed and conveniently located. I patted my chest with a little grin, grateful for my curvy build that provided this built-in hiding spot.

I stepped into the sky-high heels that matched my dress. The stilettos didn't exactly fit into my requirements for easy movement, but at barely five feet tall, I added every inch possible to offset my woeful lack of height. I was willing to sacrifice a little freedom of movement in exchange for a bit of added height and confidence. Years of practice walking in heels meant that I could walk with ease and could even run a little, when necessary. Beyond that, I could always kick them off to get them out of my way. In a real emergency, the spiky shoes might even make a decent weapon.

With a final check to be sure that I looked mature and responsible enough to join the leaders of the nation for an evening, I headed downstairs to play hostess.

I went to the library where my father and the governors would be arriving shortly. This room was ready also, but a few books out of place on the shelves against the wall caught my eye. I walked over to straighten the books and also checked that the door to the hidden safe-room behind the shelves was securely latched. I was fairly certain my father and I were the only White House residents who knew of the existence of the little rooms hidden throughout the building, but it didn't hurt to be careful.

Ever since my mother was killed in one of the war's final battles, my father had become obsessed with security. Mother had been a civilian casualty who had nowhere to run when an attacking force invaded the compound where we lived. I was not even a year old and survived only because my mother had hidden me beneath a bed and protected my location with her very life.

My father also had been a Marine back when the armed forces had been divided into separate groups of Army, Navy, Marines, and such instead of being combined into the Military Corps. Back in 2211 when he'd joined the Marines, the military still used human soldiers rather than the robotic mechanical soldiers we called "mechs" that now made up most of the armed forces. Since he'd joined the military only months before the outbreak of the Third World War, he had spent much of his life as a soldier. He'd never lost the strategic, security-conscious mindset of a fighter, even when he'd become a commander instead of a boots-on-the-ground soldier.

As a result of all this, my father was especially focused on ensuring my safety. So he had secretly brought in contractors to have these little cubbyholes installed in each of the major rooms of the new White House. I had been trained from a young age to bolt to the nearest hidden compartment on his signal, Code Red.

The books were straightened and the secret door securely closed, so I moved to the piano in the far corner. I began playing the calm, classical pieces I knew my father preferred as background music. When the door opened and my father and the governors entered the room, my fingers didn't falter for a moment. I had done this so often that I could play from sheer muscle memory and leave my mind free to listen discreetly to the conversations behind me.

I could hear my father offering his apologies that Vice-President Rodriguez would not be joining us for dinner due to another commitment, and I was disappointed to learn that Cruz Rodriguez wouldn't be attending. I'd known him for my entire life and most often referred to him as Uncle Cruz. He and my mother had grown up together; their families had even assumed that the two would marry eventually. But Angela Mercado had married my father instead, and Cruz had become a trusted family friend and political ally.

He was sly and funny and helped make boring diplomatic dinners more enjoyable with his subtle jokes and whispered commentary on the other guests. I always had a hard time stifling my laughter once he started offering red-carpet-style critiques of the outrageous fashions our guests often wore. This evening would feel much longer without his company.

"That's a shame," Governor Ruiz responded. "I was looking forward to telling Cruz about the antique handgun I recently acquired. It's very similar to one in his collection."

"Perhaps there will be time tomorrow afternoon," my father suggested. "I know Cruz always welcomes a chance to talk about his hobby."

My Uncle Cruz collected antique weaponry and loved to talk about it. I had been a captive audience many times as he told me about the many swords and guns he kept in the secured storage and display area in his suite. I couldn't even count the number of times he'd coaxed me to come upstairs and see his latest acquisition. I indulged my uncle often enough that I knew quite a bit about the old weapons he treasured. In fact, I was probably one of only a few people my age who had even seen a gun. Guns hadn't been used in many years, and most young people had only seen pictures of them in textbooks. Instead, the military had developed long-range and short-range stunners, which used a burst of targeted electricity to incapacitate someone in seconds and were much more accurate than the old guns.

It sounded as if the conversation behind me was wrapping up. I was about to bring the music to a close and announce dinner when I heard a strange sound. It was a low, continuous rumble like thunder, but not quite. My fingers faltered on the keys when I glanced out the window to see a blue, cloudless sky.

What was that sound? It was growing louder.

And then I could hear that the continual rumble was actually made up of many individual bursts of sound. Somewhere glass shattered. People began to shout and scream while that rumbling noise just grew louder and louder.

I stopped playing and looked at my father.

He met my eyes calmly and said, "Code Red. Now."

He turned to the governors and told them, "Come this way quickly, gentlemen. We'll move to a secure area until we know what's happening."

Years of drills helped me to react immediately to my father's command, and I sprinted for the far wall of the library as my father and the governors moved in the opposite direction. The governors were distracted by the sudden relocation, so my father was the only one who saw me press one very particular section of the elaborate carvings on the library shelves.

A small section of the shelving swung outward on well-oiled hinges, leaving just enough room for a single person to slide into the gap and pull the hidden door closed again. I was completely concealed from view, but tiny peepholes allowed me to see a little of what was happening in the room.

Each hidden safe-room was tiny—holding nothing more than a backpack with a small stash of food and water and a first-aid kit. There was room for only one person. My father had sent me here rather than taking the hiding spot for himself, so he could be sure I was safe while he led the governors to a larger secure area. There were so many hidden passages in this building that they would be able to simply disappear and come back for me when the coast was clear.

But there was no time. The library door burst open, and people in black and gray fatigues poured into the room. Each person carried a long, box-like thing with a narrow tube protruding from the far end. It took me a moment, but I finally recognized them as machine guns like the ones I'd seen in my Uncle Cruz's collection. I realized that these guns must have been the source of the incredible noise in the halls outside the library.

All this went through my mind in seconds as the gunmen continued to force their way into the library. Then they began to fire. The sound was like a hammer blow, forcing me to my knees. I cried out, but no one could hear me over the incredible volume of the gunshots. I crawled closer to the wall and found a peephole. It allowed me to see only glimpses of the events, but it was enough to let me see my father and the three governors fall to the ground under the hail of bullets.

I shoved my hands against my mouth to hold back my screams. If the gunmen heard me, they would only need to fire into the shelves. The small safe-room was reinforced to block the stream of a stunner, but I had no idea how well it would stand up to the deadly bits of metal flying through the air. Shaking, I stayed as still and as silent as I could, praying that the attackers would leave so I could go to my father.

When Uncle Cruz walked into the room, I wanted to scream out a warning. I couldn't let these people take the only family I had left. But I was so frightened; I could only gasp for breath. And then shock stole my breath again as the gunmen didn't fire at my uncle. Instead, a man at the front of the group stepped forward and saluted.

"Sir! Targets neutralized."

"Where is the girl?" Cruz asked. "Poppy Walker should have been here as well."

"Sir, there was no one else in the room when we arrived."

"Dammit," he said with a small frown. "Ah well, we'll track her down soon enough. It's a big building but not big enough to hide very long. I can't have her running around loose. I want the entire First Family taken care of."

I crumpled into myself on the floor of my hidey-hole, stunned. Uncle Cruz was a part of this horror? How could that be? I loved him. And he loved me—didn't he?

Yet he had apparently given the order to find and "neutralize" my father. And he wanted me out of the way too.

CHAPTER FOUR

I don't know how long I huddled there, waiting for a chance to make my escape. It felt like hours…days. Cruz—I refused to refer to him as "uncle" ever again—had set up a command post of sorts in the library.

He gestured at the bodies lying on the library floor as if they were garbage that needed to be disposed of and told his men, "Get these out of here." It was obvious from his annoyed expression that the dead meant nothing to him.

Several men followed his orders and dragged the bodies of the President and governors from the room. At that point, I was so numb from shock that I couldn't even cry again when they took my father's body away.

Cruz settled himself in one of the wingback chairs and worked intently on his tablet, reading through information and adding notes and sending emails from the looks of it. I had to force myself to stay in place instead of bursting into the room and attacking Cruz for his role in the horror I had just witnessed. Only the memory of my father's instructions should I ever find myself in a situation like this kept me still.

Stay hidden. Be silent. Gather information. Thinking of those instructions, I decided it was time to do something with the information I had. Sliding the tablet from my cleavage, I activated my message program and began texting my best friend Letty. Her father was an investigative reporter with the biggest news-holo program on screen. If he couldn't do something with this information, no one could.

Typing swiftly with silent fingers, I sent an initial text instructing Letty to get her father immediately and not to read these messages unless they were alone. A second message warned them that if anyone knew they had these emails, they would be in terrible danger. I then sent a series of follow-up messages that outlined the events of the evening and named Cruz as the man in charge.

I had just finished my last message when the door opened and another group of people in gray fatigues entered the room. Like the last group of soldiers, these people carried machine guns. But their guns were casually slung over shoulders or hanging from special harnesses rather than ready to fire.

It became apparent that these were the leaders of Cruz's armed forces as each stepped up one by one to report on his assignments.

"East wing?" Cruz asked.

"Cleared, sir."

"Good. Stand down."

The first soldier moved past my hiding spot behind the shelves as the next moved forward to answer Cruz's questions.

"West wing clear, sir."

Cruz dismissed him and motioned to the next leader.

A female soldier moved to stand at attention before Cruz as he barked, "Staff quarters?"

"Secured, sir."

"And how many of the staff were lost in the entry phase?"

"Less than a dozen, sir. Most surrendered immediately. All staff have been moved to the West Library and are guarded by mechs."

"Very good. Stand down and wait for my orders."

The soldier gave a crisp nod and marched back to stand with the others who had finished their reports as yet another group leader faced Cruz.

"Public areas and offices?" he asked.

"Cleared, sir. All civilians have been moved to the West Library to wait with the house staff."

"Excellent."

Cruz dismissed him as well, and the man walked toward me just as my tablet began to buzz with a response to my earlier messages. Though the ringer was on vibrate, I was terrified that the faint noise was enough to give me away. I clutched the tablet tightly to my chest, hoping to muffle the sound. I didn't dare move or even breathe until the soldier had moved past me with no indication that he'd heard anything. I exhaled a shaky breath when he reached the other soldiers at the far end of the library and assumed a casual stance.

I changed the settings to keep the tablet completely silent, then read the incoming message. It had only three words: Are you safe?

If I had dared to make a sound, I might have laughed. Instead, I only responded: No.

My attention was pulled back to the library as another person entered the room. It was a tall, slender woman with gray hair pulled into a severe topknot. She wore the uniform of an officer with many ribbons, medals, and other insignia to indicate that she was a big deal. I recognized her immediately as the Commander-General of the North American Alliance Military Corps, Emilie Duchéne.

"General Duchéne, are the family quarters secured?"

"Yes, Mr. President. They have been thoroughly searched. They are empty."

"Mr. President." A slow smile spread across Cruz's impassive face. "I like the sound of that."

"It suits you, sir."

"Thank you. Now, there is still no sign of Poppy anywhere? My understanding was that she would be entertaining the governors and her father here in the East Library."

"No, sir. No sign of her. We've looked everywhere and double-checked to be sure she wasn't swept up with the staff and other civilians. She's not with them in the West Library."

"Piers probably told her to run at the first sign of trouble," Cruz said, his face grim. "I want her found. If she's alive, she'll be glad to serve as hostess for dear Uncle Cruz and help legitimize the change in leadership. If she's dead…" He shrugged, "She and her father can have matching, flag-draped caskets at the state funeral next week. Frankly, I don't care which it is."

My fingernails dug bloody crescents into my palms as my fists clenched. If the force of my gaze could kill, Cruz would have dropped dead on the spot. Sadly, he was unaffected by my fierce, if unseen, glares.

General Duchéne asked, "What about the rumors of secret passages and safe rooms built into the White House? Any chance she's hiding somewhere like that?"

Cruz waved his hand dismissively. "Just rumors," he assured the general. "Piers and I laughed about those rumors any number of times. Joked about installing some secret passageways so we could escape from official functions. Believe me, if there were anything like that, I'd know about it. Piers considered me his best friend. He didn't keep anything from me."

Ha! I thought. Shows what you know. Dad obviously didn't trust you as much as you thought he did. My father had very good instincts about people. He'd trusted Cruz as a family friend and ally. But if he'd been keeping secrets from his own

Vice-President and best friend, he must have doubted Cruz on some deep subconscious level. I'd never been so grateful for my father's suspicious, security-obsessed outlook on life.

Cruz sighed. "I suppose we'll have to find her later. We don't have time to spend on that right now. We should get moving on the next phase. General, please give the order for all of our men to gather in the Ballroom for further instructions. Be sure that we have mechs guarding the room against retaliation. We don't want to lose our strike force."

As General Duchéne relayed those instructions to all their soldiers via the communicator she wore on her wrist, Cruz turned to the men standing at the end of the room and raised his voice to be heard clearly, "Gentlemen, if you'll report to the Ballroom where your troops are gathering, we'll begin Phase Two of this operation. General Duchéne and I will be there shortly."

The men saluted in near-perfect unison, then walked with haste from the room, presumably to gather with their troops in the Ballroom. I wondered what Phase Two could be. Could it possibly be worse than this?

I couldn't hear Cruz and Duchéne now. They were speaking too quietly. Duchéne was getting updates on her earpiece, and after several minutes, she turned to Cruz and told him, "All strike force teams are assembled in the Ballroom, sir. All exits are secured by mechs with additional mech soldiers posted around the perimeter as ordered."

"Excellent. Let them know that we will be there in approximately five minutes. All personnel can stand at ease until we arrive."

The general relayed that message then removed the earpiece and turned it off. "Are you sure this is necessary, sir?" she asked, her voice soft. "It's quite…final."

"It's entirely necessary. If I'm to be received as the hero who brought in the mechs and eliminated the invading forces, I can't risk having even one of these men trying to tell the world that I was involved. That I pulled them from prison, armed them with banned weapons, and gave them access to the White House. They're all murdering scum, and no one would believe them anyway but there's no reason to take chances. They won't be missed. Do it now. I want everything over with before the media gets wind of things."

The general seemed to hesitate a bit but pulled a small tablet from her breast pocket. She tapped at it for a few moments, and then looked up at Cruz. "All Ballroom mechs are armed and ready, sir."

"Go!" Cruz ordered. "Open fire!"

The general tapped one final button, and I could hear desperate cries and screams from the Ballroom, directly below our location in the East Library. A deep hum thrummed through the very walls and floors of the building, and I understood that Cruz had turned on his own troops. The mechs, ostensibly there to protect his forces, were instead using high-powered blasters to kill everyone in the ballroom. They were robots, mindlessly obeying every command transmitted by the tablet in the general's hands, so they would have no qualms about killing the very men they had been told to protect just minutes before.

I shuddered. I supposed this wasn't worse than what had come before. After all, these men had come into my home and attacked my friends and family. But still, the thought of all those people dying right below me—it was horrible. I was so caught up in my shock at this second massacre that I almost missed the next development.

But a sudden movement from Cruz caught my eye, and I looked over just in time to see him pull a blocky black object from his pocket. Duchéne looked, too. She seemed confused.

"Sir?" she asked. "What is that?"

"This little beauty is called a revolver," Cruz replied. "A banned weapon from last century. It's a bit archaic, but surprisingly effective." And without giving Duchéne another moment to react, Cruz raised the revolver to shoulder level and pulled the trigger.

From my angle, I saw only a small, neat hole appearing suddenly in Duchéne's wide forehead. But the spray of blood and bone that erupted from the back of her head left no doubt that the weapon was, indeed, very effective. I tried to stifle my gagging as Duchéne dropped to the floor like a marionette whose strings were cut.

Cruz walked to the general's body and bent to take the tablet that Duchéne still clutched in her hands. Then he walked out the door without a backward glance.

CHAPTER FIVE

I pulled myself together. I knew this might be my best chance to escape from the tiny safe-room, and I had to be calm and quiet to pull it off. Before I left my hiding place, I quickly messaged Letty with the latest details of Cruz's coup, just in case I was caught. Then I erased my contacts and sent messages so that no one could see my texts and trace them back to Letty if the tablet was found.

For extra safety, I dropped the tablet to the floor and stepped on it. The sharp heel of my stiletto easily punched through the thin screen, and I added another couple of holes for good measure. As a final step, I pulled one of the tubes of water from the backpack and poured liquid into the holes in the screen in order to thoroughly destroy the circuits inside the tablet. With that I felt confident that the data had been destroyed.

I knew that tablets were trackable via GPS, so I didn't dare take the ruined bits with me just in case the GPS chip had survived my efforts to destroy the little computer. On the other hand, I couldn't leave it in the safe room either. I didn't want the GPS to lead anyone to this hiding spot. If they found one, they would tear the White House apart to find all the rest.

I decided the best solution was to drop the ruined tablet in the library as I made my escape. After all, Cruz already knew I'd been in the library at some point tonight, so finding my tablet here would only reveal that I had been a witness. He had to suspect that much already.

Scooping the dripping tablet from the floor, I slipped the straps of the backpack over my shoulders and took a last look through the peepholes. The library remained empty. I planned my route across the room: past the open door, around the general's body—still lying on the floor—and behind the piano to the tall, carved panels beside the fireplace.

I took a deep breath, braced myself, and pressed the catch that would release the door. The soft click sounded so loud in the silence that I froze for a moment, afraid that someone would come investigate the noise. When the library and hallway beyond remained empty, I forced myself to move as quickly and as quietly as I could.

I opened the hidden door and stepped into the library, pushing the door closed behind me and then sprinting for the fireplace. The panels on each side hid entrances to some of the secret passageways that Cruz was so certain did not exist. I reached up to a corner of the panel, pressed the hidden catch, and yanked it open. Slipping behind the panel, I paused just long enough to toss my ruined tablet behind the sofa to my right, then pulled the panel securely closed behind me.

I was shaking, my heart pounding, and my knees weak. I let myself lean against the wall for a moment and listened hard for any noises from the library. All I heard was the sound of my own rough breathing. I had not been seen. Pushing off the wall, I began the next stage of my escape.

My father had overseen the design and construction of the New White House and he had personally laid out these escape routes. I had no idea how he had managed to keep them such a secret, but he had always told me that he and I were the only ones who were able to access these hidden hallways. When I was a child, my father and I had played hide-and-seek in these passages. I had seen it only as having fun with my dad, but I realized later that he had been training me even then. Thanks to him, I knew every inch of these passageways and the location of every hidden cache of supplies.

Searching my memory, I knew that if I followed the current passage to the left, I could take stairs down to the sub-basement level. At the bottom of the stairs was a niche with another packet of supplies.

Finding my way without a flashlight was a little more difficult but still manageable. The walkways were narrow, so it was easy to trail one hand over the walls to each side of me as I walked, feeling for the spots where additional hallways branched off. After a couple of minutes, I felt an opening with my right hand. Feeling my way with cautious fingers, I discovered the stairs leading down. Yes! I had remembered correctly.

I headed down the stairs. With no light, I didn't know if there were obstacles in my way or when the stairs would end, so I moved slowly. I counted ninety-seven steps before my searching toes encountered flat floor instead of another downward drop. I ran my hands over the walls until I found a rough wooden cabinet set low in the wall. Opening it, I felt around inside and was elated to feel the smooth, slim tube of a flashlight. I ran my thumb across the panel at the base of the flashlight and was rewarded with a bright, steady glow.

Shining the light inside the cabinet revealed more packets of food and water, a folding knife with several useful attachments, a small personal stunner, a basic first-aid kit, and a packet containing a decent amount of cash—because even a supposedly cashless society had places where an e-transfer wasn't welcome. At the very bottom I saw two small piles of clothing. I stuffed everything but the clothes into my backpack, then stripped out of my evening dress.

The jeans and tee left for me were a bit snug but definitely better than yards of swirling fabric. And the sturdy sneaks were even more welcome. After dressing in the more suitable clothing, I stuffed my father's stored clothes and my evening dress into the backpack as well. You never knew what might come in handy.

Just past the supply cabinet, the passageway was closed by a heavy, metal security door. It was featureless, without a knob, keyhole, or seam to enable unauthorized access. The only way to open the door was with the palm print scanner keyed to recognize only me or my father. I laid my hand on the square panel mounted next to the door. It flashed once as my hand was scanned, and the door slid noiselessly into the wall. I stepped through and used the scanner on the inside wall to close the door again.

My new flashlight made the rest of the walk through the tunnels uneventful. Since I didn't want to risk falling and getting hurt, I didn't sprint down the tunnels the way my instincts prompted. But I kept my pace brisk, stopping frequently to listen for sounds of pursuit. I heard nothing and began to hope that whoever knew about the tunnels—and surely there was someone—wasn't telling.

I walked for miles. Literally. The tunnels were an escape route, so they came out a long, long way from the White House. This was to ensure that when you finally surfaced, you were far from the emergency that forced the evacuation.

The tunnel I walked through was narrow, gray, and featureless. The only thing that changed was a new security door every mile. I scanned myself through each door and closed them all behind me. If the tunnels were discovered, the heavy metal doors would slow the pursuit.

I knew that the tunnel itself ran south for just under eleven miles, and I counted the doors I passed to track my progress. After stepping through the door at mile ten, I paused to think things through. Sliding into a cross-legged sitting position on the floor, I took a long drink from one of my water tubes as I considered my options. Thinking of how much time I had spent hiding in the library bolt-hole and then walking ten miles or so, I was sure it had to be nearing dawn—meaning it was probably growing light out with people beginning to stir.

If I left the tunnels now, would I blend in with people making their morning commute? Or would I stand out and attract attention? I could stay in the tunnels until night fell again and creep out without notice, but I risked someone in the White House finding the tunnels and sending mechs after me. I was good at hand-to-hand combat; my father had taught me himself, and we sparred regularly in our own particular combination of several martial arts and some dirty street-fighting. But I couldn't fight off a mech, let alone a group of them.

As I recalled, the tunnel came out into the basement of an abandoned building in the old city. So I wouldn't be seen emerging from the tunnel itself, and then, with a little luck, I could find a way to block the exit so no one could come through behind me. I could look at the area around the building and decide whether to hide there for the day or head out into the city. Decision made, I got to my feet and started jogging through the last stretch of tunnels.

CHAPTER SIX

At the end of the corridor was a final security door. Using the palm print scanner to open the door, I moved into a small, square room similar to the one at the beginning of the tunnel. Unlike the first room, there were no stairs here. Instead, metal rungs set into the concrete walls formed a ladder leading into the darkness above me.

I settled the backpack more firmly over my shoulders and began the climb. The first dozen rungs were not bad, but I was exhausted. My thighs ached as I continued my upward climb. Soon every muscle in my legs was burning with effort, and my hands and arms began to cramp from the struggle to pull my weary body up the narrow passageway.

When I finally reached the top, my breath came in harsh gasps as my arms and legs shook. I was barely able to keep my grip on the ladder while reaching out with my right hand to touch the palm print scanner. The final door slid open with a whisper, and I tumbled through the opening to sprawl on a dusty floor.

I lay on the floor for several minutes, trying to catch my breath and regain control of my trembling limbs. I pulled a water tube from my backpack and downed it all in a couple of huge gulps. From habit, I rolled the empty tube into a small cylinder for later recycling. I shoved the trash into my backpack and forced myself painfully to my feet to take a look at my surroundings.

I was in a large, empty room. There was not so much as a scrap of paper littering the bare floor. I wouldn't find anything to block the tunnel exit here. Instead, I used the palm print scanner to close the door behind me and made my way to the worn wooden stairs that led to an upper floor.

Moving as silently as I could, I climbed the stairs. The door at the top was ajar, and I peered through the small gap to assess the situation. This area, too, appeared completely abandoned. The dust on the floors was undisturbed by footprints, and no sounds broke the quiet of the early morning. Slipping through the door, I glanced all around. This building had originally housed a store. Empty shelves still formed orderly aisles, and the remains of peeling gold lettering on the big front windows indicated that this had been the Goodland Pharmacy & General Store.

After Goodland became the capital, the new city grew and the original city of Goodland faded away. Some neighborhoods were absorbed into the new city as "charmingly retro" housing. Some areas were demolished to make room for new growth. And some, like this one, were simply abandoned. Eventually, this neighborhood would be demolished or refurbished as well. But for now, it was a small ghost town on the edge of the urban sprawl of Goodland.

I wondered if the owners of the little store had been happy to move on to stylish new developments or sad to leave behind this bit of history. It wasn't like the original inhabitants of Goodland had gotten a say in the relocation of the government. Surely, some of them had preferred their quiet little city on the plains to the massive metropolitan area that now covered the rolling hills.

I crept through the aisles to be sure I was alone, being careful to stay in the shadows at the back of the room so I couldn't be seen through those windows at the front if anyone happened to be on the street. After confirming that the store, the area behind the pharmacy counter, and a small room at the back were deserted, I finally let myself relax a little. I closed the door to the basement and flipped the old-fashioned thumb lock on the doorknob. Granted, if someone made it through all those doors in the tunnel, this flimsy lock was not going to be much of a barrier, but I locked the door anyway.

I returned to the small room at the back of the store. It had probably been used as a break room for employees at some point, as it still contained a small square table with three metal folding chairs and a long armless couch covered in cracked brown leather. I closed and locked this door behind me, too, then flopped onto the couch. I didn't blink an eye at the cloud of dust that puffed into the air around me. I just rolled over, closed my eyes, and fell asleep.

CHAPTER SEVEN

I didn't have the luxury of waking to a moment of forgetfulness and imagining that I was still in the comfort of my beautiful rooms at the White House. Before I even opened my eyes, memory flooded me. In my mind, I heard the gunfire and saw my father fall. I felt the excruciating betrayal all over again as I realized that Cruz had been responsible for the whole thing.

A smothering cloud of depression kept me flat on the couch. What was I supposed to do now? Tears leaked from my eyes as I thought about never seeing my father again. I couldn't even bring myself to swipe them away as they rolled down the sides of my face into my ears.

I didn't know where I should go. Was there anyone I could trust? If even loyal supporters like Cruz and General Duchéne could betray us, I didn't know who to turn to. I didn't even dare contact Letty again. After all, how could I really know what she and her father would do?

Anyone could be an enemy who would turn me over to Cruz. Even a well-meaning friend could contact Cruz for help or accidentally give away information about my location. In every case, I would still be just as dead.

So what was the point in doing anything at all? Why should I move from this couch? If I had nowhere to go and no one to turn to, I could just lay here until someone eventually discovered me and put an end to the misery.

I pictured my father, so stern with others, but willing to laugh and joke around with me. More tears came as I realized that I would never joke with him again. And then a spark of anger began to burn through the fog of sadness.

My father had been a good man. He had spent his entire life protecting others. He'd been dedicated to the country and the people and spent most of his adult life fighting to preserve freedom. The people of the NAA loved and trusted him, and he had done everything possible to be worthy of that trust.

And now that service had been repaid by the worst possible betrayal. At only sixty-five years old, he should have been able to look forward to another forty or fifty years of life and service. Instead his closest friend and ally had turned on him, sending him to his death. And for what? More power and prestige? Money? A different political agenda?

That spark of anger grew into a raging fury that finally drove me off the couch. I didn't know why Cruz had done this, but I would find out. And Cruz would pay.

The first order of business was to disguise myself. Because of my father's prominent role in world politics, I had spent much of my life in the spotlight and I was recognizable. I thought my current outfit of a nondescript tee and jeans was a pretty decent start to a disguise. No one would expect to see "Perfect Poppy"—as I had been irritatingly named by the media—wearing something so ordinary. But I had to do something about my hair. It was just too noticeable.

I pulled the evening dress from my backpack and used my knife to remove a few panels of chiffon from the back of the gown. I cut one into strips and used them to braid and bind my hair around my head. I layered the other panels together for better coverage and wound them around my head like a scarf, hoping that would conceal my hair sufficiently.

I took a nutrition bar and water tube from my backpack. Though I didn't feel hungry, I knew I needed to eat and drink and forced myself to finish both. I put the trash back into my pack, then removed the stunner and slipped it into the hip pocket of my jeans. I wanted easy access to the weapon if I needed to use it.

Opening the door just a crack, I listened for any sounds indicating I was no longer alone. When I heard only silence, I moved out into the main store area and made my way to the front doors. The street outside was deserted when I slipped from the store and headed out in search of information.

I found a public square only a few blocks away. Like most public areas, this one included a holo display playing news broadcasts. A small crowd surrounded the display, everyone gathering close to hear the most recent news. Most people looked shocked. A few were crying as they watched the attractive young woman delivering the news. I sidled close enough to hear as the holo image of the newscaster looked out at me, her polished brown skin and softly waving black hair gleaming beneath the unseen studio lights. Her voice was somber, and her eyes full of sadness as she spoke.

"Grim news still emerging from the White House in the wake of last night's tragedy. The death toll continues to climb as searchers comb the house and grounds for more victims of the attempted invasion. Confirmed dead include the American, Mexican, and Canadian governors, as well as the visiting staff who traveled with the territorial governors for this informal summit with President Walker. Additional identified casualties are several members of the White House staff and many members of the president's elite security force, who were on the front lines of the assault. As we reported last night, President Walker was killed in the attack before NAA forces were able to retake control of the White House. The Commander-General of the NAA military, General Duchéne, was gunned down as she directed mech soldiers to subdue the enemy combatants. First Lady Poppy Walker remains unaccounted for at this time."

The newscaster paused and touched her earpiece, indicating without words that she was receiving updated information. After a moment, she continued smoothly. "Goodland News47 has just learned that our new president, Cruz Rodriguez, is about to address the nation. We take you now to the South Lawn of the White House for those remarks."

The holo faded to black for a moment and then the familiar image of the South Lawn faded into view. Cruz stood behind a flag-draped podium at the edge of the reflecting pool. I'd always loved that spot; it was the perfect place to sit and read a good book and enjoy the fresh air and sunshine. Cruz would often join me there, and we would talk for hours about politics, family, and the world in general.

I wondered if he had been plotting against us even then. Had he ever been our friend or only been biding his time until he could take control? I supposed I would never know. But the good memories of our times together had all turned bitter now. I would never be able to think of that spot again without remembering this moment.

I spotted Louisa in the group standing behind Cruz and breathed a sigh of relief. Though I often found her bossy and irritating, Louisa had been a big part of my life for many years. I was glad she had not been hurt or killed.

Cruz looked very impressive as he stood tall behind the podium. I sneered since I happened to know that he was not particularly tall. They had likely lowered the podium to make him look bigger and more imposing. His dark suit was tailored and pressed to perfection, but he had left his tie just a bit loose and his hair disheveled to give the appearance that he had been working and worrying. He reinforced that impression by running a hand through his hair and scrubbing it over his face before squaring his shoulders and turning to the camera.

"My fellow citizens," he began, "it is with a very heavy heart that I address you today. As you know by now, the White House was attacked by an anonymous paramilitary force last night at approximately six p.m. Because this force had sabotaged our control of the mech soldiers who guard the outer boundaries of the White House property, they were able to gain access to the White House itself. They were heavily armed with dangerous banned weapons and were able to overpower the security forces within the White House."

"I was in a meeting with General Duchéne at that time, and when she realized what was happening, she immediately attempted to send mechs to contain the situation and protect the president. This is when we realized the command center for the mechs had been hacked, rendering them unresponsive to the crisis. As I have some small skill in computer programming," Cruz explained—he had advanced degrees in computer science and robotics—with a humble expression, "I immediately attempted to regain control of our mech forces. Unfortunately, I was not able to work fast enough to save our beloved President Walker."

Cruz looked down at his hands clenched on the edges of the podium and seemed to be choking back sobs. After a moment he raised his head again, his eyes glittering with unshed tears. "I lost my closest friend and confidant. I will miss him every single day. And I can only tell you that I will do all I can to continue the good work he has done for this country. I will continue his legacy of peace and prosperity."

He was very convincing, I thought, watching him with a cynical eye. Anyone who had not seen him in that library would have no doubt of his grief and sincerity. If I had not known the truth, I was sure I would have been at his side, clutching his hand for comfort and promising to carry on my father's work. I fought down the rage that made me want to howl and scream and break everything in sight, almost panting with effort by the time I regained control of my emotions. So focused on my outrage, I'd missed part of the speech as Cruz continued.

"…was able to direct the mechs to capture the enemy soldiers and sequester them in the White House Ballroom. The plan was to take them all into custody and question them for more details about this plot and the people behind it. Unfortunately, rather than let their soldiers be questioned, one of the rebels turned the entire operation into a suicide mission. He had evaded capture by the mechs and was able to kill General Duchéne and order the ballroom mechs to kill every enemy combatant confined in the ballroom. He then killed himself to evade capture.

"While we will pursue this investigation with every resource at our command, no one is claiming responsibility for the attack at this time. We urge any citizen with information about this plot to come forward immediately. Even the smallest detail could help us learn more about the purpose of this act of violence and the people behind it.

"Finally, I have one last thing to share. As we were unable to locate Poppy Walker among the dead or wounded, we had held out hope that she had somehow escaped the awful events of last evening. Unfortunately, Poppy's body was discovered earlier this morning, another victim of this savage attack." Now he let tears run down his cheeks as he continued.

"She was a shining light and an example of the best this country had to offer. I loved her like my own child, and I will do whatever is necessary to learn exactly what happened to her and exact the vengeance deserved. So help me, God, nothing will stop me."

Pretending to break down at this point, Cruz abruptly turned and strode away from the podium. An aide stepped in to offer some closing remarks and assure the public that everything was under control and the government would continue to function normally during this terrible time as the visual faded away to be replaced with a view of two flag-draped caskets on a raised dais. Text scrolling below the caskets informed us that services for President Walker and Poppy Walker would be held the next morning. The public was welcome to attend and pay their respects.

My blood ran cold. Cruz had obviously decided that I was a threat to him. By declaring me dead, he made it easier to kill me quietly. When I disappeared forever, no one would know that I had not died in the original assault.

I couldn't go to any of my friends for help. Who would believe that the man who cried as he vowed vengeance for my death was actually my greatest danger? I had already done all I dared by sending the messages to Letty and her father. Anything more would lead Cruz right to me and make a target of anyone I contacted for help.

I didn't know what I was going to do, but I was sure that I had to get out of Goodland. I needed to be further out of Cruz's reach, so I could think and plan to bring him down.

I walked away from the news broadcast, which had moved on to a story about overpriced goods at the organic markets in the farming district. I decided to head back to the old pharmacy for the time being while I worked out my next move. I was moving fast and had almost reached safety when I turned the corner and tripped right over the feet of a mech soldier patrolling the streets. I stumbled to my knees and the fall jarred the slippery chiffon headscarf loose. It slipped backward on my head, revealing the bright color of my hair for a few seconds before I snatched it back into place and darted away. I knew that the mechs in this part of town were the type controlled by human handlers, so somewhere a human sat in a control room and saw through the mechs' eyes via a bank of monitors. I could only hope that the operator had not gotten a clear view of my face in the moment that I had looked up at the mech soldier.

I slipped inside the empty store and hid at the back of the room behind the rows of shelving. I waited for several long minutes, but there was no sign of pursuit. I had just started to hope that I hadn't been identified when I heard the innocent tinkle of a bell triggered by the opening of the front door.

I froze, listening hard to figure out who had entered, and heard the sound I'd most dreaded. It was the click-whir-thump of a mech soldier walking into the room.

My mind raced as the mech began scanning the floor. I tried to think of everything my father had ever told me about mechs. They had very little autonomy, so back at the control center, someone was telling this mech to enter the pharmacy and look around. Whether they had an idea that I would be here, or were just doing a search of every building in the area, didn't really matter at this point. If it found me, I was in deep trouble.

Mechs were big. They type used here were humanoid-shaped, six feet tall, and dressed in carbon-fiber battle armor that was virtually impenetrable. Helmets with smoked-glass visors covered their heads. The stunners they carried would paralyze an enemy instantly and could also kill, if the mechs had orders to do so. And the mechs were strong enough to break a person in half even without a stunner.

Mechs didn't run very fast and they had a hard time walking across uneven terrain, so my best bet was to knock things into its way as I ran like lightning to get out of reach of those long arms. I would have to zigzag, duck, and pray that the mech wouldn't be able to target me long enough to hit me with the long-distance stunner that compensated for the mech's lack of speed.

I could hear the mech clunking closer. In a matter of moments, it would reach the end of the row of shelves and see me in the corner. I eased my way down the aisle and around the corner. Using the shelves as cover, I stood pressed against the solid end piece so that I couldn't be seen by the mech now making its way toward the break room door. At each aisle crossing, I peeked carefully around the end of the shelves to be sure the mech was not there to see me and then dashed across the exposed space to hide behind the next end piece.

After a dozen tiny sprints, I had almost reached the exit. I just had to make it from this last shelf to the door. Once I was on the street, I would run for my life and hope to lose myself in a crowd. I sure hoped there was a crowd out there somewhere close.

I looked back one last time to be sure that the mech hadn't come around the corner, then burst from behind the shelf and raced for the door. And that's when I crashed into the second mech, which had apparently been standing quietly near the door the whole time.

Mechs were fairly light for their size, weighing in around one-hundred pounds. Despite my small size, I had a lot of hard muscle under my curves due to lifting weights, running, and practicing hand-to-hand combat. So when I slammed into the mech at full speed, there was a decent amount of weight and force behind the jolt. We both crashed to the floor and laid there, stunned. I recovered first and scrambled to my feet as the mech attempted to get up. Turtle-like, the mech couldn't seem to right itself after falling on its back.

I heard the other mech heading toward me and did the only thing I could think of. I jumped at the empty shelf in front of me, attempting to knock it over. Astonished, I watched as each shelf crashed into the next in line and knocked it over as well. It worked exactly as it had in the old cartoon that had inspired my move.

The crashing shelves pinned the mech to the ground. I knew the mech was too strong to be trapped for long, so I ran for the door again. I was almost there when a metal hand suddenly grabbed me by the ankle and yanked my feet out from under me. I belly-flopped to the floor with a startled shriek, then started kicking to free my foot from the mech's grip.

The mech pulled me backward. My fingernails tore to the quick as I grabbed at the door, the tiled floor, and pieces of fallen shelving in an attempt to hold myself back. It wasn't working, and I slid slowly closer to the mech. I could hear the mech at the back of the store trying to get loose from the pile of shelves. I didn't have much of a chance against a single mech, but once the second one was here, I would have no chance at all.

Abruptly, I stopped fighting the mech's grip. My sudden lack of resistance sent me flying toward the mech, and my outstretched feet crashed into the visor. The glass cracked and fell to the floor, revealing bare metal unprotected by the armor that covered the rest of the mech.

The sight sparked an idea. The mech was too strong; I was never going to break its grip and fight it off. But maybe... I yanked the stunner from my pocket, flipped the switch to full power, and threw myself forward.

The prongs of the stunner touched the metal surface of the mech's face, and a shock of electricity lit up the air around us. My hand spasmed as the jolt shot through my fingers, and I dropped the stunner. Luck was with me as it had already done its work, and the mech had gone limp and still, releasing its grip on my ankle.

I grabbed the stunner, scrambled to my feet, and darted for the door once again. This time I made it and burst onto the street. It was completely deserted. No help in sight, but no witnesses to tell the authorities which way I'd gone, either. I pulled the strips of cloth—dislodged during my struggle with the mechs—back up to cover my distinctive hair as I tried to decide what to do next. Unfamiliar with the area, I didn't know which way to go. I just knew I had to get moving before the second mech got free or reinforcements arrived. I went right for no particular reason and dodged into the alley beside the drugstore in order to get off the empty, exposed street.

"Pretty impressive, Red," came a whisper from the shadows. "I've never seen anyone take down two mechs and make it out alive."

I spun around, my hands flying into a defensive position, ready to fight this new danger.

"Who's there?" I asked, my voice harsh.

"Ease off, now," she said, stepping into the light with her hands in front of her. "I'm not a threat."

I looked her over. She was about my age and height but a good bit skinnier. She wasn't emaciated, but she didn't look like she'd had a lot of square meals either. Her hair was a startling neon blue and cut in a choppy, chin-length bob with a couple of candy pink streaks framing her face. She wore a lot of dark eye makeup that stood out against her cinnamon-toned skin.

"Everyone's a threat," I told her. "Get out of my way."

"Look," she hissed, "you can go if you want, but you're not going to make it far. Those mechs didn't just stumble across you, they headed straight for the store like you'd sent up a flare. They knew you were there. You take off now, and they're going to find you again. And this time, they'll send so many that you'll never get loose. Come with me. I can help you."

"Why? Why would you want to get involved?"

"Red, anyone who has a fight with those mindless killing machines is a friend of mine. And anyone who can win a fight with mindless killing machines is someone I want on my side. If you're coming, make it now. Reinforcements will be here any minute."

I hesitated, but it's not like I had anywhere else to run. I knew she was right about the reinforcements.

"I'm coming."

She nodded once. "All right, Red, I'm Sharra. Let's get moving."

CHAPTER EIGHT

I followed Sharra to the end of the alley where we bellied through a gap in the fence, jogged down another alley, and climbed a ladder attached to a crumbling brick building. We emerged in yet another alleyway, this one blocked by a tall concrete wall.

Sharra showed me the handholds to climb up and over the wall, and we suddenly found ourselves at the edge of a crowded, open-air market. People strolled through wide corridors lined with stalls selling everything from fresh fruits and vegetables to household electronics to extravagant, fancy clothing. Several vendors were doing brisk business selling mourning clothes and accessories such as black armbands and veils.

Sharra followed my gaze and made a disgusted noise. "Vultures," she said. "Trying to make a profit off the death of the president and his kid. That's just not right."

I mumbled something in agreement, then asked, "Are you sure we should be here? It's so…public. And crowded."

"Exactly. With so many people here, who's going to look twice at a couple of girls out to do a little shopping?"

I tugged at the chiffon scarves that had again slipped down around my neck, trying to pull them back into place as a meager disguise. Sharra's sharp eyes watched me for a moment before widening in startled recognition.

"Cha," she breathed. "'Perfect Poppy' Walker; I'm pretty sure I just heard that you were dead."

"Reports of my death are a little premature," I told her. "But not by much if those mechs recognize me again."

Sharra chewed on her bottom lip as she considered me and decided on her next move. A moment later, she looked down and rummaged through the tote bag she wore strapped across her chest. She pulled out a roll of fabric and gave it a brisk snap to shake out the material, revealing that the roll was actually a wide-brimmed sunhat complete with decorative netting.

As the ozone layer had thinned over the last century, it had become fashionable to wear large hats with filmy sun fabric draped from the brim. The hat and netting protected the wearer from strong UV rays and, conveniently for me, obscured my face and hid my hair as well.

I donned the hat and arranged the fall of the netting. Small beads sewn into the end of the sun fabric clinked together musically as I draped the cloth to my liking. The beads were not only decorative but also served as a weight to keep the wispy netting from blowing up at every puff of wind. It was a clever bit of disguise, as it would leave me indistinguishable from dozens of other women roaming the market in sun hats that ran the gamut from plain and serviceable to elaborately frilly and fantastic.

Sharra took my arm, and we strolled out into the market to mingle with the crowd, pausing occasionally to look at stall displays, then moving on with the busy flow of shoppers. As we walked, we were able to converse in quiet voices. The noise from the throngs of people surrounding us ensured that we wouldn't be overheard.

"Who are you?" I asked.

"No one important. The bigger question is, why is the new president claiming that you were killed in the invasion when you're clearly alive and well?"

We walked in silence as I considered my options. I didn't know this girl, but she had helped me escape the mechs. My instincts said that I could trust her, but more than that, I needed her.

She was streetwise and prepared in a way that I was not. I didn't know my way around the city, having always traveled via limousine or private copter. Though I had cut many ribbons to open new transportation stations, I'd never actually climbed aboard a commuter tram or rocket train. Simply walking the streets unescorted like this was a new adventure for me. An entourage of security officers, aides, and reporters had always dogged my every step. On my own, I was likely to get myself in trouble very quickly.

Sharra bought a couple of drinks from a convenient stall as an excuse to huddle together at a little table and continue the conversation.

"So, apparently you're supposed to be dead," she said.

"Yes, I'm supposed to be dead. And if the mechs catch up with me, I definitely will be."

"Why? President Cruz said the mechs were hacked to attack the White House; is this some kind of glitch left over from the hack? Why haven't they fixed it yet? And why are you on your own? I mean, I get that you can't just walk into the local precinct if the mechs think they are supposed to be chasing you for some reason, but surely you could call the White House, and they'd take care of things."

My laugh was bitter. I should have kept the story to myself, but I was tired and I needed help. Sharra was all I had at the moment. She'd already figured out who I was, so I wasn't risking much by telling her more. I looked her over; she seemed wiry and tough, but not as strong as me. If she tried to turn me in, I could definitely break away and run again. So I let the truth spill out.

"Oh, I'd be taken care of all right. There's no glitch. There was no hack. The whole attack was made up to get rid of my father and install Rodriguez as president. Now that he's announced I'm dead, he can't have me showing up alive and messing with his carefully planned story. He's got to make sure I stay gone."

Sharra leaned forward, her eyes intent. "Tell me the whole story."

And so I did. Mostly. I told her everything that had happened in the library and about my flight from the White House, though I stayed vague about exactly how I got off the grounds. I only told her that there was a way to leave without being seen, and finished up with finding my way to this part of the city to hide and then the fight against the mechs. When I was done, I let my head drop to my folded arms on the tabletop and just took a moment to think and try to figure out my next move.

Sharra reached out and patted me on the shoulder a couple of times. The awkward move felt like she had rarely done such a thing before. We sat in uncomfortable silence for a minute or two until Sharra suddenly asked, "How did the mechs know where you were? I told you before, they weren't just doing a search, they headed right for the old pharmacy. That's what caught my attention. They were obviously on an assignment, and I wanted to know what was up."

"I was stupid," I told her. "I looked a mech in the eye. The facial recognition software has obviously been programmed to look for me. And now that they know I'm in the area, it's just a matter of time before they flood this neighborhood with mechs to find me."

Sharra nodded. "You're right," she agreed. "You've got to get out of here." She hesitated a moment before offering, "I could take you back with me, introduce you to Lucas."

A belated sense of caution kicked in. I had already shared way too much information with this stranger, but I could just disappear and she'd never have more than a story. I wasn't prepared to follow her blindly back to wherever she came from.

"For now, I just need to get to the train station," I told her. "Do you know where it is from here?"

In answer, she stood and walked away from the table. She headed for the south end of the market at a fast trot. "This way," she called over her shoulder.

Hoping she was truly leading me to the station, I jumped to my feet and followed. "Who is Lucas?" I asked as we walked swiftly through the streets.

"He's the leader of the Resistance," Sharra told me.

"Resistance? What resistance? Who are you resisting?"

"The government, of course!" Sharra looked astonished at my lack of comprehension.

I was pretty amazed myself and more than a little angry. "What exactly are you protesting?" I asked. "The free health care? Law and order in the streets? A booming economy? Wow, I can certainly see how the oppressive government has been beating you down."

Sharra stopped in her tracks, turning to glare at me. "How about a few of those basic human freedoms laid out in the U.S. Constitution and Bill of Rights?" she demanded. "When we became a new nation, we decided to adopt those documents as the foundation of our law and government. And yet, freedom of the press? Gone. The only acceptable news outlets are official, government-sanctioned operations. The right to bear arms? Don't let anyone official catch you with that stunner or knife in your bag because you're not allowed to carry those anymore. Protection from unreasonable search and seizure? Cha! Law enforcement doesn't bother with little things like warrants anymore. If they think you're up to something, they come right in and look around. And if they take you in, forget about things like right to counsel and a speedy trial. They can keep you rotting in a holding cell for years before they bother to charge you, let alone bring you to trial. And let's not forget that we are supposed to have government 'by the people, for the people.' Do you know how many decades it's been since there has been an actual, legitimate election? The government gives us the illusion of a fair, free election, but it's just a show. The votes of ordinary people like me, and probably even you, don't count for anything."

I shook my head in heated denial. "That's not true! None of that is true! My father would never allow—"

"Your father wasn't in charge!" She cut me off with a sharp movement of her hands and an even sharper tone of voice. Making a visible effort to calm down, she lowered her voice.

"Look, I'm not saying your dad was a bad guy. From all indications, he was a really good man who was genuinely doing his best. But whether he realized it or not, he was just a figurehead. There's an entire government hiding in the shadows, and they're the ones actually pulling the strings. And they're not real concerned with little things like liberty and justice for all."

"But that's ... I mean ... What proof ...?" I couldn't even formulate a coherent sentence. Could any of this be true? It couldn't be. How could I have lived my whole life not knowing this if it were true? And yet, how could I just ignore the possibility if there was a chance they really did have proof of their claims? And if it were true, how was I supposed to accept this reversal of everything I'd always believed?

Sharra could see the confusion and conflict on my face and softened her approach.

"Listen," she said in a quiet voice. "You don't have to believe me right now. For now, we're both in agreement that you need to get out of Goodland, right?"

I nodded, and she continued, "Then let's focus on that for now. Later, maybe we get in touch, and I can take you to Lucas. He can show you the proof because we do have it. And if you see it all laid out and you're still not convinced, I can promise you that Lucas won't force you to stay. He's not that kind of guy. He'll send you safely on your way, and you'll be out of this whole mess."

I sniffled, holding back tears. "How come I feel like I'm being invited to one of those parties where they sell you kitchen gadgets or cleaning products?" I muttered. "Just come for the snacks, she says. No commitment to buy, she says. And then I'm going to walk out of there with a full set of storage containers I'll never use."

Sharra laughed. "I like that you don't lose your sense of humor under stress. That's a valuable quality in a revolutionary." She winked at me as she said it.

I only raised an eyebrow. "I like your optimism," I replied. "It's a valuable quality in a government loyalist."

She laughed again and took my arm. "Come on, Red. We've got a train to catch."

CHAPTER NINE

When we arrived at the transportation station, I automatically followed the signs directing us to the entrance, but Sharra tugged me in another direction.

"You can't walk in there and buy a ticket, Red. ID required. And you can't buy a ticket for Denver anyway."

"We're going to Denver?" I asked, my tone skeptical. "Denver doesn't actually exist anymore…you know, what with being hit with all those cluster bombs."

"Yep," Sharra agreed cheerfully. "They bombed the heck out of that whole Denver-Springs urban corridor. Anyone who was left after the bombings cleared out for fear of radiation poisoning. That means it's perfect for us."

"Because you enjoy radiation poisoning?"

"Gives us superpowers, don't you know?" She flashed me a cheeky grin before adding, "Seriously, the radiation levels were never that high to begin with, and they've declined pretty rapidly. As long as you stay away from certain areas, you're just fine. The major benefit is no mechs and no government peacekeepers to avoid. We take care of ourselves and keep to ourselves, and anyone else out there does the same."

We'd been walking casually along the fence line for the transportation center, heading nowhere in particular. Or so it seemed until Sharra pushed against a section of the fencing, causing it to swing open just a bit. The two of us shimmied through the opening—Sharra had an easier time of it than I did. She had the nerve to laugh when my generous upper chest got me wedged in the opening for a few moments.

"I always figured those things were more trouble than they were worth," she chortled.

"Ha, ha," I responded as I managed to wiggle free. "Very funny, A-Cup."

She laughed, not taking offense at my mild jibe, and together we pushed the fencing closed. She led me through a maze of outbuildings until we reached one labeled Baggage Terminal C. Pulling a security tag from her bag, she tapped it on the lock, which released with a quiet thunk.

She strode with confidence through the mostly empty halls, moving as if she had every right to be there. I tried to mimic her attitude. It must have worked because no one questioned our presence. We walked down two corridors and a short flight of stairs before the way was blocked by a door marked "Authorized Personnel Only."

Sharra's security tag opened this door too, and we entered a huge open area filled with machines and conveyor belts whipping luggage this way and that and filling giant bins with suitcases and packs en route to other destinations. The noise was incredible. The machinery rumbled with a deep, bass that shook you to the bone accompanied by a counterpoint of higher-pitched squeaks and squeals from the various moving parts and a constant thump-thump-thump of baggage dropping into the transport containers.

I looked at Sharra with wide eyes, and she grinned at me and motioned that I should follow her into the locker room beside us. The walls and door must have been very thick because when she closed the door behind us, the noise level immediately dropped to bearable background levels.

Sharra moved to the last locker on the row and opened it with another tap of her security tag. She pulled out a small backpack and extracted a plastic makeup case.

"Sit," she told me. "We're gonna make sure no one looking at you would mistake you for 'Perfect Poppy.'"

"Blech. I've always hated that nickname."

"You see? There's a silver lining in everything, at least you can ditch the "Perfect Poppy" image. From what I've learned about you already, I can tell that you're not the plastic Politician Barbie Doll we'd all figured you for."

"Um, thanks?"

Sharra only laughed and began applying makeup to match my look to hers. She added dark shadows and liners around the eyes and layered on the mascara. Then she pulled out a tiny paintbrush and a small pot of blue paint. With light, feathery strokes she drew intricate designs in a strip down the right side of my face from forehead to chin.

"With this 'tattoo' down the side of your face, people will be so busy staring at it that they won't pay much attention to the rest of your face. Cuts down on the probability that they'll recognize you. I'll give you this pot of dye so you can refresh the design when you need to."

I nodded, agreeing with her logic. I was completely on board with her disguise plans until she pulled out a knife. "It's time to do something with the hair. It's way too recognizable."

I clutched at my hair in denial. I loved my hair. But after a moment, I forced myself to drop my hands and nod. She was right. The hair was too distinctive. I screwed my eyes shut and clenched my fists in my lap as Sharra flipped open the knife and started chopping off long sections of hair. She cut it ruthlessly short, about a fingertip in length over most of my head and a little bit longer on top with a small, asymmetric fringe over my forehead.

When she finished, she directed me to the mirror hanging at the end of the row of lockers. My mouth dropped open in shock as I took in my changed appearance. A tattooed stranger with short-cropped hair and dramatically smoky eyes stared back at me.

Running my fingers through my short hair, I pulled it into rough spikes. Sharra had done a pretty decent job of making it look like my jagged haircut was a deliberate style choice instead of an obvious attempt to change my appearance. As a bonus, I hadn't had time to touch up the color lately, so the roots exposed by my super-short cut were noticeably lighter. My hair was now a fiery orange.

I had always considered my face rather plain. I was well put-together and nicely groomed, but overall quite ordinary. That's probably why I liked my hair so much. It was the only thing about me that wasn't average. But now…now I looked fierce. The dark eyes and the striking tattoo gave me a dangerous air. The spiky hair was rebellious and wild. I seemed like someone you wouldn't want to run into in a dark alley.

I liked it. Even my close friends would have trouble recognizing me right now. Between the changed hair color, radically new hairstyle, and plain wardrobe, I definitely didn't look like "Perfect Poppy" anymore.

Turning to Sharra, I nodded in approval. "You know what I really need?" I asked. "Black leather. That would really complete the bad-ass image."

She nodded, managing to keep a straight face. "Black leather, check. I'll take care of it," then she snickered as she tossed me a pair of bright orange coveralls instead. "This will have to do for now."

CHAPTER TEN

We made our way through the harsh clamor of the baggage floor to find a tall man in an orange jumpsuit and ear protectors supervising the loading of a several vac-trains. Sharra waved to catch his attention, and he turned, acknowledging us with a short nod, and pointing at the last of the trains lined up at the entrance to the vac-tunnels.

It was a short train, only an engine and six freight capsules. Sharra led me to the last capsule. She pressed a button on the side of the capsule and a round door opened. We stepped inside, and welcome silence descended as Sharra closed the door behind us.

I looked around with interest since I'd never been inside a vac-train capsule before. I was a bit disappointed that it was so ordinary. The sleek, shiny chrome exterior of the ovoid capsule was much more interesting than the prosaic interior. The inside was simply matte gray metal with no real distinction between ceiling, floor, and walls. The capsule was mostly empty, but there were a few boxes strapped down near the back of the pod.

"Make yourself at home in our luxury accommodations, Red. The trip isn't long, but we'll be here for a while waiting for our turn through the tubes."

The vac-trains—shorthand for vacuum tube trains—ran through airless tubes and tunnels. With no air resistance, the trains could travel at extremely high speeds, and the two-hundred-mile trip from Goodland to Denver would take less than fifteen minutes. Since the vac-trains had to run through the specialized tunnels, much more time was spent waiting for an available tunnel than actually traveling. It could be several hours before our train left the loading station.

I sat on the floor next to the cargo, so I could use the boxes as back support, and Sharra joined me. "How do you have access to all this?" I asked, waving my hand around in an attempt to encompass the train station, the cargo capsule we sat in, and the makeup and clothing she'd provided to disguise me.

Sharra bit her lip as she hummed. "I don't think I can tell you that yet," she said apologetically. "It's not really my secret to share. I'll just say that we have contacts in the city who can get us some of the things we need in exchange for things that can only be found around Denver."

Her response only made me more curious, but politeness—and the sense that she wouldn't give me any further information—obliged me to drop the conversation. Instead, I only nodded and let silence fall.

I dozed off slumped against the wall and the stacked boxes and slept until a high-pitched chime that rang through the cars. Sharra was startled awake as well and pulled herself together enough to warn me, "That's the signal that it's our turn to go. Brace yourself."

The warning came just in time as the train suddenly began to move. It accelerated so quickly that the G-forces pinned me back against the boxes and forced the breath from my lungs with a quick huff of air. After a few seconds the acceleration leveled off, and I was able to catch my breath.

I wished there was a window in the capsule, so I could see how fast we were traveling. Of course, since the blank concrete walls of the tunnel were the only scenery, I supposed it wouldn't be much of a view.

Sharra sat up and stretched, then got to her feet.

"We need to be at the front of the pod when the train slows down," she told me. "Otherwise the G-forces will throw you across the capsule when we start to brake."

Thinking of how much force had pinned me against the boxes as we accelerated, I knew I wanted something solid to brace against during deceleration. Sharra and I moved to the front of the capsule and sat against the smoothly curved gray wall.

"So the vac-train is headed for the Denver hub to change tracks, I assume?" I asked Sharra. There was a major transportation hub in the mountains above the old city of Denver. Picture the vac-tube system as a series of bicycle wheels spread across the continent. Tubes headed to—or arriving from—many destinations radiated out from a center hub. To reach your final stopping point, you took a tube from one hub to another, switching directions at each hub as needed until you reached the station you were headed for.

The Denver hub was one of the major transportation centers with tubes to hundreds of other hubs and stations. The transport center had been built deep within the Rocky Mountains because there was no surface land available. The massive Denver-Springs megalopolis had covered every acre up to and spreading into the mountains. Since the transport hub was so far underground, it was one of the few things in the Denver area to survive the crippling bombing strikes during the war. The miles of bedrock surrounding the installation also protected it from the radiation of the dirty bombs that had been detonated at the old NORAD base. A small army of workers kept the transport center running, but they commuted in on the vac-trains. No one lived in Denver anymore. Or at least, that's what I'd always thought.

The chime sounded again to warn us that the train was preparing to stop. We braced ourselves for the deceleration and were pinned to the wall again as the train came to a smooth halt at the station.

Sharra blew out a breath. "I never get used to that," she commented as she grabbed her packs and opened the capsule door.

The transport hub was, if possible, even louder and busier than the baggage depot back in Goodland. The machines clanked and squealed and loud blasts of pressurized air escaped from the vac-tubes each time a train entered or left a tunnel. With hundreds of trains and tunnels in use at any given moment, the sound of rushing air was almost constant.

Stepping onto the platform, I saw that all the workers here wore orange coveralls like ours. With so many people dressed alike, we were able to blend right in—just another couple of commuters coming in to work the next shift.

I followed Sharra to the end of the platform and up a set of metal stairs. I was relieved when I saw that the first two doors at the top of the stairs were bathrooms. Sharra and I took advantage of the chance to use the facilities, then stepped out into the long, empty corridor. Though every light along the hallway was shining, the sullen glow seemed to ooze down the walls, barely reaching the floor. The entire passage had an aura of gloomy hopelessness.

"Cha," I muttered. "Talk about creepy."

Sharra just nodded, body tense, and hurried down the hallway. We weren't quite running, but we weren't far from it. I wasn't sure what had her so worried, but her fear was infectious. I found myself looking back anxiously to be sure no one was behind us. It was hard to see far in the dim light, which just made me more paranoid.

Sharra stopped at a door labeled "MAINTENANCE" and used that all-purpose security tag to open the lock. We slipped inside and closed the door behind us. Sharra leaned against the door and pulled in a shaky breath as the lock clicked behind us.

"What were we running from?" I asked Sharra.

"Probably nothing," she said tersely. "I just…don't like that section. There's something off about it. Live in this city long enough and you learn to trust your instincts on stuff like that. Or you don't. And then you die."

She straightened away from the door and started down the stairs. I stayed where I was for a moment—startled into immobility by her words, which was why I was still close enough to the door to hear a wet snuffling sound along the bottom edge. I froze, terrified that whatever was on the other side of that door knew I was standing there.

My heart was pounding, and I broke into a cold sweat. Sharra was already out of sight. Without knowing exactly what was on the other side of the door, I didn't dare call out to warn her. I eased down the stairs as quietly as I could. I really wanted to get away from that door. I moved down the stairs one slow, backwards step at a time, afraid to take my eyes off the door.

I was nearing the bottom of the stairs when my backward step bumped me into something solid. My panicked shriek was muffled by a hand clamping over my mouth. Just as I started to drive my elbow back into my assailant's ribs, a voice hissed, "It's Sharra,"

I stopped the blow and reached up to pull her hand away from my mouth.

"Why are you sneaking up on me?" I asked in an angry whisper.

"Why are you paying so much attention to what's up there that you didn't notice me coming up behind you?" she whispered back.

"There was something at the door," I breathed. "It was sniffing at the crack like it was trying to track us. I don't know what it was … but it sounded big."

Sharra's eyes were wide and frightened as she looked past me to the door at the top of the stairs.

"It must not be sure we're here," she said, "or it would be trying to come through the door after us. Come on … quietly."

We slipped down the rest of the stairs, throwing glances over our shoulders all the way down. I didn't even know what I was watching for, but if the previously fearless Sharra was scared of it, I wasn't sure I even wanted to know what it was.

Another steel door blocked the bottom of the stairs. I expected Sharra to relax a bit once we had closed it behind us, but she remained tense and watchful. Following her lead, I stayed silent and moved carefully through the next section of tunnels. This area looked like it had been abandoned years ago. A few long-life safety bulbs flickered in their sockets, but the dim pools of illumination only served to make the surrounding shadows look even darker.

We crept through the shadows doing our best not to disturb the silence. I listened hard for any indication that we weren't alone in the tunnels. All I heard was our own footsteps until a piercing shriek suddenly rang through the tunnels. It sounded close, and I wasted precious seconds frantically looking for the source of the cry, certain it must be about to leap out at me.

Sharra grabbed my arm and yanked me into a stumbling run. We sprinted through the darkness—no longer attempting stealth—just trying to escape from the animal lurking in the gloom. In the dim glow of the tunnel lights, I could just see the outline of a door. Sharra yanked it open, and we dove inside and slammed it behind us.

Another of those small lights clung to the wall revealing a small, square room. There were a few boxes stacked randomly against the walls, a rack holding a few more orange coveralls, and something large and lumpy covered with an oil-stained tarp. There was no sign of a big, hungry animal inside, and the doors—both the one we leaned against and the large, rolling garage door at the end of the room—seemed sturdy enough to keep the predator at bay.

Judging from the way Sharra slumped against the door to catch her breath, I assumed she also felt that the doors would stop the animal from getting to us.

"What was that?" I asked her.

"Shadows," she told me wearily. "That's the only name I know for them. Shadows because they like to hide in the shadows. Come at you from the dark." She shook her head. "They're getting braver. I haven't seen them this close to the work areas before."

"But what are they? Animals of some kind, right?"

"Yeah. They're dogs ... or what used to be dogs. Best we can figure is that the radiation changed them, sped up evolution, messed up the DNA, something. So they're more like a cross between a dog and a lizard. Size and shape of a Great Dane with tough, scaly skin like a reptile. Red eyes that glow in the dark like something out of a nightmare. They're fast and strong and scary smart."

I tried to speak but couldn't force sound through my suddenly dry throat. I swallowed hard and tried again.

"How do you fight them?"

"Don't," Sharra said. "Run. If at all possible, you want to avoid fighting them because they're quick and vicious and almost always hunt in packs, so you won't be fighting just one. The good news is that they're generally impatient and easily distracted. If you can get out of their immediate territory, they won't follow you for long. If you do get forced into a fight with a pack, your best bet is to injure one of them badly enough to incapacitate it. Once it's down, the others will turn on the easy prey and hopefully give you a chance to get away."

"Wow. Have I thanked you yet for inviting me to visit your lovely city?"

CHAPTER ELEVEN

Though I had no desire to ever set foot in the dark again, Sharra said we couldn't leave the storage unit until after sunset. Though these storage pods were no longer used by the transportation depot, if someone saw us leave, he or she might investigate and find the things Sharra's group had stashed here. After stripping out of the orange coveralls and adding them to those hanging on the rack, we filled the time by sharing some of the food and water from my pack and napping.

There was a small window high in the outside wall. Neither of us was tall enough to look out the window, but we could watch the light change with the coming of night. As Sharra judged that it was almost dark enough to leave, she removed the cover from the large objects near the door.

I hurried over for a closer look when a pair of mag-lev bikes were revealed. Mag-lev bikes were built to look like the motorcycles that were popular back in the days of fossil fuels with lots of shiny enameled paint and glittering chrome. The bikes were fast, maneuverable, and lots of fun.

There were a couple of bikes in the White House garages, which my father and I had occasionally used when we could sneak away from our security details. A hidden exit from the garage let us slip away from the White House and into the streaming traffic on the streets of Goodland, our helmets rendering us faceless and as anonymous as any other citizen.

I let myself enjoy the happy memory of my father for just a moment, and then pushed it away before it could hurt too much.

"The mag-lev rails are still intact?" I asked. "Didn't the bomb strikes tear up the streets?"

"Sure, some of them," Sharra replied, "but Denver was pretty progressive and had fully converted to mag-lev back before the war. Every street has multiple rails, so it's usually pretty easy to find a way around any damage or blockage. Have you ever ridden a bike? Because it doesn't really seem like the kind of thing First Ladies get up to. You can ride double with me if you're nervous about riding on your own."

"I'll be fine on my own," I told her as I went over to inspect the bikes. The paint was scratched and the chrome dull instead of shiny, but the machines were in good shape with large, solar-powered engines and an almost full charge, despite sitting inside for at least a day or so.

I threw a leg over the bike and bounced a little on the black leather seat as I inspected the controls. Push-button start, a switch to convert from off-rail rolling to full mag-lev mode, throttle and brakes in the handlebars. It was all similar enough to what I was used to that I was sure I could handle the bike without trouble.

Sharra watched me inspect the bike and said, "You don't look like a newbie. Can I assume you've driven a bike before?"

"I have one a lot like this back at home," I responded. "I can handle myself."

"Good to hear. It's always best to move fast out there."

I tightened the straps on my backpack, pulled on the helmet that was strapped to the back of the bike, and settled myself more comfortably on the seat.

"Ready when you are."

Sharra pulled on her own helmet and pressed the button to turn on the engine. It started with a quiet rumble. Solar engines, even powerful ones, didn't make a lot of noise. I started mine as well and we used the rollers to move up next to the big sliding door that led to the outside world.

"Stick close to me," Sharra said. "The first stretch is the most dangerous since we'll be on rollers and can't move as fast. Keep a close eye out for Shadows and Lurkers until we—"

"What are Lurkers?"

"Street thugs, basically. They're city people who hang around looking for an easy mark; then they beat or kill the mark and take anything they can get. They'll just see two girls and figure us for easy targets. They'd be wrong, but better to just avoid the situation than to have to fight and prove it."

I nodded in understanding, and she continued, "So keep an eye out for Shadows and Lurkers until we can get to the first mag-lev rail. It's about 200 yards west of here. Once we catch that, we can slide right on into the city. Lurkers keep to their own territory, so they won't chase us and risk running into someone else's zone. And the Shadows are fast, but not fast enough to catch a bike on an open rail."

We exchanged tight grins of anticipation. I was so excited I could've probably levitated even without a bike. In spite of the sadness, fear, and anger I still felt over the events of the last few days, there was no denying that this was an adventure. I had never experienced anything like this in my safe, restricted life. This new life that I'd stumbled into was frightening and confusing, but it was definitely not boring.

My heart was pounding as I watched the sliding door roll soundlessly out of our way. I gave the throttle a small twist and my bike slid forward in one smooth motion onto the rolling casters. As soon as we were clear of the door, Sharra did something to make it roll closed again while I looked around us for any sign of Lurkers or Shadows.

I saw nothing, and Sharra didn't seem to see anything amiss either as she headed west and signaled for me to follow. It was a short, but tense, ride to reach the end of the row of storage units. I think we both breathed a sigh of relief when we saw a mag-lev rail gleaming in the moonlight just ahead of us.

The rails were set flush with the hard surface of the roads, so all we had to do was roll over the line and flip the switch to turn on the electromagnets. I felt a small jolt as the magnets engaged and the bike rose to hover a scant few inches above the road.

Sharra turned her head to look at me, or so I assumed since I couldn't see her face behind the shadow of her visor. But I could clearly see the thumbs-up signal she gave me before she turned forward again and gave the throttle a healthy turn. Her bike shot away down the line, and I could hear her happy whoop floating on the air behind her as she sped away.

I shouted with joy myself as I opened up the engine and flew after her. I felt the wind whipping against my exposed skin and plucking at my clothes as I soared through the cool, dark night. The light from the moon and the headlights were the only signs of life to be seen. At that moment, we could have been the only people in the entire world.

For a few minutes, I reveled in the sense of freedom. I wasn't a girl on a mission. I wasn't on the run from assassins and thugs and demonic lizard-dogs. I was just part of the night.

I revved the engine and caught up to Sharra, then leaned to the left and felt the bike pull loose from the rail I was on and skate sideways for a moment before clicking onto the next lane. With a challenging cry, I zipped past Sharra. She responded by speeding up to catch and pass me. We continued our impromptu game of leapfrog as the miles sped by, hopping from one rail to another and weaving in and out of small obstacles in the road when necessary. It just might have been the most fun I'd ever had in my life.

I was sharply disappointed when Sharra signaled that she was pulling over and came to a stop at the side of the road but obediently pulled over beside her. She flipped up her visor to reveal a wide grin.

"You've got some skills, Red! That was insane … you know, in the good way."

I flipped up my visor and beamed back at her. "Completely marvi," I agreed. "Let's do it some more."

She laughed. "Definitely, but I just wanted to get you oriented so you know where we are and where we're headed. We've been moving pretty much due east coming down out of the mountainous region. Now, we're starting into the flatlands where most of the actual city was … is."

She pointed to the north. "We're just passing the Boulder area now. There's pretty much nothing but rubble left there. A few packs have taken over that section, but as long as you stay out of their way, they'll leave you alone. The big, empty area you can see over that way is Rocky Flats. I don't know what all went on there, but it's freaky contaminated. Like glow-in-the-dark bad. We'll skirt around it to head into Denver, but just know that if you ever have to go that way you don't stop for anything you see. If it's living in Rocky Flats, there's definitely something wrong and probably very scary about it. I've heard that some of the stuff that lives there makes the Shadows look like house pets."

I shuddered and promised to avoid Rocky Flats like the plague. Sharra nodded in satisfaction and then pointed east.

"We're going to head due east for about another twenty miles to get to the old freeway, then take it south into Denver. There's plenty of packs with territory between here and there, but the plan is to just get through fast before they have a chance to react and be out of sight before they even think to chase us. Got it?"

I nodded. "How many people are living here, anyway? Everything I've ever been taught says that this is all deserted wasteland, but you talk like there are people everywhere."

"It's not populated like it was before the war, but it's definitely not empty. There are a lot more people living rough than anyone wants to officially admit."

I flipped my visor down, not wanting her to see my facial expression as I wondered just who knew about this and why it was such a secret. Sharra didn't press; she only slid her own visor into place and pulled her bike back onto the nearest rail. I followed close behind as we headed for Denver.

We still traveled fast, but there were no more playful swoops and passes. Sharra was concentrating on getting us through unnoticed. We almost managed it, too. We had just passed the battered remains of an exit sign for Denver Downtown when we were suddenly no longer the only ones on the road.

Mag-lev bikes were so quiet that it was possible for us to sneak through areas without being detected, but their quiet engines also meant that this group had been able to sneak right up on us without warning. We were surrounded by almost a dozen bikes, some of them carrying double. They closed in, trying to force us to stop. Sharra revved her engine and shot through a small gap between two riders, taking off down the exit ramp onto the smaller surface streets. I followed, trying desperately to keep Sharra in sight since I didn't know where we were going.

We sped through the streets, taking turns recklessly fast as we tried to lose the bikes on our tails. As we flew around yet another corner, one of the bikes caught up to me and slapped into the back of my bike. It wasn't a particularly hard collision, but it popped my bike loose from the mag-lev rail, and I went skidding sideways across the pavement. When the base of the bike hit the curb at the edge of the road, I was flung over the handlebars to land in a crumpled heap on the cracked sidewalk.

All I could do was lie there, staring blankly at a weed growing inches from my nose as I tried to catch my breath. From the corner of my eye I saw Sharra slow and look back, trying to decide if she could help me. Then she leaned low over the handlebars and shot off into the dark streets, leaving me behind.

A million small aches and pains made themselves known as I rolled slowly to my knees. I didn't bother to get up any further than that. I was completely surrounded, and I knew I wouldn't be able to move fast enough to break loose from all of these people and retrieve my downed bike. Instead, I waited in silence to see what would happen next and watched for an opportunity to escape.

A tall man dressed in ragged jeans and a leather jacket at least a size too small came to the front of the group and reached down to roughly jerk the helmet from my head and drop it on the ground at his feet. His hair and bushy beard were iron gray and stood out in a frizzy halo around his head, making me think of a dandelion gone to seed. Keeping that image in my head helped me feel less intimidated as he loomed over me, clearly trying to frighten me.

I tilted my head back to look him squarely in the eyes, which seemed to startle him. I took advantage of the moment and got smoothly to my feet. I didn't want to stay in such a vulnerable position.

With an angry snarl, he reached out with one meaty paw and slapped my cheek. "You'd oughta be more respectful of your betters, little girl," he growled. "I din't tell you to stand up."

I knew this man. Oh, not his name or his background, but I knew his type. He was a bully through and through, and I had encountered plenty of bullies in my years of playing politics with my father. I had no tolerance for bullies and refused to play along with their little power games. Maybe this was more physical than the social maneuvering I was used to, but the principles were the same at the core.

So I ignored my throbbing cheek as I stared at him in the eyes again and replied, "I didn't ask your permission. And I certainly wouldn't consider you my better in any way." I sneered at him, knowing that it would make him angrier.

Steam practically rolled from his ears as he snarled, "What'r you doin' in our patch? Yer trespassin' and you gots to pay the fine."

As he shouted, he revealed a mouth full of missing, rotting teeth and a few drops of saliva flew from his lips. I pulled a disgusted face and made a show of wiping at the drops of spittle that had hit my cheeks.

"Oh really?" I asked coolly. "And just what exactly makes this your territory?"

"Because I said so!"

"Oh, certainly. If such a fine, upstanding man as yourself says so, it must be true," I replied, voice mocking.

I could see from the faces of the men and women standing behind Dandelion Man that this kind of defiance was unheard of. Almost all of them were staring at me with wide eyes, and several mouths had actually dropped open in shock. Only one person, a boy about my age, seemed more amused than astonished. His shoulder-length dark hair fell in perfect waves around his face as he ducked his head, trying hard to hide a grin at my insolence.

I tore my eyes away from Laughing Boy. Nice as he was to look at, this was hardly the time to be ogling a cute boy. I needed to focus on the man in front of me who was sputtering in fury.

Dandelion Man reached out to slap me again. I was ready for it this time and shot my arm up to block the strike. I took the hit on my forearm, toughened from many years of practicing this exact move, and let the blow slide off to the side. Before he could recover from his surprise and try again, I took the offensive.

My right hand darted forward to grab a handful of greasy beard, and I yanked hard to bring his face closer to mine. "I let you get away with hitting me once," I hissed, "but don't try it again."

I shoved him backward as I released my hold on his beard and wiped my hand on my jeans, knowing this was going to enrage him. I was correct, and he gave a wordless roar of rage as he charged me.

He was so blindly focused on his anger that it was even easier than I had anticipated. I simply stepped out of his way. He couldn't react quickly enough to my change in position, and he crashed into the brick wall behind me. He fell to the ground without a sound, knocked unconscious by the force of his own attack.

While his people were still reacting to this strange turn of events, I took advantage of the confusion and ran. They were blocking my path to the bike, so I took off into the dark streets and hoped that I could find somewhere to hide before they could get themselves together and track me down. Within seconds I heard shouts and pounding feet behind me as they realized I was getting away.

I was a fast runner, but they had the advantage of familiarity with the area while I was running blind. Someone behind me was barking orders to split up and cut me off at the next corner.

I zigged and zagged through the streets, trying to lose my pursuers, but they always seemed to find me again. At one point I caught a glimpse of Dandelion Man, apparently recovered enough to rejoin the chase. I knew that if he caught me again he would take out his frustrations very painfully on my tender skin.

I ducked into an alleyway and stopped to rest for a moment, hands on my knees and sucking gasps of air as quietly as I could manage. A tall, slender figure stepped out of the shadows and stopped just out of my reach. It was the boy who had laughed at my impudent response to Dandelion Man.

Laughing Boy made no move to capture me. Instead, he leaned forward and softly told me, "Every one of these idiots took off chasing you. They left the bikes unguarded. If you can make it back there, you should be able to grab your bike and get out of here."

I narrowed my eyes at him. "As far as I can tell, you're one of those idiots. Why would you help me?"

"Because chasing down a couple of girls and hassling them—and probably worse—just because they crossed the wrong road is not the right thing to do. And I try to do the right thing where I can."

I gazed deep into his eyes, trying to get a read on whether he was telling me the truth or playing some game of his own. Mostly what I noticed is that he had beautiful, deep brown eyes with tiny flecks of gold. Heavy, dark brows were lowered in concern as he leaned in closer. And unlike Dandelion Man, this boy had a full set of nice teeth in his attractive mouth.

"I want to help you get out of here," he said. "These are not nice people. You don't want them to catch up with you." He lightly touched the pattern inked on my cheek. "Just get to the bikes and then go south. That will take you into unclaimed territory."

I put my hand on his arm. Even under these circumstances, I could appreciate the strong muscles beneath the thin material of his shirt.

"Come with me then!" I urged. "If they're that bad, you shouldn't be here with them either. Help me get loose and come with me to find my friend. She can get you in with her group."

"Nah." He stood up straight again. "I have my reasons for staying. This is a bunch of worthless bastards, but there are others back at home who need looking after. Get outta here before someone sees you and I have to take you prisoner to save face."

"Like you could," I scoffed. "I've taken down bigger, better men than you, Laughing Boy."

He chuckled and gave me a nickname of my own in response. "I believe you probably have, Little Bit. Go on now. Run for it." He melted back into the shadows, and I left the alley, trying to find my bearings and figure out which direction would take me back to the bikes.

Just as I had figured out that I needed to head straight through the alley on the other side of the street, I saw something that made my blood run cold. One of the shadows in the mouth of the alley stirred, and I caught a quick gleam of red eyes shining in the darkness and a glint of moonlight on scaly black skin.

I froze in the middle of the street, not sure what to do next. Sharra had told me that if I was faced with a Shadow I should run. But running blindly to get away from this animal could put me right back in the arms of the men I was trying to escape. I was still trying to decide my next move when pounding footsteps came racing toward me.

Dandelion Man and two of his flunkies were running flat out, trying to reach me before I took off again. They were blocking the road to my left. I knew that going right would just take me back into the maze of streets and further from the unguarded bikes. And the Shadow in the alley in front of me moved as if gathering itself to leap out at me.

I decided to do something no one would expect; I ran straight toward the Shadow. It didn't seem to know how to react to my full-speed approach and stopped to watch me hurtling toward its hiding place. Taking advantage of the animal's surprise, I dodged left as I got to the mouth of the alley and leapt up to grab the bars of the fire escape directly above my head.

Dandelion Man and his friends were so intent on catching me that they didn't even notice the Shadow until they literally ran into it. The lizard-dog immediately started to rip and tear at the men who had fallen into its hiding place. I tried my best not to hear their screams behind me as I dropped to the ground and ran for the bikes.

Just as Laughing Boy had said, the bikes were unguarded. I ran straight to my bike, tipped drunkenly against the curb. With a sturdy push, I was able to stand it upright and slide it back over to the mag-lev rails. I hit the start button before I was even completely astride the bike and was racing away before anyone could see me go.

CHAPTER TWELVE

Taking Laughing Boy's advice, I followed the compass on my instrument panel and did my best to head south but the streets in this part of the city ran at strange angles instead of a more reasonable north/south/east/west pattern. To make matters worse, many streets were completely blocked by the rubble of collapsed buildings, so I had to keep turning onto new streets in order to continue heading south.

I wasn't sure how far I needed to go before I was in neutral territory, but eventually I came to a neighborhood that looked more intact than many of the others I had seen. Though most buildings on the west side of the street were reduced to rubble overgrown with a wild tangle of thorny vines, several small shops on the east side seemed largely intact. At this point, I was exhausted and decided my best move was to stop and find a place to rest.

I turned off the magnets on the bike and it dropped the half-inch to rest on the rollers as I steered it away from the mag-lev rail. I dismounted and wrestled the bike onto the sidewalk in front of a shop that looked like it had been a café. I parked the bike in front of the cracked and dusty window and cupped my hands against the glass to peer inside.

I couldn't see much in the dim moonlight that filtered through the window, but I could make out a few tables and chairs and a front counter with built-in stools for seating. I saw no signs that anyone or anything was inside. I tried the door, which opened easily but with a loud screech to announce my entrance. So much for taking a quiet look around.

Since there was no longer any value in being quiet, I stepped inside and called out, "Hello? Anyone in here?"

I listened intently but heard nothing in response. I ventured in a little further to look around. The tables and counter-top were coated in a thick layer of dust and grime that appeared undisturbed except for tracks from some kind of small animals. I grimaced. Probably rats.

Moving past the front counter, I found a small kitchen. It had long ago been ransacked for any food left behind. Doors to the cupboards and refrigerator hung open to reveal empty shelves. All the surfaces here were also coated in dust. It had been a long time since anyone had been here.

I saw another door in a shadowy niche beside the refrigerator and across from the old stove. The doorknob turned smoothly, and I inched the door open, ready to slam it closed again if there was anything alarming on the other side. Fortunately, the only thing outside the door was a small, dank alleyway. It was crowded with old trash and building debris, but there was just enough space that I would be able to maneuver the bike down the alley and out to the street.

I closed the door again and flipped the deadbolt above the doorknob. The second exit had me decided; I would make a space for myself here for now. The front entrance was not particularly secure, but at least the screaming hinges would give me warning if someone came in, so I could duck out the back entrance.

I went out to the sidewalk to retrieve my bike. I wasn't going to risk leaving it outside without me. Wheeling it through the dining room and into the kitchen, I positioned it behind the stove so that it formed a barrier between me and the rest of the room. The kitchen was small enough that the bike would slow down an intruder long enough to let me get out the back door.

I kicked a few dented, empty cans out of my way to clear a space for myself against the back wall. I shrugged off my backpack and pulled it into my lap as I sat cross-legged on the floor. I removed a tube of water and hunk of beef jerky and tried to make them last as long as possible to convince my grumbling stomach that they were enough to satisfy my hunger. It didn't work, but it did take the edge off enough to allow other needs to take precedence over my hunger.

I got to my feet again to look for something that would serve as a bathroom. An empty bucket underneath the front counter worked for the time being, though I would have to find a better solution if I stayed here for long. For now, though, I had taken care of the most urgent issues, and I really needed some sleep.

I closed up the backpack again and plumped it up as best I could, lying my head on it. I had a moment to be grateful that it was a warm summer night, since I had no blankets, and then I was asleep.

CHAPTER THIRTEEN

I woke the next morning, alerted by some small noise that told me I was no longer alone. My eyes flew open to meet a pair of golden eyes with slit-pupils only inches from my own. I gasped and scrambled backward as the large gray tomcat hissed at me, startled by my sudden movements.

My heart was still pounding in reaction, but I started laughing at myself. Hard to believe I'd been so scared of a harmless cat. He was still staring at me, ears flattened against his head. Feeling lonely and in need of a friend, I tried to coax the cat toward me. I stretched out my hand, calling, "Hey, kitty, kitty, kitty."

Instead of coming to me for petting and hugs, the cat hissed again and swiped at me with his front paw. I jerked my hand back just in time to avoid the sharp claws. He darted forward and began digging at my backpack, and I realized he could probably smell the jerky I'd eaten for dinner last night. That was undoubtedly the reason he'd approached in the first place.

I pulled the backpack away from him. I didn't want the cat clawing through my meager possessions. It was foolish to share; I had barely any food for myself. But still, I tore off a piece of my remaining jerky and tossed it to the big cat. His sharp white teeth snatched up the food before it hit the floor, and he ran away with his prize.

I broke off a piece of jerky for my own breakfast and chased it with one of my few remaining tubes of water. Finding a source of water had to be high on my priority list today. And since I was already awake, thanks to my early-morning visitor, I might as well get to work.

I made use of the bucket again, and then cautiously opened the back door. After looking around and listening hard for a couple of minutes, I felt fairly sure that there was no one around. I took my bucket outside and found a trench at the back of the alley where I could dump it. Judging from the stale odor lingering there, this was not the first time the trench had been used for this purpose.

Back inside I found a piece of twine on one of the dusty shelves and used it to tie the front door closed as tightly as I could manage. If anyone else came exploring while I was gone, I hoped it would discourage them from coming inside and discovering my bike. I was going to check out the neighborhood on foot today. The bike was simply too conspicuous if I wanted to stay unnoticed.

I removed the ignition stick and tucked it into my pocket to make it a little harder for anyone to make off with the bike. Stepping out the back door, I wound another piece of twine about the doorknob and a metal latch on the doorjamb using a series of complicated knots that would be hard for most people to recreate. If my knots were disturbed when I returned, I would know that someone might have entered the café. That was the only alarm system available to me, so it would have to do.

I checked out the rest of the shops along the short street. There were only three more intact enough to explore, and they were all as empty as my little hidey-hole. Clearly, these buildings had long since been raided for anything useful and abandoned once again. Though I saw another cat or two prowling in the alleys, I saw no sign of other people anywhere.

I couldn't remember the last time I had been truly alone. Even when I slept or visited the bathroom, I knew that a Secret Service agent was only a few feet away, ready to protect me from any sudden threat. I found the empty silence here oddly soothing and enjoyed knowing that for once there were no cameras or judgmental eyes trained on my every move.

After exploring the shops on the east side of the street and discovering nothing useful, I stood in the center of the street for a few minutes and looked around. It was the middle of the day, the sun high in the sky, yet somehow it still felt gloomy in contrast to the dazzling brightness of the white streets and buildings in Goodland. Here, the mounds of debris from fallen skyscrapers and razed neighborhoods cast long shadows over the streets even when the sun was shining brightly.

The pockets of shadow made it hard to pick out details in the mounds of rubble and twisted vines on the other side of the street, but after studying the section in front of me, I could just make out a door leading into a building that was only partially destroyed. Although I needed to go searching for a water source, I decided to check out that last shop building first, just in case the half-collapsed building hadn't been as thoroughly emptied as the rest.

Shoving some tendrils of hanging vines out of my way, I ducked inside the doorway I'd spotted. It was hard to see in the darkened hallway, but I made my way further inside, searching for anything useful.

Two doors off the hallway were already ajar. I poked my head inside each but didn't see anything worth grabbing. These rooms had been stripped down already. There was one more door at the end of the hall. A dusty plaque glued to the sturdy steel door declared that it was a storeroom. A collection of dents and pry marks announced that people had tried to force the door open, but it didn't look like anyone had been successful.

Feeling grateful for my father's unconventional training, I pulled the folding knife from my backpack. It had a couple of attachments that weren't exactly standard issue; they looked like a nail file and a small pry bar, but if you knew how to use them, they were a pretty efficient set of picks for most standard locks.

I set to work and was quite proud of myself for getting the lock to release after only a couple of minutes. I opened the door and grinned. These shelves were full!

The storeroom had apparently belonged to some sort of alternative lifestyle store because the stock on the shelves was not exactly standard fare. One entire wall was devoted to whips, chains, and cuffs of various styles. I actually took a whip and attempted to flick it a few times, wondering if I could use it as a weapon. Since the whip flopped limply as I waved it, I decided to leave it behind. I did grab a couple of lengths of chain and locks, though; they'd be better than twine for securing the doors of the café, and the chain could serve as a weapon as well.

The other two walls held shelves of clothing. To my amusement, most of it was black leather, just as I'd joked about with Sharra back at the train station. Pushing back the twinge of sadness that I'd lost my new friend so quickly, I sorted through the clothes to see if there was anything I could use.

The shelves nearest me had stacks of underwear and t-shirts. Though the underwear was certainly more risqué than I would have ever worn before, slutty underwear was still better than no underwear, and I tossed half a dozen sets into a pile by the door. I added a small stack of thin t-shirts in shades ranging from black to dark gray.

Next, I found several pairs of leather pants that fit reasonably well. They weren't really leather, of course. No one had used real leather in decades. The faux leather that was used instead was actually tougher and easier to care for than genuine leather, looked just as good, and was more breathable and less likely to chafe, making it much more comfortable to wear. Few people complained when true leather was outlawed.

I found a pair of knee-high boots that were a perfect fit and couldn't resist leaving them on. They looked so good even with my dirty jeans. I tossed my sneaks into the pile of things to take back to the café, then moved to the last shelf and grabbed some leather vests to wear over the thin t-shirts.

My wardrobe selections weren't just to appear more intimidating—though I hoped it would have that effect. The tough material would offer protection against any hazards I encountered.

The last thing I found was a couple of long, swirling black capes. Rolling my eyes at the thought of anyone walking around in a cape, I grabbed them anyway. The capes were made from heavy fabric, so they would work nicely as blankets for my bedroll.

I bundled all my treasures together in the capes and slung the makeshift pack over my shoulder. Stepping into the hallway, I closed the storeroom door with care behind me. I wanted to keep my discovery a secret from anyone else who might come this way, just in case I needed to come back for something.

I walked up the hall to the doorway where I'd entered and frowned. I remembered pushing a couple of hanging vines aside to go through the door, but there were a lot more vines crowding the only exit now. Since I could see thick thorns studding the vines, pushing them aside with my bare hands felt like a bad idea.

Instead, I used my new bundle of clothing as a sort of battering ram, slapping the vines out of my way and rushing through before they could swing back at me. Though it seemed likely that my overstressed brain was seeing things, I could have sworn that the thick vines deliberately twisted as they fell, reaching out for me. I ran for the street, only to trip and almost land on my face because one of the vines had somehow gotten twined around my ankle.

I yanked my foot free, glad that I had worn the leather boots. If I'd been wearing my jeans and sneaks, the thorns would have bitten deep into my leg. Thanks to my bundle of clothes and new boots, I'd gotten free of the clinging vines with only one scratch, an angry red line running from my left wrist almost to my elbow.

I realized that I was standing still in the center of the street, just staring at the scratch on my arm and watching the drops of blood well up and drip to the cracked pavement. I wasn't sure how long I'd been doing that; it felt like my thoughts were suddenly muffled in fog. I was so tired that my head was spinning. I just wanted to lie down and take a nap.

I caught myself as I almost sat down right there on the street and forced myself to place one foot in front of the other to make my way back to the café. The short trip back seemed to take hours as I staggered with exhaustion and confusion.

When I arrived at the back door, I found it nearly impossible to undo my own knots. I almost pulled out my knife to slice through the twine in order to get back inside. But after struggling with the rope for several long minutes, I managed to untie the knots and open the door. I lurched inside, slammed the door closed behind me, and fumbled the locks closed.

I dropped to my knees, unable to walk another step. I was barely able to crawl to the spot where I'd slept the previous night. I dropped my backpack and the bundled clothes and slumped to the floor beside them. I had the distant thought that I should probably clean the scratch but couldn't follow through enough to pull out my first-aid kit. Instead, I finally closed my eyes and let the whirling darkness in my head pull me under.

CHAPTER FOURTEEN

I felt an instant sense of déjà vu as I opened my eyes to see the gray cat staring at me. He leaned in close, and I thought for a moment that he was going to rub his head against my face. I smiled, anticipating the soft brush of fur along my cheek. Instead, the cat darted in, snagged the pack of jerky that was spilling from my backpack, and sauntered away.

He didn't bother to run, seeming to realize that I didn't have the ability to chase him. No, he trotted out of the kitchen, ears and tail cheerfully elevated as he clutched his prize in his teeth.

He was right, too. I was unable to chase him down and retrieve the jerky. In fact, it was a major effort just to drag myself to a sitting position, my head spinning as I leaned against the wall for support. My left arm throbbed, the pain making me grit my teeth, but I couldn't manage to lift the heavy limb so that my eyes could focus on the injury. I bent my head to look at the arm and almost fell onto my face when I overbalanced.

I pulled myself upright until I could lean against the wall again. In the back of my mind, I was aware that something was very wrong but couldn't focus my attention enough to worry about it. Instead, I concentrated on getting a good look at my painful scratch. I held my left wrist with my right hand and pulled the uncooperative arm closer to my face with great effort.

My vision swam, and I blinked fiercely to bring things back into focus. Finally, I got a good look at my arm and confirmed that the wound was not deep. It was only a scratch. But the scratch was swollen and oozing with yellow pus. I gagged a little. Disgusting.

There was no one here to help me, so I knew I had to care for it myself. Slowly, every movement feeling as if I were pushing through deep water, I pulled the backpack onto my lap and fumbled through it to find the first-aid kit.

I opened the kit and pulled out a tube of Derma-Seal. I set it aside for the moment. I couldn't apply the wound sealant until I had dealt with the infection. Deeper in the kit I found a jet-can of sterilizing solution. The jet-can used a blast of pressurized air to propel the sterilizing solution into a wound, cleaning the exposed tissue even as it applied a dose of anti-microbial medicine to fight infection.

I knew it was going to hurt. Gritting my teeth, I pushed the button. The medicated air shot out to scour the infected scratch clean. I almost dropped the jet-can at the screaming pain but forced myself to grimly hang on and finish the job. By the time I had cleaned the entire wound, I was panting and dripping with sweat. My whole body was shaking with reaction. I didn't know how a simple scratch could cause so much trouble.

I surveyed the injury with bleary eyes and was gratified to see that, though it was bleeding freely again, there was no longer any sign of the oozing infection. I smeared my arm with Derma-Seal to close the wound and stop the bleeding, and then applied a sterile pressure sleeve to further protect the injured area. I felt immediate relief as the pain-relieving medication that infused the bandage material started to numb my aching arm.

The pain had temporarily cleared my head, but now that it was easing, I felt my thinking turn fuzzy again. Working as fast as I was able, I reassembled the first aid kit and replaced it in the backpack. I removed one of my last precious water tubes and drank it thirstily. After stashing the flattened tube in the backpack, I closed all the latches. I didn't want that thieving cat to take any more of my limited supplies.

Exhausted, I laid down with the backpack as my pillow. I dragged one of the cloaks from the storeroom close enough to pull the edge over my body and let myself drift into sleep once again.

CHAPTER FIFTEEN

I opened my eyes to see the damn cat staring at me again. He probably hoped I would still be in a stupor that would leave him free to steal more of my food. But my mind was finally free of that smothering drowsiness, and I could think clearly again. My arm hurt, but not with the same intensity as before, and I felt like I would be able to get up and move around without falling over this time.

Still staring at the cat, I noticed that his muzzle and front paws were damp. My eyes widened with excitement. If the cat was still wet, there must be water somewhere nearby. If I could just track the cat back to the source, I would have drinking water. I knew cats were picky about the cleanliness of their drinking water, so if the cat could drink it, it was clean enough for me to drink as well.

I sat up slowly, not wanting to spook the cat into running away. He crouched, ears flattened, tail lashing, ready to bolt at the slightest threat. When I reached for the backpack, his whiskers twitched with interest. He knew that was where I kept the food. I dug through the small pack of food, looking for something else that would interest a cat. I rejected the protein bars in favor of a small plasti-pack of tuna and opened it with the pull tab.

The cat rose to his feet, nose twitching madly at the smell of the tuna. He was almost quivering as his desire to come investigate the scent fought with his instincts to stay out of reach. I wasn't generous enough to give all the tuna away; I needed food, too. So I used my fingers to dig out a small chunk of fish and flicked it to the eagerly waiting cat, then scooped a chunk into my own mouth.

We shared the container of fish, and it was gone far too soon. I slid the empty plasti-pack across the floor in his direction and let him lick out the remaining scraps and juices. I hoped the salty fish had made him as thirsty as it made me.

I watched him as he finished licking the container and then gave himself a good washing. Finally, he finished his meticulous grooming and got to his feet. As he walked away, I quietly got to my feet and followed. He looked back to see me following him but didn't seem particularly threatened. Maybe it was the presence of the backpack, that magical source of tasty treats, which reassured him.

He trotted through the kitchen to the front of the café and leapt onto the counter and from there onto a high shelf. I saw that there was a small window set high in the wall next to the shelf. The glass had long since broken out, making it a perfect doorway for an agile cat, but much too undersized for even a small human like myself. I turned and ran for the back door, hoping that I would be able to spot the cat again once I was outside.

I secured the door as quickly as possible, safety-conscious even in a hurry, and rounded the side of the building. My eyes searched the wall for the tiny window and spotted it just in time to see my feline friend leap from the window to a crumbling wall next to the café building. I trailed behind him as he walked to the end of the building and pushed through a barrier of thick, brushy vegetation. Lucky for me, these seemed to be normal, everyday kinds of plants instead of the vicious vines I'd encountered across the street. Behind the bushes, a small stream ran across the rocks. It looked well-established, like it was an offshoot of a regular water source, not just runoff from any recent rainstorms.

The cat leaned down to lap at the water, enjoying a long, leisurely drink. He turned and looked at me, as though to say: There, now we're even. Then he sauntered away and disappeared into the brush beyond the stream. I didn't follow him any further. I'd found what I was looking for. I dropped to my belly and used my hands to scoop up water, drinking from my cupped palms. The water tasted sweet and refreshing.

I chanced giving myself a makeshift bath while I was there, bathing in my clothes in order to give them a wash as well. I dripped my way back to the café, where I stripped out of the wet clothes and hung them across the kitchen appliances to let them dry.

I pulled on new clothes from my stash, added my boots, and used the makeup kit and tiny mirror that Sharra had given me at the train depot to repair my makeup and touch up the inked pattern on my face. Just because I hadn't seen anyone yet didn't mean I wouldn't, and I didn't want to be too recognizable if that happened.

I inspected myself as much as I could in the faint reflection on the stainless steel kitchen surfaces. The leather pants fit well and were actually quite comfortable. I'd also pulled on a thin black tee and one of the leather vests.

I smiled a little. With my short, spiky hair, dramatic face, and the black leather clothing, I looked tough and dangerous. Nothing at all like "Perfect Poppy," the First Lady. Even better, my appearance helped me feel tough and dangerous as well. I felt ready to take on the wild city where I now found myself. I shouldered my backpack and went out to explore and figure out my next steps.

I inspected the vines across the street from a safe distance. They looked still and benign in the morning sun, but I remembered how they had seemed to move toward me as I tried to leave. I found a stick on the ground and tossed it into the mound of plants then watched in fascination as the trailing vines immediately drew in around the stick, grabbing it tight.

The giant plant must be some type of Venus flytrap, I reasoned. The thorns had some kind of poison that muddled your thinking and left you inclined to just lie down and let the vines have their way. I was lucky that I hadn't been scratched until I was almost out of the plant's reach. If it had taken me any longer to move away, the creeping vines would have pulled me down and deep inside the plant, never to be seen again.

I shuddered and skirted widely around the vines. I would not be going back into that storeroom again. I would make do with what I had pulled out the first time.

I continued my exploration of the neighborhood. Now that I had clothing and water, my next priority was food. My small stock of supplies was shrinking rapidly, and I needed to find something more to eat. I had a firestarter attachment on my folding knife, so I could build a fire and cook my food if I could just find something edible.

I saw signs of small animals around the neighborhood. Rabbits maybe, or large rats. Either one should be edible. I retrieved the twine that I had been using on the doors—now replaced with the chains I'd found in the storeroom—and used it to make a few clumsy snares. My father had shown me how to do this, but it wasn't anything I'd practiced often. I thought I had the basic technique right, though.

I left the snares, knowing that I had to wait and see if they would catch anything. I kept exploring and eventually came across an old city park. Now, it was a wide stretch of overgrown lawn and trees. There was even an old playset still sitting there, just waiting for children to return and play again.

The grass was studded with dandelions and I plucked them with eager fingers, seeing that there were plenty here to provide a large handful of the edible leaves. Dandelions grew quickly, too. The ones I picked today would be ready to harvest again in a matter of days. Even better, when I cautiously investigated a clump of bushes at the edge of the park, I found that they bore clusters of wild strawberries. I sat down right there and ate my dinner, a tasty salad of dandelion greens and strawberries.

Afterward, I checked the trees growing in the park and found that several of them had ripe apples and another was covered in plums. I picked as many of each as I could cram into my backpack and headed "home" feeling happy and hopeful. I checked the snares on the way back and saw that they were still empty, but I wasn't bothered. I had everything I needed to survive for the moment.

CHAPTER SIXTEEN

It was hard to keep track of time, but I thought that I had been living in my little café for about three weeks. I had fallen into a daily routine that included eating my fill of fruit for breakfast before washing up at the stream, foraging for edible plants for lunch and dinner, practicing my martial arts routine in order to stay fit, and checking my snares. The snares were almost always empty, but twice I had caught a small rabbit with my carefully-placed traps.

Skinning and gutting the animals was a struggle. In theory it seemed simple enough to remove the skin and innards, but I found it much more difficult than expected when I tried it. It was worth it, though, when I got to roast the chunks of meat over a tiny fire.

I didn't want to have the fire and scent of cooking meat too close to where I slept, just in case they attracted attention, so I'd built a little fire ring beneath an apple tree at the park. I spitted the meat on long sticks and broiled them over the flames before devouring the protein. I even shared little bits of the meat with the gray cat, who continued to show up sporadically hoping for treats. He still wouldn't let me pet him, but he was willing to take any food I tossed his way.

I drifted through the days, focusing on nothing more than filling my basic needs. Honestly, I knew I should probably put some effort into finding Sharra, but I had been in the spotlight for almost my entire life. It was so nice to be able to do what I wanted when I wanted. No one was watching my every move, ready to judge and criticize me. No one was scheduling every minute of my day with activities that were supposedly important but only felt trivial.

When I'd first run from the White House, I had burned with fervor to somehow regroup and return to make Cruz pay. But that was before I'd realized how much effort was required to simply survive out here on my own. And remembering what had happened to my beloved father sent me spiraling into crushing sadness that made it hard to even function, so I'd chosen instead to not think about it. Besides, what could I do? I was one girl. I had barely managed to escape in the first place; what made me think I could do anything but die if I went back?

An unexpected sound pulled me free of my thoughts and I froze to listen. Faint voices were drifting in my direction. People! I hadn't seen another person since escaping from Dandelion Man and his band of merry men. I had been on my own for so long that the idea of talking to someone other than the cat was exciting. At the same time, my last encounter with people in this city had almost gotten me killed. I wasn't going to just pop out and introduce myself without getting a feel for what kind of people they were. Instead, I followed the voices, keeping to the shadows so that the people wouldn't spot me.

The voices led me to Kalamath Street, where the remains of a large roundabout left a fairly clear space among the dilapidated buildings. Creeping forward, I moved close enough to get a look at the men who were speaking. To my surprise, I recognized one of them. It was the guy I'd called Laughing Boy. The last time we'd met he'd been kind and helpful. After a moment's hesitation, I stepped out where the approaching men could see me.

As soon as Laughing Boy spotted me, his eyes lit up. "Hey!" he exclaimed. "Hey!" He waved at me in greeting.

I smiled and gave a small wave in return as I walked closer.

"I wondered where you'd disappeared to," he said. "It looks like you've been managing okay. No more run-ins with mutant dogs?"

I laughed a little. "No mutant dogs, luckily, though I did have an encounter with some kind of mutant plant." I held up my arm to display the angry red scar running from wrist to elbow.

"Man-eating vines," I told them. "There's some kind of poison on the thorns that will make you happy to just lie down and let the vines keep you."

"They are terrible, those plants," the second man commented. He had a deep voice and a lilting Spanish accent that caught my attention immediately. I turned to study him as he continued, "I have come across these vines before. It is best to simply burn them out. When the winter cold comes, the vines will dry up. They burn more easily then."

I nodded, recognizing a good idea when I heard it. I would toss a few firebrands into the nest of vines as soon as they started to dry up. That is, assuming I was still here at that point.

"Thanks for the tip," I said, as I held out my hand to introduce myself. "I'm Poppy," I told him. It hadn't occurred to me until the words left my mouth that maybe I should use a different name. But it was too late now. I would only draw more attention to myself if I tried to backtrack now. At least I'd only offered my first name.

"Mateo, of the Liberty pack," he replied, taking my hand. He didn't shake it as I'd expected, just held it firmly in his own large hand as he looked me over. Since he didn't seem inclined to stop his close inspection any time soon, I returned the favor and scrutinized him in return.

He was only four inches taller than my own five foot nothing, making him fairly short for a man. But his stocky build was muscled and looked powerful, so it wouldn't do to underestimate him. Shiny black hair waved around a swarthy, handsome face, and a thin mustache defined his upper lip. He was quite attractive, except for the way he kept my hand clutched in his own damp palm despite my efforts to discreetly pull away.

He stepped closer, still holding on to my hand. "So, Poppy, are you on your own out here? This is not a good area for a little girl to be all by herself."

I frowned at him and stepped back, finally managing to pull my hand free. No matter how attractive he was, I didn't like the way he looked at me and didn't feel inclined to share any personal information with him, so I simply turned to my left and focused on Laughing Boy instead.

"What about you?" I asked. "Do you have a name?"

He smiled, his teeth a bright flash in the deepening twilight and a dimple appeared in one bronzed cheek. "Rivers, from the Wolf pack," he told me, holding out a hand for me to shake. "Eric Rivers, actually, but no one calls me Eric."

Unlike Mateo's sweaty, prolonged grip, Rivers simply gave my hand a quick shake and let go again. My heart stuttered a little as I touched his calloused palm. His cheerful smile and friendly gaze were a stark contrast to Mateo's slick grin and oily stare. Rivers felt safe and trustworthy, even on short acquaintance, while Mateo's attention felt slightly threatening.

Deciding that I would rather no one knew exactly where I was based, I smiled at the men and changed the subject. "So is this your territory? I've come through this neighborhood a time or two and haven't run across anyone before."

"No one really claims this area," Rivers told me. "There's just not much here to make it worth setting up a base."

I nodded. "I noticed the same thing," I lied. "That's why I found a place to hole up down that way instead." I jerked a thumb over my shoulder to imply that I had a place to stay that was in the opposite direction of my little café. "After my run-in with those vines my first time through here, I didn't want to stay anywhere close to them!"

Mateo's eyes gleamed. "No, it wouldn't be safe for a little thing like you to stay in this neighborhood by yourself. It is too empty. Isolated."

I just stared at him for a moment. Was he trying to scare me? Or was he really just that socially awkward? It was just possible that he didn't realize how it sounded when he said things like that. Rivers caught it, though he didn't seem concerned.

He clapped his companion on the shoulder. "Cut it out, Matty. You're starting to sound like a creeper."

Mateo looked startled, then turned back to me with the intensity dialed way down. "I apologize," he told me. "I was concerned for your safety; I did not mean to make you uncomfortable."

I smiled at him, relieved that it appeared he was just bad with social norms after all. "No problem," I assured him. "I appreciate the concern." Switching subjects, I asked Rivers, "So if this isn't your territory, what brings you this way?"

"Hunting," Rivers replied easily. "I have snares set up around here that catch the occasional rabbit or squirrel. Sometimes a nice fat rat. Mateo's out hunting for his pack, too."

I wrinkled my nose. I hadn't been able to bring myself to try eating rat yet even though they were more common than the rabbits I was sometimes able to catch. Rivers saw the look on my face and laughed.

"City girl," he teased. "Try living rough for another couple of months, and you'll be happy for a bit of rat for dinner."

I smiled and shook my head. "Maybe," I agreed, "but not yet. For now, I'm doing okay without the rat."

"So you're on your own?" Rivers asked. "I thought you were joining a pack?"

"My friend and I got separated the night we met," I told him. I glanced sideways at Mateo. I didn't know what he knew about my first encounter with Rivers. Maybe it was best not to mention anything. However, Rivers didn't hesitate to mention it.

"Mat, this is the girl I told you about, the one who helped Eddie beat himself up and then fed him to a Shadow hound."

I blushed a little at his admiring tone.

"She is not so large as I expected," Mateo said thoughtfully. "I have heard Eddie speak of this, and in his telling, she is a hulking warrior woman." He winked at me, and I laughed a little, charmed.

"He's okay, then?" I asked. "I wouldn't wish a dog attack on anyone, really. I just didn't have many options at the time."

"The Shadow took down Dirty Jin, but he's definitely no loss," Rivers told me. "Eddie got a little torn up, and he's still getting over the bites. He'll probably survive, though, once the poison works its way out of his system."

I winced a little. "Sorry?" I wasn't exactly sorry, but I wasn't happy to hear that someone had died, either.

"Don't be," Rivers said bluntly. "It's nothing more than they deserved. Most people around here are decent, but there are a few who like to think that living rough means there are no rules. That group was outside our territory, deliberately setting up an ambush, and they didn't have any good intentions for anyone they caught. I found out what they were up to and tracked them down. I was trying to send them home when you and your friend came through."

"I just want you know," he added earnestly, "I wouldn't have just stood by and let them go at you. I was just figuring out what I should do next when you took care of things on your own."

"That's good to know," I told him. "I've wondered what you were doing with that group. Why are you with people like that?"

"They're my pack," he said. "They're not perfect, but they're family. Eddie is our pack leader, but I'm his second, so I can head off most of his crazy ideas. One of these days he'll get himself killed and then I can really straighten things out. Until then, I do what I can."

"Should I avoid this area? I don't want to run into any of them again." Even the memory of that night was enough to make me break into a cold sweat; I certainly didn't want to repeat the experience.

"I'd stay south of Kalamath just to be on the safe side, but none of that group comes this far south. They like to hunt closer to home."

I filed that away for future reference and changed the subject since I didn't want to dwell on the whole unpleasant encounter any longer. I turned the conversation back to where it had started.

"So yeah, I lost track of the friend I was with, and I'm not with her pack after all. I don't know if you'd know her; her name is Sharra. She had pink and blue hair the last time I saw her." I motioned vaguely around my face as I added, "Kind of dusky gold skin tone and brown eyes, I think. Very pretty. She said her pack was somewhere downtown, but that's as much detail as I have."

Rivers shook his head. "Not ringing any bells," he told me. "But I've only recently moved up in the pack to the point that I interact with anyone outside our pack. I don't know many people outside my immediate neighborhood yet. And what we consider the downtown area is pretty big. There are quite a few packs around. But I'll keep my ears open for someone fitting that description."

I glanced at Mateo. He was shaking his head also, but something about the look in his eyes made me wonder if he knew more than he was saying. I didn't press, though. I wasn't actually ready to find Sharra yet. I needed time on my own to heal before I went back to living with people again. However, I didn't think I should let Mateo know that I was living alone.

I told the men, "I'm not on my own though. I met up with someone and we're sharing space ... kind of a roommate, I guess. We help each other get food and water. It's working out pretty well."

They didn't need to know that my roommate was actually only a moody tomcat who, other than leading me to water that first time, really didn't bother to help out around the place.

"That's good," Rivers said, looking relieved. "It's always better to have someone around to watch your back. Listen, though ... if you need help, you can come to Wolf pack. I'll protect you from Eddie and his buddies."

"Or to the Liberty pack," Mateo added. "I would be glad to speak to the pack leaders on behalf of a ... friend." He licked his full lips and lingered suggestively over the last word as his gaze slid over my curves.

Ick. I could just imagine the friendly favors that Mateo would expect in return for that recommendation. No thank you. I was better off on my own.

"Well, thanks for the offers, guys, but things are okay for now. I'm just going to head home before it gets much later. I don't want my roommate to get worried." I wasn't sure the cat would notice my absence, much less worry about me, but it didn't hurt to reinforce the idea that I wasn't alone.

I raised my hand in a quick wave as I started walking northeast; my café was actually due south from here, but I stuck with the misdirection I'd used earlier about where I was staying.

"Take care," Rivers called to me. "I come around this way once a week or so to check my traps. Maybe we'll bump into each other again?"

"Maybe," I agreed. "See you. Later, Mateo."

Mateo only nodded, his dark eyes tracking my path through the rubble-crowded street. I faded into the shadows as soon as possible, trying to be sure they couldn't see exactly where I had gone. Moving on silent feet, I crept up the back of a tumbled stack of cinderblocks and drywall and tucked in behind a heap of debris.

I could just barely see Mateo and Rivers standing together in the street where I'd left them, and I couldn't hear their conversation at all. They finished speaking and headed off in separate directions. Rivers went west, Mateo moved north, and both disappeared from view.

Trained by my father to be excessively cautious, I stayed where I was. My restraint paid off after a few minutes when Mateo silently reappeared in the street where we had met. He prowled the area, obviously looking for something. I couldn't be sure that he was trying to find where I had gone, but it sure looked that way.

I watched Mateo pick his way through the cluttered street in the direction I had gone. He passed directly below me, gazing intently into the shadows and peering at the nooks and crannies that could have hidden a small person. Like most people, he never thought to look up, so he didn't catch a glimpse of me.

I waited until he was out of sight and then waited a few minutes more. Finally satisfied that he was gone for now, I made my way back to my café. I blocked the doors with extra care once I was inside. Something about Mateo had spooked me, and I needed to feel like my little home was still a safe retreat.

Once I was convinced that the café was as secure as I could make it, I settled into my bedroll for a night of restless sleep.

CHAPTER SEVENTEEN

The next few weeks slid by in blur of routine. I focused on the routine so that I didn't have to think about anything else. Every memory of my father or the events of that horrible night brought a wave of pain that threatened to incapacitate me, so I pushed the memories away. I didn't consider about my next steps or what might be happening in Goodland. I didn't worry about the resistance movement that Sharra had mentioned. I refused to think about anything but my day-to-day survival.

I wouldn't call my days monotonous because it seems like a ridiculous description for days that regularly included a chance of death or grievous injury. Still, every day included the same tasks again and again: collect water, forage for food, check traps for game, practice my self-defense skills, and most importantly, avoid deadly plants, mutant animals, and dodgy people.

I ran into Rivers every three or four days. I had the impression he was deliberately checking in on me. I didn't mind that, but Mateo was coming around as well. I didn't enjoy seeing Mateo. He was always staring at me like a predator sizing up prey and took every opportunity to brush up against me, touch my arm, or stroke my hair when Rivers wasn't around.

Though I had told him repeatedly to keep his hands to himself, the message never stuck. Even worse, I'd caught him trying to follow me home again just yesterday and turned back to confront him over it.

"What do you think you're doing, Mateo?" I'd asked.

"Nothing, my love. I am only trying to be sure that you reach your home safely," he'd told me, all innocent eyes and charming smile.

I hadn't been fooled.

"I'm not your love," I'd told him firmly. "And I don't need you to see me safely home. Turn around and go back to your own home." I'd glared at him, arms crossed and jaw clenched in anger. As usual, Mateo hadn't taken me seriously and only smiled and shook his head.

"As you say, my dear. I will see you another day." He'd started to walk away, but at the last minute turned around and bent to kiss me. I'd jerked my head to the side so his lips only grazed my cheek and shoved him away with both hands on his broad chest. He let himself be pushed back but only so he had a better view of my cleavage.

"Go. Home." I'd gritted out. "Do not follow me again, or I will make you regret it."

Mateo had stroked his hand over my right cheek and then let it slide down my neck, across the outside curve of my breast and onto my hip. I'd shoved him again, this time with plenty of force, and he lost his grip on me as he stumbled back a step.

To my dismay, he'd only laughed as if my resistance was a flirtatious game. He whistled cheerfully as he finally turned and walked away. He hadn't been at all discouraged by my anger. I wasn't sure what it would take to convince him that I wasn't interested. I'd about decided I was going to have to break a finger or his nose or something in order to really get his attention.

I hadn't yet resorted to really getting physical with him, because I didn't want to make an outright enemy of him. I was sure he could be vicious, and I would rather have him trying to be friendly—in his own nasty way—than actively trying to harm me. I had considered asking Rivers to intervene, but it went against the grain to show weakness by going to him for help.

A rumble of thunder startled me out of my reverie. I glanced at the sky and confirmed that the usual afternoon storm was rolling in. Black clouds were racing east from the mountains, and I knew that I had only twenty or thirty minutes before the soaking rains began. Abandoning plans to check more trap lines, I headed for home in an attempt to beat the rain. In spite of my hurry, I was careful to keep watch behind me to be sure that Mateo was not around. I didn't want him to follow me home.

As summer eased into fall, I had learned that autumn in Denver involved lots of rain. It was practically guaranteed that a booming thunderstorm complete with wind, rain, and hail would hit the city every afternoon. The regular rain made it easy to keep my water supply full even though the afternoon storms cut down on my time for gathering food. The rain also dropped the afternoon temperature abruptly, leading to some uncomfortably cold nights already. I was not looking forward to winter. If the autumn storms continued into winter, they would leave a lot of snow behind.

Not for the first time, I thought about trying to track down Sharra and her pack. Presumably they were set up to make it through the winter, where I was not. I hadn't done anything about it so far because I wanted to be alone, but I was starting to think that I would soon have no choice. I wasn't sure I could deal with a long, cold winter on my own, and Mateo was becoming more of a problem every day.

Looking for Sharra's pack was probably my best option. I didn't want to join Rivers' pack because it meant I would have to deal with Eddie and his friends. And I certainly wasn't going to ask Mateo to take me back to join his pack.

I had a third friend of sorts out here, a woman in her fifties or sixties who lived packless. Leeza didn't exactly dislike other people; she was friendly enough whenever we met. She just didn't want to live with people all the time. She and I often saw each other when we were gathering berries down by the creek, and we talked while we worked. I'd told her part of my story—the part about coming to town with Sharra and then losing her—and learned that she actually knew Sharra.

Leeza and Sharra had known each other when Sharra had first arrived in Denver and was living rough, much like me. When Sharra had decided to join a pack, Leeza had declined. She preferred to stay on her own. But Leeza knew the general area that Sharra's pack claimed as territory and had told me how to find the neighborhood if I decided to go looking.

I shook my head and pushed the thoughts of my father and winter away as I always did. I wasn't ready to go searching for a pack yet. I preferred the solitude in spite of the hardships. I wasn't sure I was willing to follow Leeza's example and stay solo for the long term, but for right now it suited me. Maybe in another couple of weeks I would be ready to be with other people full-time again.

CHAPTER EIGHTEEN

As the last weeks of fall slipped away, Rivers and I settled into a routine of meeting in the Kalamath roundabout every three days for lunch. We'd each bring a bit of food to contribute and share it to make a meal. Mateo sometimes showed up to join us, but he had finally backed off and seemed willing to accept that I wasn't interested in any sort of relationship. I didn't enjoy spending time with him, but I could deal with an occasional meeting.

I kept my guard up and kept my distance and was grateful to accept the food they shared. They regularly brought meat saved from the previous evening's meal. My traps hadn't gotten any better, and it was getting harder to find fruit and other edible plants as the weather grew colder. I wasn't starving exactly, but those leather pants were fitting more loosely than they used to.

Based on the way they gave the largest portions of lunch to me each time we met, I was sure Rivers and Mateo realized that I was running short on food. I was hungry enough not to argue, though.

As usual our mealtime conversation consisted of gossip about the local packs and our version of current events.

"I saw a bear over by the river," I offered. "It was clearing out the last of the blackberries from that patch of bushes under the freeway overpass."

"Did it give you any trouble?" Rivers asked.

"Nope," I said around a mouthful of roasted rabbit. "I saw the bear before it saw me, so I turned and hightailed it out of there."

The men laughed as I'd intended. Though Rivers had seen me scuffle with Eddie a little on the first night we'd met, and I'd had very small altercations with Mateo, neither man really knew that I could fight. Instead, I'd used an old strategy I'd learned from my father and cultivated an image of myself as someone less capable and competent than I really was. Let them think that I was a little weak and needed taking care of; it just meant they would underestimate me if we ever found ourselves at odds.

Mateo offered his local news next. "You should avoid the Monarch pack's territory. They have found a way to collect and store flammable gasses. I do not know where they are storing it, so it would be best to stay far away from the territory altogether. The rumor is that the containers are not very stable and tend to explode without notice."

Rivers looked profoundly unhappy at this news. "They're going to burn the city down around our ears," he complained. "Even Eddie thinks it's a bad idea to try bottling that stuff. And Eddie's not exactly a voice of reason."

"What are they doing with it?" I asked, mystified. "Why do they need bottles of flammable gas in the first place?"

"Well, you know, in case of revolution," Rivers said, as if it were the most obvious thing in the world.

"Revolution?"

"Against the corrupt government," Mateo proclaimed vehemently, his eyes alight with fervor. "Someone must bring them down. We cannot just continue to let the government turn the citizens into sheep … into puppets. We must stop them at any cost!"

"I don't know about any cost," Rivers disagreed. "There have to be limits."

"Um, yeah," I agreed. "This whole idea is crazy. You want to blow up the government? That's ridiculous! Our system of government may not be perfect, but it's certainly better than chaos and anarchy! Without a stable government in place, everyone is in danger. And how do you decide who makes up 'the government' in the first place? Is it everyone in the White House? The Capitol? Everyone in Goodland? Where do you draw that line?"

Now Rivers leaned forward, his words quick and intense. "Look, Poppy, I don't know your exact background, but I get the impression that you weren't exactly struggling along in the middle class before you ended up in Denver. So I get it that you've been living in your little ivory tower world, above all the petty little annoyances we real people have to deal with, but here's a news flash for you. The government is not a noble, kindly, overseer looking out for all the citizens with love and care. It's a machine. And the people running the machine don't know or care how many ordinary people get run over as the machine moves along its way. It just may be that in order to make things better for everyone, we have to start by taking that machine out of the picture."

"An ivory tower world, huh?" I replied. "Well maybe so, but you live in a world full of paranoid, guerrilla-warrior wannabes, so here's a news flash for you. That government machine you rail against is just a lot of people. People just like you who love their friends and families and who are just doing a job. They're not gleefully plotting the downfall of all the so-called regular people; they are regular people. And if you go in there with

129

plots and schemes and scarily-unstable homemade bombs to bring down the government, those are the people who are going to get hurt. Now, if you want to do something to go after corruption at the top and bring that down, I'm right there with you. But you will never convince me that there is a good reason to slaughter innocent people just to get to the people you think you need to eliminate."

I got to my feet, unwilling to spend another moment with Rivers. I suddenly felt like I didn't even know him, someone I'd come to feel was a real friend. Judging from the look on his face, he was feeling similar disappointment in me.

"I'll see you in a few days," I told them abruptly, and stalked away. I was so disturbed by our argument that I forgot to head off in the wrong direction and walked south toward my café. For all these weeks, I'd been careful to not give any clues to the location of my home base and now I'd stomped off directly toward it. I swore under my breath at my own stupidity, but there was nothing to be done about it now.

I hid and watched my back trail to be sure that no one was following me, but when neither of the men appeared after several long minutes, I relaxed a little. I watched for a few minutes longer, then more carefully worked my way back home.

I sulked inside my café for an hour or so, rehearsing our short argument over and over in my mind. Of course, I was able to come up with much better responses now. The gray tomcat was the one to finally break me out of my brooding. He had come in through the window, hoping to find something to eat. After I'd ignored him for too long, he proceeded to get my attention with a few ear-splitting yowls.

Forced to focus on him, I shook myself out of my bad-temper. "Hey, Roomie," I said. "Don't worry, I didn't forget about you." I rooted through my ever-present backpack to find the bits of rabbit that I had saved from my lunch and wrapped in a couple of large leaves. Pulling the small package from the side pocket, I made kissy-noises at Roomie, trying to convince him to come closer. I laid the rabbit on the floor near my leg and sat very still so I wouldn't spook him. He slowly belly-crawled toward me, inching tentatively closer to his treat. When he finally reached the rabbit, he pounced on the shreds of meat.

He was so busy enjoying the food that he didn't bother to shy away when I reached out to scratch between his ears. He only allowed me to pet him when I brought food, but that small bit of affection was better than nothing. For a change, he didn't bolt away the moment he'd finished eating. He tolerated my petting for an extra minute or so, then jumped onto the countertop and began to wash.

Buoyed a little by Roomie's near-friendliness, I pulled myself together and got ready to go back out to check my trap lines. Shouldering my backpack, I said goodbye to the cat and headed out to look for food.

Two hours later I trudged back home, discouraged. I'd caught nothing in my snares and found only a few withered berries left on my usual bushes. Even the dandelions were starting to die off for the season; they had been a major staple of my diet since I'd settled in here. I wasn't sure what I could replace them with. A flash of movement from the corner of my eye snagged my attention from my food worries.

I snapped my head left, looking for threats—and saw Mateo.

"Hello, my love," he called. "It appears I have finally found your home."

"Why did you follow me, Mateo?"

"I only want to get to know you better, little one," he said in a coaxing voice. "We could be such good friends if you would just give me the chance." He crossed the street toward me as he talked.

I wanted to back away, but I also didn't want to appear intimidated, so I stood my ground. I let the backpack slide off my shoulders to hit the pavement and used my foot to nudge it aside so it wouldn't get in my way. I settled my weight on the balls of my feet, my muscles tensed and ready to spring into action.

"Mateo," I said evenly. "I've made it very clear to you that I'm not interested in that kind of friendship. You need to leave now."

"I have been very patient with you, querida. But it is time to stop playing games."

"This isn't a game, Mateo! Go away. Go now."

"I am very disappointed to hear this. You are being very unkind, and I have been nothing but pleasant to you."

I was furious, and in my anger I let my guard down for just a moment. He took immediate advantage, lunging forward to wrap his arms around me. He was not a big man, but he was solid and very strong. His arms were like steel bands holding me against him and trapping my arms and hands between our chests.

He ground his mouth into mine, kissing me roughly. When I tried to turn my head away, he reached up with one hand to painfully grab a handful of my short hair and hold my head still. This loosened his grip on my arms, and I was able to pull my right hand free. I punched him in the side of the throat as I stomped on his instep with my booted foot. I didn't do much damage, but I did startle him enough that he stopped kissing me.

"Stop this, Poppy," he snarled. "You will not win this fight."

Before I could respond, I heard a familiar yowling cry and Roomie leapt from the crumbling wall behind us to land on Mateo's shoulders. His wicked claws slashed at Mateo's back, causing him to finally release me as he flailed at the cat. Before I could intervene, Mateo got a good grip on Roomie and flung him violently through the air.

The cat hit the front window of the café with a sickening crunch, followed by the dissonant clatter of breaking glass. The entire front window collapsed into jagged shards, burying Roomie in the sharp pile of glass fragments. He didn't move or make a sound.

I rounded on Mateo, ready to beat him to a pulp. I punched him twice in the stomach before he could react, and he doubled over, gasping for breath. I would have continued if I hadn't heard a faint, pathetic meow.

I ran back to the café and started to unearth Roomie from the pile of glass. I hadn't forgotten Mateo though, so he didn't take me by surprise when he rushed up behind me. I moved to the side, sticking out a foot to tangle his legs and trip him up. He fell, striking his head on the pavement. He wasn't unconscious, but he was definitely woozy and seemed unable to focus enough to get up and attack again.

I left him where he was and turned back to my cat. I knew Roomie was hurt when he actually let me pick him up and carry him to the sidewalk. I knelt on the ground with him, gently running my hands over him to try and locate his injuries. But I wasn't a veterinarian. I couldn't find any open wounds or obvious deformities, so I had no idea what might be wrong. I could only stroke him gently and try to comfort him.

Mateo was still lying dazed, so I cradled Roomie in my arms, scooped my backpack off the street, and walked back inside the café. I settled the cat inside the backpack, trying to make him as comfortable as possible. I left him there to rest while I quickly gathered my sparse belongings and bundled them into one of the large cloaks. I used some of my twine to tie the bundle to the back of the mag-lev bike. I pulled the backpack onto my shoulders, moving slowly and gently so I wouldn't disturb Roomie.

I grabbed the handlebars of the bike and rolled it out of the kitchen, through the shattered glass littering the floor of the front room, and out the front door. Now that Mateo had discovered my refuge, I knew it would never feel safe again. I was leaving.

I swung my leg over the bike and settled onto the seat as I inserted the ignition stick and turned on the engine. I rolled right past Mateo's prone form without a second thought. He was still groaning. He wasn't dead, so he'd just have to take care of himself.

I clicked onto the first clear mag-lev rail I came to and switched the bike to full mag-lev mode. The engine purred to life. I twisted the accelerator and shot forward, leaving my first home in Denver behind.

CHAPTER NINETEEN

During the past few months, I'd scoped out a few potential places for refuge in case my home base was compromised. Now, I maneuvered my bike through the debris-strewn streets on my way to one of my backup shelters. I moved northwest, headed for the old football stadium.

I had learned that while the stadium itself was held by the small La Soltura pack, the neighborhoods around the stadium were unclaimed territory. These buildings were in serious disrepair, discouraging most people from using them as shelter, and any building still standing had been explored and cleared useful items long ago. No one around here would care if I spent a few nights in the area, and I was far enough from my previous neighborhood that Mateo would be unlikely to stumble across me. For the moment, that was all I was looking for.

I worked my way deeper into the neighborhood, stopping occasionally to move chunks of concrete or other rubble blocking my path. Finally, I reached the small set of doctor's offices I had chosen as my hideaway. Though the front lobby area no longer existed, it was just barely possible to walk my bike through an unroofed hallway to reach the lone treatment room that still boasted four walls, a door, and most of the roof.

I wheeled the bike into the tiny room and squeezed past it to enter the room myself. I had to shift the bike around a couple of times to make space for the door to close, but I managed to shut the door behind me and flipped the small thumb lock on the doorknob for the small bit of extra security that it offered.

A chunk of ceiling and the walls were missing in the southwest corner of the room, letting in the last bit of light from the setting sun. Soon it would be completely dark, so I knew I needed to unpack quickly if I wanted any light to work with.

I climbed onto the exam table that was still bolted to the center of the floor. Though the faux leather covering was aged and cracked, at least the table was slightly padded. It was probably a better bed than the corner of the kitchen floor I'd used back in my café.

Sitting cross-legged on the table, I took off my backpack and pulled it into my lap. Opening the flap, I peered inside to check on Roomie. The poor cat opened his eyes and meowed pitifully. I knew he was in rough shape when he didn't even try to swipe at me as I cautiously put my hand inside the pack to stroke his head.

"I'm sorry, buddy," I murmured. "I wish I knew how to help you feel better. If it helps any, I stomped Mateo hard for what he did to you." Though it was only a coincidence, I liked to think that the reason Roomie began to purr at that moment was because he was glad to hear that I'd made Mateo pay for his rough treatment.

I rummaged in the front pocket of the bag for a moment and found the last bits of rabbit from lunch. I had saved this small packet when I'd shared my leftovers earlier, thinking I could give it to Roomie as a dinnertime treat. Plucking the shreds of meat from the leaves it was wrapped in, I hand-fed the little pieces to the lethargic cat. When he had finished the rabbit, he licked my fingers clean of grease and then fell asleep.

I wrapped myself in both of my cloaks, then settled the backpack at the top of the exam table and curled myself around it to sleep.

CHAPTER TWENTY

I woke up shaking with cold the next morning. Small snowflakes drifted lazily through the gap in the ceiling to land on my face, which certainly didn't help. I wrapped myself more tightly in my cloaks and hugged the backpack to my chest hoping for some extra warmth from Roomie's body heat. He grumbled a little at the jostling but didn't try to escape my embrace.

I snaked one hand into the opening at the top of the bag, lightly stroking Roomie's head and chin while I thought about my options. I hated running from Mateo, but I wasn't willing to stay and make a target of myself either. He was going to be very angry now. Well fine, I was angry too. I wanted to fight him again. I wanted to break his face for what he'd done to my cat and what he'd tried to do to me.

But I was also sensible enough that I wasn't going to go searching for another confrontation. Better to just get out of the situation, especially since I'd already started to think about leaving.

Since winter had begun approaching in earnest, I'd come to realize that I wouldn't be able to continue on my own. Food was getting hard to find and resources would only be getting scarcer. And this first taste of really cold weather had me shivering so violently that the exam table rattled a little. Two heavy cloaks and my trusty boots made up the sum total of my winter gear. This wasn't going to protect me against any extreme weather or cold. I needed to team up with one of the local packs for protection. I just had to decide who to approach. In spite of my friendship with Rivers, recent argument notwithstanding, I wasn't willing to join his pack. Voluntarily putting myself in Eddie's reach was just as bad as hanging out with Mateo.

Liberty pack was the largest alliance in the downtown area and controlled the largest territory. But Mateo was a Liberty pack member, so that was a definite no.

I'd learned about various other packs during my lunches with Rivers, and none of them stood out as great options. I hadn't met anyone from those groups, so I didn't have connections that would help me join up.

Really, my only choice was to find Sharra. Though Leeza didn't know which pack Sharra belonged to, she had given me directions that would probably lead me to Sharra, eventually. If I started asking around once I was in that northeast neighborhood, chances were good that I could track her down. There weren't so many people living rough that you could just disappear as part of the crowd, and that bright aqua and pink hair would make her pretty memorable.

I didn't know Sharra well, but she had helped me get out of Goodland. I had felt an immediate connection with her when we met—enough to make me follow her here to Denver. Now that I needed to abandon my solitary lifestyle, finding Sharra felt like the right thing to do. After all, nothing was going to force me to stay with her if I didn't like her or her pack. I would stay here for a day or two to nurse Roomie back to health, and then I would go looking for a friend and a pack to take me in.

Decision made, I supposed it was time to drag myself out of my slightly warm bed, so I pushed the cloak aside and slid off the exam table. I did a few stretches and jogged in place for a couple of minutes to warm up a little and work out the kinks of sleeping on a hard table. Even for someone of my short stature, the table was too short and narrow to be comfortable.

I needed to scout around for water. I was hungry too, but we could go longer without food than without water. Grabbing one of my cloaks, I bundled up against the cold. I managed to tie the cloak around me in such a way that it looked odd but kept me fairly warm and didn't impede movement too much.

I peeked into the backpack to check on Roomie. He was sleeping but woke as soon as I lifted the flap. I petted his head gingerly, encouraged when he actually tilted his chin to give me better access to stroke his ears. I ran careful fingers along his sides and down each of his legs. He growled once and snapped at me when I gently pressed on what I thought were probably his ribs. That made sense—his ribs could certainly be bruised from crashing through the window.

He was still lethargic but otherwise seemed okay, so I just tried not to disturb him too much as I reached past him to find the small bowl I had scavenged from a house near my old location. It wasn't large, but it would hold a little water to bring back for Roomie.

I left the remains of the medical clinic and chose a direction at random, hoping to find water before I'd gone too far. The odds were in my favor. I'd learned from Rivers that several dams in the area had been destroyed in the bombings. The resulting floods as the reservoirs emptied had destroyed even more of the city. But with the water no longer held in reservoirs, many small creeks and streams had reestablished themselves across the landscape. There was plenty of water to be found in Denver; most of it was even clean enough to drink.

I only had to walk a few blocks before I found what I was looking for. A decent-sized stream tumbled through the rubble. It looked clear and clean. It seemed safe to give it a try.

I dipped my bowl into the stream and lifted it to my lips. I took a sip, holding the water in my mouth for a moment to check for any strange taste. Nothing seemed off. The water was cold and refreshing. Since I had no way to check any more than this, I simply tipped the bowl and drank the rest of the water. I even refilled it and had another big drink. I was parched after having nothing to drink since last night.

Normally, I would have taken this chance for a sponge bath at the very least, but the air was cold and the water frigid. I also didn't know the area well enough to be sure there was no one around to see me. But I felt grimy, and after a few minutes of thought, I hit upon a solution and quickly stripped off my tank top before wrapping myself in the cloak again. I rinsed the tank top thoroughly in the rushing water and balled up the dripping fabric in one hand. With the other hand I scooped up another bowl of water to take back for Roomie.

Thanks to the cold water dripping from the cloth in my left hand and the water sloshing over the edges of the bowl in my right hand, my fingers felt frozen by the time I made it back to the clinic. Every time a gust of wind brushed over my hands, the sharp prickles of cold made my fingers cramp. As soon as I was inside the exam room, I dropped the bowl and tank top onto the table and tucked my icy hands into my armpits to warm them.

It took longer than I'd hoped, but my hands eventually stopped aching with cold. They were a little stiff, but I didn't think I'd picked up any frostbite from my short time in the bitter cold. It was cold inside too, but there was still a little insulation in the old walls that held off the worst of the chill.

Just having walls and most of a ceiling to block the wind was a huge help.

Roomie crawled out of the backpack to lap at the water in the bowl. He drank for several minutes, emptying the bowl. While he busied himself with the water dish, I used my still sodden tank top as a washcloth for a quick but thorough sponge bath and searched out a set of clean, dry clothes from my bundle of belongings. They looked pretty much identical to the clothing I'd just removed but smelled a lot better.

After changing into the clean clothing, I pulled out my makeup and mirror to apply the dramatic eye makeup I'd come to favor and freshened the inked pattern running down the right side of my face. I even used my knife to trim my hair. I'd kept up with this pretty regularly, so I needed only a few minutes to take care of a few patches that had grown out a little too far. Getting cleaned up helped me feel much better, with the added benefit that looking more put together would help make a better first impression when I went looking for Sharra.

My touch-ups complete, I bundled up in the cloak again and headed out to look for food. My stomach was aching with hunger, and I knew Roomie needed food, too. His recovery would be faster if he had enough to eat. I didn't know what I might be able to find in this area, but I had to give it a try.

Since I'd seen nothing promising on my water-gathering excursion earlier, I headed in the opposite direction this time. Food was scarce now. I found only a few dandelion plants withered by the snow and cold and a scant handful of berries remaining on a couple of bushes. This wasn't going to do much to fill our empty bellies. I sat to rest for a few minutes as I tried to think of more options for finding food. A quiet scratching and scurrying in the debris to my right interrupted my thoughts.

Turning only my head in order to avoid frightening whatever little animal was in the rubble, I saw it—a big, fat rat.

I smiled wryly as I recalled Rivers' prediction that eventually I would be glad to eat rat and realized that day had come. If I could catch that rat, I would happily roast it for my dinner. I moved my hand very, very slowly across the ground where I sat until my fingers encountered a palm-sized rock. My fingers closed around the stone, my muscles tensed in anticipation as I watched the rat's every move. Finally, it moved into plain sight as it scurried across the bare ground only a few feet away from me. In one smooth move, I lifted the stone and hurled it at the rat.

I was astonished when I actually hit the little animal and knocked it to the ground. I leapt to my feet and raced over to grab the rat before it recovered from the stun. My time living rough had forced away any squeamishness I'd had initially, and I broke the rat's neck with brutal efficiently then skinned and gutted it in preparation for cooking. I wrapped it in leaves as best I could. Although most of the leaves were too dry and brittle to be of use, I managed to scrounge enough bits of greenery to package the meat. Elated by my success, I headed back to the clinic to share the bounty with Roomie.

Roomie was still sleeping in the backpack when I returned. I'd made a quick detour to the stream on my way back to the clinic, so I had a fresh bowl of water for the cat. I sat the water on the exam table next to the backpack and took the food with me into the room directly across the hallway. This exam room had three walls. The fourth wall and the ceiling were just tumbled piles of drywall and concrete. Lucky for me, there were also splintered remains of the wood braces that had originally formed the walls. These would make excellent kindling and fuel for the little cooking fire I needed, and the open wall and ceiling meant the smoke could easily escape.

I gathered the smallest bits of wood and stacked them in an open spot on the floor, and then pulled out my handy folding knife with its firestarting attachment. I used the firestarter to generate sparks until the kindling began to smolder. I blew on the tiny flickers of flame until they caught hold and began burning. The heat from this minuscule fire was already warming me nicely; it felt even better as I added larger pieces of wood to create my cooking fire.

I found a stick to use as a spit and suspended the rat above the flames. It didn't take long at all before the delicious smell of the cooking meat overcame any reservations I was still holding over eating rat meat. As soon as the meat was done, I pulled it from the spit and devoured it along with the withered dandelion greens and berries I'd found this morning. I actually had to force myself to stop when I'd finished about half of the rat. Hunger really did make anything more palatable.

I pulled off enough shreds of meat to make a decent meal for Roomie and re-wrapped the rest of the meat in the leaves I'd used before. Earlier on in my time here, I'd have been pickier about finding clean leaves, but now I just shrugged and accepted the fact that I didn't have any clean leaves so these would have to do. Mostly, I was just happy that the rat had been big enough that I could make two meals of it.

As much as I was loving the warmth of the fire, I didn't dare leave it burning any longer. The light would be a beacon to anyone who happened to look in this direction, and I didn't want anyone to come investigating and find me here. Regretfully, I scattered the coals and stomped out the burning embers. I scraped dirt over the remains of the fire to be sure it was out before I went back across the hall.

I tucked the leftover meat into an outside pocket of the backpack and securely fastened the flap before I laid Roomie's shredded meat on the exam table next to the water bowl. The cat poked his head out of the backpack, nose and whiskers twitching madly at the scent of roasted meat. The aroma was tempting enough that Roomie eased his way out of the bag and pounced on the food. He ate with gusto and then lapped up about half the water. When he had finished, he settled himself on the table for a long, leisurely wash. His movements were stiff, but I was happy to see him feeling well enough to attend to his grooming.

When he had finished washing, I assumed he probably needed to relieve himself. I moved slowly to avoid startling the cat and slid my hands under his haunches to pick him up. A low, growling rumble informed me that he wasn't entirely happy with this handling, but he didn't bite or claw me. I carried him outside and set him down on a grassy patch.

I left him there for a few minutes as I took care of my own needs. When we were both done, I picked him up again. He didn't protest this time and calmly let me carry him inside and set him on the exam table. He immediately climbed back inside the backpack and curled up to go back to sleep.

A few minutes later, I had wrapped myself in both of the cloaks and climbed onto the table. I curled myself around the backpack again and did my best to sleep in spite of the cold.

CHAPTER TWENTY-ONE

I woke stiff and cold again in the morning. The snow flurries had ended, though the morning light was still gray and muted by the continuing cloud cover. I gave up on trying to sleep and slid off the uncomfortable exam table.

Deciding the best remedy was to get moving, I left Roomie sleeping in the tiny exam room and found my way to the old parking lot for the clinic. It was strewn with debris, as most places in the city were, but there was a patch along the west side that was mostly empty. I picked up a few rocks, bits of trash, and chunks of concrete and tossed them aside to clear out the space. I needed some room to complete the exercises that would help reduce some of the achy stiffness and practice my fighting skills.

I began with a slow series of yoga poses. As my sore muscles stretched and loosened, I moved to more complicated stretches in preparation for the next phase of my workout routine—martial arts exercises called katas. The katas were detailed patterns of choreographed movements used to practice combat skills. I'd learned them from my father. We had run through them together every morning, usually enjoying a quick breakfast afterward before one or both of us was dragged away by assistants intent on lists of meetings and responsibilities for the day. The morning katas were sometimes the only time we got to spend together.

I had to fight back tears at the memories of my father. Although it had been months since his death, sometimes the memories still threatened to overwhelm me. Unwilling to deal with my feelings, I shoved the memories away again and channeled my sadness into fierce attention to my form.

I ran through the kata at full force: whirling, leaping, kicking and punching. I moved faster and faster as I neared the end of the drill, then slowly again as I brought the exercise to a close. I finished the routine with a series of three backward hops and a bow, remaining bent at the waist with my hands on my knees for a moment as I caught my breath.

Straightening, I saw Roomie sitting at the edge of the square, watching me as he did most mornings. He seemed to find my daily exercise routine fascinating and rarely missed the chance to stare with unblinking eyes while I practiced. Sometimes I found his intense gaze a little unnerving. As I'd noticed even on the day we first met, there was more intelligence behind those eyes than I'd ever seen in a cat before. Given the existence of the bizarrely changed lizard-dogs called Shadows, I supposed it wouldn't be too unlikely that other animals had been changed as well.

Perhaps Roomie was some sort of mutant cat with human-level intelligence but no way to communicate with people. Or maybe I was letting my long, mostly-sleepless night get to me and read far more into his actions than was sensible.

Right this moment though, I was just thrilled to see him up and moving around. His movements were slow and stiff, but at least he had felt well enough to climb out of my backpack and go looking for company—or more likely, looking for food.

I walked over and crouched in front of him, tentatively reaching out to rub the top of his head. He accepted my petting, not ducking away or growling at me as he had often done before.

"Cha, are we actually friends now, then?" I murmured, keeping my voice quiet and soothing. "I'm a pretty nice person, you know. You could do worse."

I gave one last scratch beneath his chin before standing again. I needed to keep moving or my muscles would grow stiff. Roomie continued to watch me as I walked around the parking lot a few times to cool down. He followed me when I walked back to the exam room and hopped up onto the table when he saw me rummaging through the backpack. I opened the side pocket and pulled out a small chunk of meat for each of us to eat. I fastened the pocket securely again and told Roomie, "This has to last us for another meal, so don't go helping yourself to the leftovers."

He stared back at me, then gave a long, slow blink. I chose to take this as understanding that he should leave the food alone.

We each ate our breakfast of cold rat, and then Roomie crawled back into the backpack. I reminded him again not to eat the rest of the food and left him curled up in the backpack while I took the bowl and my damp tank top from yesterday and headed for the stream for water. I drank my fill and drenched the tank again. I carried the bowl and the dripping cloth back to the clinic where I had a quick sponge-bath while Roomie drank his water.

Roomie seemed well on his way to recovery, and I didn't want to spend any more nights in this frigid shelter. I decided it was time to head out and look for Sharra. I tucked the wet tank into another of the outside pockets on the backpack before I gathered the rest of my belongings. I coaxed Roomie back into the backpack and gently shrugged it onto my shoulders, then muscled the bike out of the little room, through the remaining bits of hallway, and across the parking lot.

I clicked back on to the mag-lev rail I'd come in on and headed for the downtown area where I hoped to track down Sharra. My route took me very close to the circle on Kalamath where Rivers, Mateo, and I liked to meet up. I impulsively turned the bike that way, just hoping that Rivers might be there looking for me. I hated to leave things between us with a fight. No matter how much I disagreed with him, he had been a good friend. If we could stay in touch, maybe he could eventually be something more than a friend. I wanted a chance to make up.

The path to Kalamath was slow going. Several times I had to get off the bike to clear the road enough to let me through. Even where there was a path through the tumbled debris, it was narrow and harder to navigate on the bike that on foot. I slowly worked my way through the streets until I emerged into the mostly empty area that was the former traffic circle on Kalamath Street. And sitting on the blocks of tumbled concrete where we usually ate our lunch, Rivers was waiting for me.

CHAPTER TWENTY-TWO

I followed the rail around the edge of the traffic circle until I reached Rivers. He got to his feet as I got close, and I realized that with the helmet hiding my face, he didn't know it was me. I stopped the bike and removed the helmet as I slid off the seat. I left the helmet hanging from the handlebars and walked over to Rivers.

He had visibly relaxed once he recognized me, and now he walked up to me and inspected the bike.

"I'd almost forgotten you had this," he commented. "I haven't seen you ride it since the night we met."

"Mostly I just walk. The roads are pretty hard to drive around here."

He nodded. I nodded. We both just stood there in awkward silence, staring at the bike and refusing to meet each other's eyes. I cleared my throat a little just as Rivers coughed. I laughed.

"Cha, this is ridiculous. I'm sorry, okay? I don't want to fight with you."

The relief on his face was clear. "I don't want to fight with you either," he assured me. "I just got carried away. I'm really not some kind of a hardcore rebel, ready to burn down the city and everyone in it. I came over to the circle first thing this morning, hoping you would come looking for me so I could apologize. I don't want to lose you."

"I'm not lost," I told him with a smile. I took a step forward and wrapped my arms around his waist in a hug. His arms closed around my back, and he hugged me fiercely. I rested my cheek against his chest. The thumping of his heart beneath my ear was comforting. I realized that it had been months since I touched another person like this. Mateo's forced embraces certainly didn't count.

I relaxed into his hold. His arms tightened, holding me close. He spoke, and I felt the rumble of his voice as much as I heard it.

"Poppy," he said softly.

I pulled back just enough to meet his eyes. His face was so close to mine that I felt the soft puff of his breath against my skin. His lips parted slightly, and he leaned down toward me. My heart was pounding; I was sure he could feel it thumping against his chest. His lips were moments away from brushing mine.

Roomie chose that moment to pop his head out of the backpack. Rivers was startled by the sudden appearance of this furry face, complete with sharp teeth bared in an annoyed growl, so close to his own. He yelped and let go of me as he stumbled back a few steps.

"Cha!" he shouted. "What the hell?" His eyes were wide as he tried to make sense of what had just happened. I couldn't help myself and started laughing.

"I'm sorry!" I managed between fits of giggles. "Really, I am. I forgot he was there. You ... your face ..."

I could barely form a complete sentence. I was laughing so hard that my legs were weak. I sat down right there on the ground, still cackling. I only laughed harder when I saw the combination of shock and confusion on Rivers' face.

As I finally managed to get my snickers under control, Rivers dropped down to sit on the cracked concrete beside me.

"So who's your friend?" he asked with a smile.

"This is the roommate that I mentioned to you," I explained. "Appropriately enough, I call him Roomie."

Rivers cautiously held out a hand for Roomie to sniff. Still poking his head out of the backpack, Roomie gave Rivers a dismissive glance and settled in for a wash instead. Rejected by the cat, Rivers dropped his hand with a small smile. Since that hand landed on my knee with a warm squeeze, I saw no reason to complain.

"This is the roommate, huh? I had hoped it was someone a little larger and more intimidating. I pictured you having somebody around to watch your back."

"Roomie does his best," I told Rivers defensively. "Actually, that's why he's in my backpack. He was hurt trying to defend me, so now I'm trying to take care of him and be sure he's okay."

The hand on my knee tightened briefly. I could tell that Rivers was forcing his voice to stay casual as he asked, "What was he defending you from?"

"Mateo," I told him bluntly. "I wasn't as careful as I usually am when I went home the other night, and Mateo followed me back. Mateo wanted to get really friendly; Roomie and I disagreed."

I twisted one hand back over my shoulder and stroked Roomie's broad head. He tolerated it but didn't interrupt his grooming.

"Roomie jumped onto Mateo's back, and Mat grabbed him and threw him through a big window. I thought he was dead for a minute, but he pulled through. He seems to be doing a lot better today."

"How's Mateo?" Rivers asked grimly. "Did you throw him through a window of his own?" He hesitated a moment before asking, "Did he…? Are you…?"

"I'm fine," I assured him. "Roomie interrupted before things went very far. Mateo was not entirely conscious when Roomie and I left him, but I imagine he survived and slinked home to pretend he didn't lose a fight to a girl and her cat."

Rivers blew out a relieved breath. "Good. Good." His hands were fisted on his thighs, and his jaw was so tightly clenched that I could see a muscle twitching in his cheek. "When I see him…"

I laid my hand on his gently. "Just let it go," I told him. "I can take care of myself. And like I said, I'm fine."

"You're leaving," he pointed out. "That doesn't say 'fine' to me."

"I've been thinking about it for a while," I told him. "My place was not ready for winter. I'm cold, and I'm running low on food. It's time to quit being such a loner and join a pack … I'll have more than just Roomie to watch my back."

Rivers turned his hand over to clasp mine and looked into my eyes. "Come with me," he said, his voice earnest. "I can look out for you."

I shook my head. "You can't be with me every minute," I pointed out gently. "And you know that Eddie and his buddies would not just accept me into the pack. Not after Eddie got torn up and Dirty Jin died. It wouldn't be safe for me there."

Rivers' shoulders slumped. "I know," he admitted. "You're right. Otherwise, I would have tried to convince you to come back with me weeks ago."

"And you still can't leave?" I asked. "You could come with me. With two of us we might not even need a pack; we could watch out for each other."

"I can't," Rivers said, his expression sad. "I'm the one who makes sure that no one goes hungry and that the pack stays safe. I have responsibilities, and I can't just leave. Eddie and his friends are the minority. Most of our pack members are decent people. They need me."

I was disappointed but not surprised. I knew that Rivers felt very responsible for his pack. I'd never really expected him to be willing to leave. I sighed.

"I know. I understand. I'm going to go looking for Sharra. I talked to Leeza a while back, and she was able to tell me Sharra's general neighborhood is north and east of here, but she doesn't know which pack Sharra joined. At least I have a starting point, so I figure if I head northeast I'll eventually run into someone who can tell me where to find Sharra. The blue and pink hair is memorable. Someone is sure to recognize the description."

Rivers nodded. "It's a good strategy," he agreed. He let go of my hand to point at a road that split off Kalamath circle to the north.

"Follow that road," he told me. "It runs northeast through Wolf territory, and it's a pretty safe area. Follow it until you hit a guard checkpoint for Liberty territory. It's just a couple of guys on mag-lev bikes, but they're pretty cautious in Liberty. They have a lot more elders, kids, and general noncombatant types than most packs, and they're very protective of them. Let them know I sent you that way. They'll recognize my name. Just tell them who you're looking for. If they don't know her, they should be willing to give you directions and an introduction to the next pack."

"Liberty is Mat's pack, right?" I asked.

"Right. He never said anything about recognizing your description of your friend, did he?"

"He said he didn't, but I think maybe he was lying," I admitted. "I didn't push. It seemed too much like asking a favor, and I didn't want to owe him anything."

Rivers bit his lip. "I'm kind of worried that Sharra is Liberty Pack," he confessed. "From everything you've said, it sounds like she was well-funded and very well-connected. Those are definitely words that describe Liberty. They're the biggest and most successful pack. What are you going to do if you find Sharra and she's in Mateo's pack?"

"I'm going to ignore Mateo and watch my back," I assured him. "That's pretty much my plan no matter which pack I connect with. And on that note…" I got to my feet, careful not to jostle Roomie too much. "The day is moving quickly. I'd better get going."

Rivers stood as well and walked over to the bike with me. After I climbed on, he leaned in and brushed a light kiss on to my cheek. It wasn't the kiss we'd almost had earlier, but Roomie had thoroughly broken the mood for that one.

Rivers took the helmet from the handlebars and gently settled it onto my head. "Be careful," he told me, face serious. "Even the safe areas have some iffy spots."

"I will. I'll try to come back to the circle in three days to check in, okay? To let you know where I end up."

He squeezed my hand on the bike's grip and then stepped back. "See ya later, Little Bit," he told me softly.

"Later, Laughing Boy." I grinned, starting the bike. I raised my hand in a wave as the bike's magnets grabbed the rail and started pulling me away.

CHAPTER TWENTY-THREE

I followed the road Rivers had indicated. It was slow going as it wound through cluttered neighborhoods and decimated business districts. I had to detour from the main road more than a few times when the street was impassable. Sometimes, I had to go several blocks out of my way before I could find a path back to the road I needed.

My growling stomach told me it was well past lunchtime when I came to the remains of an enormous building of some kind that completely blocked the road. The wreckage stretched for blocks in each direction. I was afraid I would lose my way completely if I tried to go around. I decided to take a break while I considered my options.

I climbed off the bike with a wince. My backside and legs felt stiff and sore after riding for so long, but the discomfort eased once I moved around a little. I set my backpack on the ground with the flap open so Roomie could climb out. He wandered off for a minute to find a place to relieve himself. I did the same.

Another of the small streams that were so common in this city ran alongside the road; it looked clean, if a little gritty. I washed my hands in the stream and discovered that the water was so cold it made my fingers tingle.

Retrieving the little bowl from my backpack, I got myself a drink. I could taste a little silt in the water, but I was thirsty enough to not complain. Roomie didn't seem bothered either and lapped up the water as if he hadn't drank for days.

When we'd both drunk our fill, I pulled out the last of our food supplies. Roomie had obligingly left the remaining rat alone overnight, so I was able to share it with him now. Cold and greasy rat meat was not exactly appetizing, but it did ease the gnawing hunger. A little searching around the edges of the stream produced a handful of dandelion greens to accompany the meal. I offered some of the greens to Roomie, but he just stared at me in disdain and turned his nose up at them. Looking at the wilted leaves, curled and browning at the edges, I couldn't blame him. But knowing I needed the fuel, I shoved the greens into my mouth. I chewed and swallowed as quickly as I could and went back to the stream to rinse the lingering bitter taste from my mouth.

Bio needs taken care of, I returned my attention to the problem of how to get past the fallen building. I studied the area before me, hoping to spot a path around the jumbled wreckage. Unfortunately, the rubble stretched as far as I could see in both directions. I didn't want to move so far off my route, so it appeared that my only choice was to find my way through the remains of the building.

Roomie had already settled himself into the backpack. My shoulders ached from carrying the big cat, so I picked up the bag and twisted the straps around the handlebars to fasten it securely to the bike. Roomie didn't appear to care. He was probably already sleeping, enjoying his relaxing trip through the city.

The ground wasn't clear enough to ride, so I grasped the bike by the handlebars and pushed it instead. Ahead of me, a large sign had fallen from the building to lie across the stream and form a bridge. I read the sign as I rolled the bike across the water and learned that the building had once been a hotel and convention center, which accounted for its size.

To find my way through, I had to look for the clearest path and then remove enough obstacles to make the route passable. It seemed that every inch of progress was a struggle. Sweat rolled down my back, and I was breathing hard by the time I had muscled the bike over a pile of lumber and shingles in one area and wound my way through half-standing walls in another.

Bizarrely at one point, I encountered a mountain of tangled metal and plastic piled higher than my head that covered most of a city block. I cocked my head to the side, wondering if looking at it from a different perspective would cause the strange sight to make more sense. I realized that the strange heap was made up of hundreds of chairs jumbled together and piled high, then rusted into place over time.

It looked as if one of the floods that had hit this area had swept through the building, bringing down walls, destroying rooms, and collecting the chairs that must have been set out in preparation for some large event. Now all those chairs had fused into an odd sort of sculpture. Strange.

I moved on, continuing to pick my way through the detritus of the ruined convention complex. After a long, hard trek, I finally reached the other side of the debris field and found a clear rail. I rolled the bike over to the exposed rail and wearily climbed on.

Clicking on to the rail, I headed north again, hoping that I was still on the right path. Nighttime fell early in the shadow of the Rocky Mountains, and it was already starting to get dark.

If I didn't find the border soon, I would have to make camp somewhere here in Wolf territory.

Five minutes later, I learned that I was indeed on the right track when my progress was blocked by two men leaning on bikes that looked a lot like mine. My heart jumped in my chest. I hoped that these were decent Liberty pack guards rather than gangers from MS-13 or unaffiliated Roamers, who could be dangerous. Of course, since I was currently an unaffiliated Roamer myself, I really shouldn't judge.

I came to a stop, as they obviously intended, but stayed on guard and ready to take off again at a moment's notice.

"You need to turn back, Miss," one of the men said sternly. "This is Liberty territory. No trespassing allowed."

Relieved to learn that I had found my way to Liberty territory, I pulled off my helmet so I could talk more easily and gave them a wide, sunny smile. My years in the political realm meant that I was used to dealing with suspicious or unfriendly people and turning their attitude around. After so much time alone lately, my skills felt rusty, but I did my best to exude a non-threatening, trustworthy vibe. The dimples helped. Who could distrust a girl with dimples?

I could see the guards' defenses start to crumble. I had gone from an unknown, possible threat in a faceless visor to a small girl with a big smile. The man on the left was a tall, broad-shouldered blonde with a short, military-style haircut. He relaxed his stance a little and smiled back at me.

Continuing with the sweet, girly persona, I blew out an explosive breath of relief. "Oh, good! I've been looking for you guys!"

"For us?" the second man asked, a little confused.

He was tall also but lean where his partner was muscular. His hair was an explosion of tight brown curls standing out from his head for several inches in every direction, and his skin was tanned a dark gold from plenty of time outdoors. Physically the two men were completely unalike, but the way they stood, moved, and reacted similarly told me that they were well-trained and disciplined. It might take a little work to convince them to let me through.

I turned my high-wattage smile on him and maybe batted my eyelashes, just a little. "Well, not for you specifically, of course. I didn't know you would be here. But I was looking for someone from Liberty pack. My friend Rivers from Wolf pack sent me this way to find you. He thought you would be able to help me find someone."

Both men looked bewildered at the flood of words tumbling from my mouth, but they had both relaxed now. Neither of them viewed me as a threat anymore, which was the first step in getting them to let me pass through their territory. I kept talking before they could gather themselves to interrupt.

"I'm looking for another friend of mine. Her name is Sharra. She's four or five inches taller than me and pretty skinny. And when I saw her last, she had bright blue hair with a couple of pink streaks."

I saw surprised recognition in both their eyes. They knew who I was talking about. But there was suspicion, too. They weren't going to help me find Sharra without a little convincing that I wasn't dangerous. The dark-haired man gave the tiniest glance to the right, making me think there just might be someone else back there. I raised my voice a little to be sure that everyone could hear me clearly.

"Sharra and I met in Goodland a few months … no … Cha! It has to be more like six months ago now! She helped me out of a jam and brought me back to Denver with her. But as we were headed to her home base, we got ambushed by Eddie the Dandelion Man. We both got away okay, but we got separated.

"Eddie the Dandelion Man?" the blonde guard asked, obviously amused.

I laughed. "A little habit of mine," I admitted. "I tend to assign nicknames to people based on something I notice about them. Eddie has all that fuzzy hair and a crazy beard standing out all around his face. It made me think of a dandelion gone to seed."

A deep laugh echoed through the canyons formed by the battered buildings and piles of rubble surrounding us. A mountain of a man stepped out of the shadows, just where I'd suspected someone might be waiting. He walked toward us, still chuckling. His teeth were a bright flash of white in the deep chocolate of his face, and his shaved head gleamed in the small bit of sunset light that made it to street level.

He spoke, his voice a bass rumble deep in his massive chest. "A dandelion gone to seed; that's about the best description of Eddie that I've ever heard."

He looked me over with shrewd, dark eyes before nodding in satisfaction. "Short redhead with blue designs drawn on her face … you must be Poppy?"

"Yes!" I exclaimed. "You know Sharra!"

"I do. She told me all about making a new friend in Goodland back in May and then losing you when the two of you were ambushed. She came back to base and took a rescue party back to find you, but there was no sign of you by the time we got there. We knew you were okay though. There were enough witnesses to the whole thing that I think everyone in Denver has heard the story of how you let Eddie beat himself up and then fed him to a Shadow."

He grinned. "Sharra was pretty proud of you for that one. Since we knew you'd kicked loose of Wolf pack, we had patrols watching for you, hoping to bring you in to base but no luck. After all this time, we'd started to think ... well, that bad things had happened. Where have you been hiding?"

"Not hiding, really. There just wasn't anyone much around to see me. After I got away from Eddie's crew, I managed to get myself thoroughly lost. I ended up way south and west of here in an area that's pretty much deserted.

"I found myself a safe place to hole up. Just for a day or so, you know, until I figured out how to track down Sharra. Then I got poisoned by some carnivorous vines." I held up my left arm with its long red scar as demonstration. I could tell from the look on their faces that they knew the plants I was talking about.

"Nasty things," the big man agreed. "We call them creepers. We try to burn them out whenever we can because they're pretty toxic. It looks like the creeper got you pretty good; you're lucky you survived."

"It took a while to recover," I admitted. "By the time I finally felt better, I'd pretty much settled in to my little place and felt safe there. I decided to stay there on my own and take some time to get my feet under me."

I met his gaze squarely, and if my knees weakened just a little when I started into his gorgeous, deep brown eyes, well, that was no one's business but my own.

"Since you know Sharra," I said, "then you may know that I have had some fairly major life changes recently."

He nodded. "I'm aware," he confirmed.

"Well then, I'm sure you understand that I felt like being alone for a while."

He folded his arms over his wide chest. I was distracted by those arms for a minute, wondering if I could manage to circle one of those massive biceps even with both hands. I was pretty sure I couldn't.

I realized he was speaking and pulled my attention back to his words in time to hear him ask, "What brings you looking for Sharra now?"

I answered honestly. "It's cold. I managed okay during the summer, but for winter," I shook my head, "I'm just not equipped."

He gave me a searching look and then nodded. "Reasonable enough," he agreed. "I can't blame you for looking for someplace warm and safe."

He held out his hand, and I shook it warmly, feeling a little thrill as our hands touched. "So you know I'm Poppy," I said. "I'm going to make a wild guess that you're Lucas?"

"I am."

"So why is the pack leader hanging out in an abandoned building on the edge of your territory? Just hoping to run into me?"

He laughed and gestured to a mag-lev bike sitting in the road behind him. "I like to make the loop through our territory once a month or so to see for myself how things are going. I was just about to head back home when you drove up. So just a happy coincidence I was here, I guess, since these guys would have sent for me to come talk to you anyway. Why don't you follow me back to base? I'll take you to Sharra."

Everything I'd heard about the leader of Liberty pack told me Lucas was trustworthy, so I didn't hesitate to go with him. I slung my leg over the bike and reached to turn it on when a thought struck me.

"Wait, Mateo is in your pack, right? Did he ever say anything to Sharra about knowing me? I mean, he knew I was looking for her."

Lucas raised one eyebrow, a skill I wished I had. "You're friends with Mateo?"

"I know him," I clarified. "I wouldn't say we're friends."

"And why is that?" Lucas asked.

I hesitated for a moment but decided to keep silent. With no proof of Mateo's behavior, I didn't want to start a match of he said/she said before I'd even set foot inside pack headquarters. I was going to do just as I'd told Rivers and ignore Mateo as much as possible.

I shrugged one shoulder. "Cha, he doesn't get along with my cat," I told him. As if on cue, Roomie chose that moment to pop his head out of the backpack and glared over my shoulder at the three men. I snickered as all three of these big, brave men jumped back at the surprise appearance of my cat.

"What the ... You have a cat in your backpack?" the blonde asked incredulously.

"What? You don't?"

CHAPTER TWENTY-FOUR

I'd followed Lucas through a maze of city streets for what felt like an hour. I was pretty sure it hadn't actually been that long, but in the dark with icy wind whipping at every bit of exposed skin, time seemed to move crawl. By the time Lucas pulled off the street into a small, fenced parking lot, my body was stiff with cold. Only the center of my back was still warm since Roomie was curled up inside my backpack again. I pulled into the lot behind him and dragged myself off the bike, muscles protesting. I fumbled with the twine tying my bundle of belongings to the bike, unable to get my fingers to cooperate. Lucas stepped in to untie the knots and lifted my bundle off the bike.

"I'll take it," he told me. He patted me on the back with one huge hand, shaking my whole body with that casual gesture. "Come on inside. We'll get you a space to rest up for a bit before we talk about what you plan to do next."

I was grateful for the offer. It had been a long couple of days, and I was ready to drop in my tracks. Right now I wanted nothing more than a place to lie down and close my eyes. Lucas led me to the base of a glass tower. In the light of the moon, I could see that it had been very tall and graceful at one time, but it now ended in a jagged border against the sky about twenty floors up.

It was hard to tell in the dark, but I was pretty sure I saw the tell-tale shimmer of Solaris-Web running through the glass walls of the tower. Solaris-Web had been developed about fifty years ago as an alternative to bulky solar panels. The webbing was embedded in the very materials that made up the outside of the building and soaked up solar energy all day. The Solaris fibers carried the energy through the walls to provide power inside the building. Since the technology had been very new when the war started, this must have been one of the first buildings ever built using the solar-powered webbing.

I pulled my attention back to ground level to avoid tripping over the large cracks and bumps in the sidewalk beneath my feet. There were also piles of debris cluttering the sidewalk and hugging the foundations of the building. We stopped at a break in the rubble where a man was standing guard. He was short and broad with wiry dark hair and three long parallel scars running down his left cheek.

He had obviously seen us coming because he immediately pulled open the door, which was formed by a large piece of plywood blocking a gaping hole in the wall behind him. Lucas and I slipped past him with a murmured thanks, and he pushed the wood back into place behind us.

I paused to take a good look around as Lucas turned to speak to another guard who was on duty inside the building. After a few murmured sentences, the guard slipped away on an errand for Lucas, leaving us alone in the quiet shadows. We appeared to be standing in an open lobby area that filled much of the ground level. Perhaps this had been a hotel or a very nice bank? Whatever its original purpose, this had obviously been a very posh building before the war turned so much of it to rubble.

As I'd suspected there would be, soft lights shone inside, almost certainly powered by the Solaris-Web. Engraved wall sconces around the edges of the room created small pools of golden light in the cavernous darkness of the enormous lobby. To still work after so many years meant they were very well made.

The building was warm, too, much warmer than just being inside would account for. The solar power must have been providing heat to the building as well. After so many months living a Spartan existence, the thought of these modern conveniences in the middle of the blighted city was miraculous. Before I could ask Lucas about these luxuries, I heard the sound of footsteps racing down the wide staircase leading into the lobby. I looked over and saw Sharra, blue and pink hair exploding from a high ponytail atop her head. She beamed as she ran across the lobby and snatched me into a fierce hug.

"Poppy! I'm so, so happy to see you. I felt so terrible leaving you behind! I've been feeling so guilty. Now to see you here and looking okay, well, what a relief! Do you forgive me for dragging you off to Denver and then abandoning you?"

I hugged her back. "Not your fault," I insisted. "I knew why you took off. And hey, I managed to handle things myself."

"That's for sure," Sharra agreed with a wide grin. "Every pack in the city has been talking about that encounter for months. Eddie is generally considered pretty tough, and this tiny bit of a girl took him down? Cha, even his own friends couldn't keep quiet about it, though I'm sure he wished they would."

Sharra laughed and finally turned me loose. "I was not at all surprised by the story. After all, I saw you take out a mech fighter. Eddie was hardly going to be a challenge compared to that."

"He wasn't expecting me to push back," I explained, "and I think maybe he'd been drinking. That made it easier. I was lucky, really."

"So modest," she said, shaking her head. "Allow me to continue enjoying my mental image of you beating him up without breaking a sweat. It makes me happy."

I rolled my eyes but smiled. "You can keep any illusions you want to hang on to if you'll just let me stay here where it's warm and point me to a flat space where I can pass out for a few hours."

Lucas passed my bundle of belongings to Sharra. "Why don't you give her a five-minute orientation for now and get her settled for the night? You can give her the full tour tomorrow."

Sharra nodded. "Sounds good. See you tomorrow."

Lucas gave me another staggering pat on the back and left us. We watched him go for a moment before Sharra turned back to me. "I'll show you just the basics for now, so you can find your way around a little. Should we start with the restrooms?"

With so much going on, I actually hadn't even thought about that, but now that Sharra brought it up, I suddenly needed to pee so badly I could barely control myself. "Yes, please," I begged. "I really need to find a bathroom."

Sharra led me down a short hallway to the remains of a state-of-the-art—as of twenty years ago—gym. The various machines had been dismantled now, only pieces of them remaining. They had probably been scavenged for parts to fix machinery more useful than old workout equipment.

We walked through the former gym to reach a pair of side-by-side doors in glossy black. The engraved silver medallions at the center of each door proved to be palm print scanners, though the dull colors of the security displays indicated that the scanners were no longer active. That was no surprise; the scanners would need electricity to operate. The solar lighting in the old building could operate without a working electrical system, but complex electronics like scanner locks would require a stable source of power.

"Locker rooms," Sharra informed me as she pushed open the door etched with an elaborately fashioned female stick figure. The second door boasted a similarly styled male stick figure.

The women's locker room was tiled in stark black with gleaming white fixtures and shining silver hardware. While the other areas I'd seen had a coating of dust and rubble, this room had been scrubbed ruthlessly clean.

Sharra pointed to the left. "Showers," she said and then to the right, "Toilets."

My eyes widened in surprise. "Running water?" I asked. "How is that possible? Hold that thought. Tell me after I pee."

I dashed into one of the little cubicles on the right and availed myself of the working plumbing. Much relieved I returned to the sink area and washed my hands, then splashed some water on my face and ran my fingers through my hair. That was all the effort I was willing to put into freshening up at the moment. I was just too tired.

Sharra could see my weariness. She grabbed my elbow to steer me from the room. "We'll walk and talk so you can get your explanation on your way to bed."

"Bed," I half moaned. "That sounds amazing."

Sharra smirked. "I don't know that amazing is the right word. The mattresses here are all at least twenty years old, but there's no shortage of them at least. This place was a huge hotel back in the day. We think most of the meeting rooms and conference spaces were on the upper floors, probably to take advantage of the view, so there are a lot of relatively undamaged bedrooms in the lower levels that didn't collapse."

We walked back to the lobby as Sharra continued her explanation. The floors were covered in fine marble tiles and the furniture, while dusty and worn after all this time, had obviously been of high quality. There were a number of chairs and loveseats scattered around the large room; most were occupied by sleeping people. A few raised their heads to watch us through curious eyes.

Sharra ignored them, so I did my best to do the same as we started up a dramatic set of dusty marble stairs to the second floor. "Lucas' dad Daryn founded this pack shortly after the city was bombed out and abandoned. Since no one else was really here yet, he got to take his pick when it came to choosing a home base. Even though this building looks like a wreck, it still has good bones. And of course, there's the Solaris-Web, which made a huge difference. Daryn was one of the engineers who installed the Solaris-Web when the building was built, so he knew enough about the system to repair some of the infrastructure. He and the pack rigged up a whole cistern and filter system on the top level and managed to patch it into existing plumbing. It's all gravity fed, so it doesn't need much power to operate. The pipes only lead to the locker rooms and the kitchens though. The rest of the building is dry."

"So it's just running on rainwater?" I asked with interest. "I guess Denver gets enough precip for that to work. It seems to pour here every afternoon."

"Thanks to climate change," Sharra agreed. "This whole area used to have a lot of trouble with drought; we would have had a much harder time making it without easy access to water. But these days, there's so much rain and snow that we really never have to worry about water here."

That made sense. Global climate change had already been an issue before the war, but the way the war had added gasses and particulates to the atmosphere had changed the landscape of entire regions and drastically altered weather patterns over much of the world. The results in Denver had obviously led to more rain and snow than had previously been common for the area.

We reached the top of the stairs and turned left. Sharra led me to an open door a few steps down the hallway. I saw a small desk and chair and a wide, soft-looking bed. I didn't even wait for Sharra to tell me that I could use the room before I stumbled inside, plopped my backpack on the desk, and climbed into the bed. I was asleep before she closed the door.

CHAPTER TWENTY-FIVE

I don't know how long I slept, but when I woke sunshine peeked through small tears and holes in the ancient curtains. A hundred aches and pains made themselves known as I climbed out of bed, reminders of my work making a path through the old convention center yesterday.

I walked over to the desk to check on Roomie, but he wasn't in the backpack. I did a quick search of the small room, but he was nowhere to be found. I assumed he had found a way out of the room, and he would find his way back later if he wanted to. He seemed to be feeling better now; he might just decide not to be friendly anymore. I hoped he would come back, but there was nothing I could do about it. Either he would or he wouldn't. In the meantime, I decided to do a few katas to try and stretch my stiff muscles. Then I would find my way back downstairs to those wonderful bathrooms. After six months of living in primitive conditions, toilets and showers seemed like incredible luxuries.

I shoved the bed and desk to the edges of the room to make space for my workout and leapt into the complicated pattern. My hands and feet flew through the air at top speed until the kata ended with a dramatic backward roll into a low foot sweep and a backfist throat punch. Holding my final position for a moment, I grinned with the exhilaration of a well-executed routine. It was always fun to do a complicated set and get it exactly right.

I got to my feet and turned when I heard the applause. Sharra and Lucas stood in the doorway, clapping in appreciation for my performance. For once I was grateful for my pale red-head's complexion, which caused my face to flush beet-red at the mere hint of exercise. Being able to blame my rosy cheeks on the energetic kata allowed me to play it cool in response to their attention.

"Good morning," I said, my voice cheerful.

"Good morning," Lucas rumbled in response. "I begin to see how you walked away from a skirmish with Eddie and took care of yourself in the rough for six months."

"You're definitely not the soft townie that I would have expected," Sharra agreed as they stepped inside and closed the door behind them. "I doubt anyone who ever watched Miss "Perfect Poppy" on the evening news holo would believe you could do that."

The room had seemed plenty big enough a few minutes ago, but the space felt very small now that Lucas was standing so close. At my height, I was used to having people look down at me, though generally I was wearing one of my many pairs of high heels to lessen the effect. Without those confidence-boosters, I felt dwarfed by his proximity. As usual when I felt threatened, I took the offensive.

"Cha," I muttered, tipping my head back absurdly far to overemphasize his height. "How tall are you, anyway? You are freakishly large."

He grinned at me, the cheerful expression taking him from just nice looking to seriously gorgeous, and my heart skipped a beat. "Maybe you're freakishly small? My size is very useful when I'm standing guard or fighting off a rival pack. Or just to intimidate others so that I don't have to actually fight. I'm not sure what benefit your tiny size would bring."

"It does help others underestimate me," I said, just before aiming a blow at his chiseled chin.

He instinctively moved to block me, but it had been just a feint, and I had already redirected my blow to strike him in the stomach. I pulled most of the force since I didn't really want to hurt him, using just enough strength to let him know that I could have done worse if I'd chosen to. Even at that reduced speed, I bruised my hand a little striking his muscular abdomen. The man was seriously ripped.

He let out a small "oof" but didn't otherwise react to my attack.

"Are you always so ready to fight, little Red?" he asked.

I thought about his question. My father's death and living in the rough for six months had changed me. In the past I'd fought with words, but now I was more likely to get physical. To be honest, after the last few months of being on my own, I had started to crave the adrenaline rush brought on by danger. I looked Lucas in the eye and nodded. "Yes. Pretty much."

He smiled. "Excellent."

Sharra took a seat on the bed. Patting the spot beside her, she instructed me to sit with her and directed Lucas to take the armless chair from the desk. Flipping it around, Lucas sat backward on the chair, leaning his folded arms on the back.

"So," he said. "Poppy Walker. What are we going to do with you, then? According to all the news coming out of Goodland, you're currently lying in a crypt in the National Cemetery. And yet … here you are. The new President has mourned your death quite dramatically. Does he know that you're here instead of there?"

"He doesn't know where I am now," I assured him, "but he is quite aware that I'm not in that tomb."

He nodded thoughtfully. "I see. Why, then, is he pretending that you are?"

I glanced at Sharra who gave me an encouraging nod. Really, what other options did I have? If I was going to survive long enough to get revenge on Cruz for his betrayal, I would need to ally myself with someone.

I had already decided to trust Sharra, and she obviously trusted Lucas. Ideally, I would've liked to move slowly and get to know more about them before making a decision to align myself with this group, but I didn't have that luxury. As Poppy Walker, I'd been able to dance delicately around relationships without making a commitment. But the old rules no longer applied.

I had learned that this new world in which I found myself was much more direct. Playing games and withholding information from an ally here would be considered untrustworthy. My best shot at getting the shelter I needed, and maybe help with Cruz, was to tell them both the whole story. Besides, Sharra had surely told him everything she knew about me already.

When I'd finished my recitation of the events from the last several months, Lucas was silent. He stared at the wall behind my head and chewed on his bottom lip as he considered my story.

Finally, he turned to me. "I would suggest that we keep the whole 'president's daughter' thing under wraps for now. Hard to know how some folks might react. The pack leadership knows—Sharra told us about you when she returned from Goodland. But as far as anyone else here needs to know for now, you're just Poppy—no last name. You joined up with

Sharra in Goodland, and you're just one of the pack here. That work for you?"

"I am just one of the pack," I pointed out. "Unless you need someone to arrange a dinner reception for visiting dignitaries, my political skill set isn't exactly in demand here."

"You might be surprised," he said enigmatically.

I waited for him to elaborate, but he said nothing more as he got to his feet and walked to the door.

"We'll talk more," he promised me. "But for now, I leave you in Sharra's capable hands. You wanted her for guard rotation?" he asked Sharra.

"Definitely," she agreed. "I've got five on medical right now, which puts the patrol levels a lot lower than I'm comfortable with. I've seen Red in action, and she has some serious skills. I need her a lot more than they need another veggie chopper in the kitchens."

Turning to me she explained, "I'm the guard captain, so I'm conscripting you for duty. Otherwise, you'd be put on a domestic rotation to scrub toilets. They always make the newbies scrub toilets for a while."

"Well, then, I'm glad you're sparing me that. What do I do on guard duty?"

"The guards patrol our borders and territory. We keep our streets clear of scary beasties, Lurkers, and intruders from other packs. It's not for the faint of heart, and you need to be able to deal with trouble when it comes your way. I know you can handle yourself; you'd be wasted on domestic."

I flushed with pleasure. I'd never been praised for my fighting ability before; it had always been a secret between me and my father. Now that I didn't have to hide my skills I just might enjoy it if a little trouble came my way.

"Sure," I told Sharra. "Put me in the rotation."

"Marvi," she said with satisfaction. "Now, how about a shower? Some breakfast?"

"That sounds great!" I said. I was sweaty and dirty from my trek through the streets yesterday and my workout this morning. And I hadn't eaten since my sad lunch with Roomie yesterday afternoon. My stomach was cramping with hunger.

Grabbing some clean clothing from my backpack, I followed Sharra out of the room. I hoped Roomie would be there when I got back. Descending the wide staircase, we entered the lobby I remembered from the night before. In the daylight, it was dilapidated and worn. It looked as if the entire front wall of the two-story atrium had originally been composed of glass. Now a massive pile of rubble formed a barrier to the outside. The other three walls seemed to be intact, making this a reasonably protected shelter.

"This is just a commons area," Sharra explained. "Some people sleep here if they don't like to be closed up in a room. Most people use it as a place to go if they don't feel like being alone. There's usually someone here at any time."

"How many people do you have in the pack?"

"We're a fairly large pack as far as these things go. One-seventy-two at last count. That's why we took over such a large building even though it's harder to secure. The pack didn't set out to have such a big group, but there are a lot of people who can't really take care of themselves. Most packs around here are pretty rough, and if you're not a fighter or you have little kids, it can get bad for you. We've become known for taking care of our own, so Roamers ask to join up with us. We won't usually turn them away as long as they're not defecting from another pack. We try to stay neutral in pack skirmishes so we would only take someone from another pack in extreme cases."

We turned left as we entered the women's locker room, and I saw a half dozen shower cubicles with frosted plexi-glass doors. There were also a few deep sinks on the back wall.

Sharra pointed them out, explaining, "Everyone is responsible for washing their own clothes. There are containers of soap powder on the shelves above the sinks. There's a domestic rotation that takes care of bedding, towels, and other group laundry. Drop things to be laundered in those bins on the other side of the room and pick up clean stuff from the shelves next to the bins."

She walked over and pulled a couple of towels from the shelf. She handed me one, and I added it to the bundle in my arms. Sharra opened the door to one of the shower cubicles and showed me the lever installed about waist high.

She demonstrated how to turn on the water, which only lasted for a minute or so before it stopped. She grinned wickedly. "You probably won't want more. The water is cold. Bad enough now when we're using rainwater. Just wait another month until we're getting straight snowmelt a degree or so above freezing."

I shivered and mentally calculated how fast I could wash and jump back out.

She indicated a closed container sitting on a high shelf in the corner of the cubicle. "There's the soap." With a showy wave of her arm she stepped out of the cubicle. "Enjoy."

The door clicked closed behind her, leaving me in the tiny dressing area in front of the shower itself. I stripped off my dirty clothing and stepped into the shower area. I braced myself and then shoved the lever upward. I did my best to muffle my shocked yelp when the icy water poured over me, but I heard Sharra laughing at me.

After my frigid shower, I grabbed my towel from the hook and dried off as quickly as I could, anxious to get dressed and warm up. I pulled on underwear and another set of my now-standard uniform of leather pants, dark tee, and dark leather vest.

Sliding my feet back into my boots, I stepped out of the cubicle, damp towel and dirty clothes in hand. Sharra was waiting for me, and I followed her out of the locker room, still clutching my old clothes. We took a quick detour upstairs to leave the grubby clothes in our rooms for later cleaning—Sharra's room was just a few doors down from mine. Then it was back down the stairs to find the dining hall.

"We have set hours for meals," Sharra told me as we crossed the lobby again, this time turning to the left instead of moving straight through to the gym area.

On the far side of the lobby, we entered a large open room. It had probably been some sort of ballroom or convention space. Now it served as a dining hall for the Liberty pack, with round tables set up around the room where people could sit to eat and a few long tables at the front used as the serving area.

"Breakfast is available from six to eight," Sharra continued. "Lunch is eleven to one, and dinner is from six to eight. Get yourself here during those hours or you're out of luck … unless," she held up a finger to emphasize her point, "you're out on guard patrols during meal hours." She pointed to a pair of swinging doors behind the serving tables. "In that case, you can go to the kitchens when you get back and they'll get you something."

We walked to the serving tables and helped ourselves to big bowls of oatmeal. There was no cream or brown sugar to doctor it up, but it had been so long since I'd had anything resembling a real meal that I certainly wasn't going to complain. My stomach growled in anticipation.

Sharra and I seated ourselves at one of the round tables. There were four people already there, and they didn't seem particularly friendly. Unlike most of the people I had seen so far, this group wasn't dressed in casual jeans and tees. Instead, they wore lots of leather, most of it black. Their gazes were cool and assessing as Sharra made the introductions.

"Guys, this is Poppy. She's the new recruit I brought back from Goodland. We finally found her again. Poppy will be in the guard rotation because she's got mag skills. When I met her, she was fighting two mechs and took them both down, too." They looked impressed at that information. "And I'm sure you've heard the stories about how she beat up Eddie from Wolf pack and fed him to a Shadow when he tried to hijack her. Help her out and give her the lay of the land where you can."

Sharra turned to me and reversed the introductions. "Poppy, these are four of my guards. You'll probably be partnered with one of them when you go out on patrol. Gabe is the big guy on the end," she pointed at a large man with the dusky skin and broad features that marked him as a Native Canadian, "and his brother is Len. They're not actually twins even though they look like they ought to be." The men nodded at me in greeting but didn't stop eating to speak.

"On Len's right is Marcii; she's a full-on Coloradan. Her family lived here when the city was destroyed, and they just never left."

Marcii was a heavyset brunette who looked like she could snap someone in two without breaking a sweat. Her intimidating appearance was enhanced by the hair buzzed close to the scalp, piercings in both eyebrows and her bottom lip, and colorful sleeve tattoos covering both impressively muscular arms from wrist to shoulder. Despite her menacing look, the grin she shot me was friendly.

"Two mechs?" she asked, her voice unexpectedly light and feminine. "That's damned impressive. And gossip's been all over the streets about some slip of a kid taking down Eddie and half his pack. Nice work there, couldn't have happened to a better guy. Nice t'meetcha."

"Thanks," I replied. "Gossip travels fast around here. I didn't realize the packs interacted so much."

"Well, not that much really," Marcii explained, "but this was big news. We bump into guards from other packs often enough, and we all like to trade a story or two. This story has been in the rotation a lot lately. Did you really feed Eddie to a Shadow?"

"I just ran faster is all," I demurred. "Got lucky that the Shadow went for the guys instead of deciding to chase me."

"Cha," scoffed the fourth guard at the table. He looked small in comparison to Marcii, Len, and Gabe but closer inspection showed him to be of average height, around five foot eight. He was wiry instead of bulky, but he looked strong enough to hold his own in a fight.

He held out a hand across the table, and I shook it. "Nathan," he said, "of approximately nowhere. I tend to drift from place to place, wherever things look interesting. Right now, Denver is pretty interesting." He flashed an engaging grin, dark eyes sparkling with mischief. "From what I hear, you did a leapfrog over the top of that Shadow and dumped Eddie and company right on top of it."

"Something like that," I admitted. "But really, it was all just a lot of lucky timing. I haven't really heard much about what happened to the men. The Shadow ... it killed one. But did the other men recovered?"

"One dead," Nathan confirmed. His friendly expression hardened as he continued, "Slimy guy called Dirty Jin. He is no loss, believe me. I'll spare you the stories of the things I know he'd done, but believe me, if he'd gotten hold of you, he'd have killed you as sure as that Shadow."

The others at the table nodded solemnly.

"Guy was a nasty piece of work," Marcii confirmed. "From what I hear, Eddie and the two other guys managed to get free when the Shadow stopped to eat Dirty Jin. Poor dog probably got food poisoning from that meal."

Nathan chortled and gave Marcii a playful shot in the arm, then turned back to me. "Eddie is still laid up with some bad bites. A lot of the Shadows are venomous, you know, so he's fighting that off. But he'll probably be okay eventually, more's the pity. Two other guys got mostly minor injuries, and they recovered just fine."

I nodded and dug into my oatmeal, thinking about this strange new world in which I now found myself. I still had many more questions than answers. This probably wasn't the best time to ask about the resistance group Sharra had mentioned so long ago, but I could get some information about logistics.

"So where do you get all this?" I asked, waving my hand vaguely around the room. "The food, the clothes … where does it come from?"

"We raise most of our own food," Sharra said. "We have gardens and greenhouses in the safe zones. We raise animals for food and send out hunting parties for wild game. There's plenty of that in and around the city. For things that we can't easily raise ourselves, we have contacts who help us trade or buy what we need.

"Money, goods, clothing and that sort of thing we mostly get by scavenging. There are still a lot of buildings and homes in the city that haven't been explored. We send teams in to look around and see what's useful and bring it back to our storage area in the basement. And again, we can trade for things that we can't find by scavenging."

"And no one cares? I mean, doesn't someone own those buildings and the things in them?" I asked.

"Honey, no one is left who has a claim to any of it. They were either killed in the bombings or evacuated afterward. They're long gone, and we're here and we need it." Nathan's voice was blunt but not unkind, and I nodded in understanding.

In my old world this would have seemed strange to me, but hadn't I been doing the same thing on a smaller scale? The old rules just didn't apply here. I fell silent again as we finished our meal, and Sharra and the others turned to casual conversation, letting me stay quiet as I tried to adjust to my new life as part of a pack.

Sharra finished eating before me and left me at the table to eat my breakfast at a more leisurely pace. I would have a few days to acclimate to my new home before beginning my guard duties. I was listening to the others trade stories about their recent patrol when I felt a shiver between my shoulder blades. I casually turned my head to look around and saw Mateo sitting at a table on the other side of the room, glaring daggers at me.

Marcii had noticed his malevolent stare, too. Speaking quietly enough to not be heard by the men, she asked, "So do you know Mateo, or did he just take a dislike to you from a distance?"

"We're acquainted," I told her. "We're not very fond of each other."

She nodded, still staring across the room at Mateo. "I don't have any firsthand knowledge, but I hear rumors that he can get a bit nasty when he thinks no one is watching."

I hesitated to badmouth an established pack member, but Marcii had created an opening. In a low voice I told her what had happened with Mateo. She looked sympathetic but her words were firm.

"You're going to have to watch your back, then. The guy's a total bottom-feeder, but you have to just deal with it and move on. This isn't some fancy-ass Goodland tea party, y'know? When you're living rough, good manners and basic human decency are a bonus, not a requirement. Even in a good pack you're expected to be able to look out for yourself."

She shrugged her wide shoulders. "I'll pass it on so people know what happened, but don't expect anything to change. That's not the way things work around here. But feel free to give him another beat-down if he makes a move." She grinned, her lip piercing glinting in the morning light.

I nodded. It wasn't what I was used to, but nothing in Denver was. We turned back to our breakfasts and ignored Mateo until he left the room.

CHAPTER TWENTY-SIX

I spent the next few days exploring the home base and the local neighborhood. I learned the routines for mealtimes, laundry, and showering and started to make some friends among the pack members. Roomie was a big help when it came to getting to know everyone. Though he often left to roam the streets at night, during the day he preferred to ride around in my backpack as often as possible. If I left my room without him on my back he would follow me, yowling until I gave in. People were so astonished to see one of the famously fierce street cats acting this way that they would make conversation with me to learn more, which let me meet a lot of the pack members.

After all my time alone, I found that I actually enjoyed being around people again. It was freeing to be able to be myself and not worry about being "Perfect Poppy" the First Lady all the time. Still, I was used to being busy. Now that I didn't have to spend all of my time managing political events or struggling for survival, I didn't know what to do with myself. I was wandering the halls of the base looking for something interesting to explore when rough hands suddenly yanked me into an empty room. My arms were pinned to my sides making it harder to strike back. Mateo shoved me against the wall before letting me go and stepping back out of my reach.

"And hello to you, too, Matty," I said. I didn't want to give him the satisfaction of knowing he'd rattled me, so I forced myself to act cool and calm.

"What did you tell them?" he demanded. "Lucas and Sharra both came around asking me how I knew you and why I didn't tell them where you were. They're both watching me like hawks now."

"I told them that we'd run into each other sometimes when I was living rough, that's all. Anything else going on is completely unrelated."

He glared down at me, and I had to restrain myself from punching his obnoxious face. "That had better be it, you little—"

"There's no need to threaten me, Mateo. I have no plans other than to ignore your existence. You leave me alone, and I'll leave you alone, okay?" I left the room without waiting for his response, slamming the door behind me.

I stomped down the hall still fuming and muttering to myself as I thought of better things I should have said to Mateo. My anger had me so distracted that I didn't notice someone walking up beside me until a hand touched my elbow. I jumped in surprise and whirled, hands poised to strike out.

"Whoa!" Lucas exclaimed, putting his hands in the air and taking a step back. "I didn't mean to startle you."

"Sorry," I said. "I was off in my own world, I guess." I smiled up at him, shaking off my foul mood. "What can I do for you?"

"Walk with me," he suggested. "I thought I'd take you up to the guard room. Sharra is short on guards for patrol duty today, so she wondered if you were ready to take on a patrol route."

"Yes!" I exclaimed. "I am so ready to get back to being useful."

Lucas chuckled. "Feeling a bit bored, are you?"

"It was really nice to relax for the first couple of days, but now I'm ready to be busy again."

"Well, I think I can guarantee that patrol will keep your boredom under control. It's more likely to be a bit too exciting. Guards on patrol are injured too often for anyone's liking, which is why Sharra is often shorthanded. Stay sharp. I'd hate to have you get hurt."

Lucas dropped me off at a small conference room on the second floor. It had large windows that looked over the bleak gray wreckage of the city with snow-capped mountains looming in the distance. A battered square table in the corner had seating for four and was piled with papers and books. Sharra sat there with Marcii, Len, and Gabe. I gave them a quick wave.

My attention was pulled to the east wall, which was covered with a huge map of the city. Judging by the logo in the corner of the big signboard, the map had once been on display at the Denver Chamber of Commerce. It had now been repurposed to track the various packs in the area. A thin wash of color had been applied in some areas, apparently to color-code sections of the city. I looked at the map with great interest, wanting a clearer picture of my position in the ruined city.

Sharra walked over as I inspected the map. "Blue areas mark Liberty territory. Other packs are marked in different colors," she explained.

The center of the downtown area was all held by Liberty. It was a sizeable territory. The packs around us were significantly smaller. There were also quite a few areas marked in sullen red. I tapped my finger on a red section nearly surrounded by Liberty blue. "What's this?" I asked.

"Wild territory," Sharra told me. "It's a section that's still hazardous. That particular spot has some dangerous plant life, venomous and carnivorous and thoroughly unfriendly. But we can't wipe it out without also destroying some plants that are good for healing. So we just keep people clear of it.

"Give me a few minutes to get the rest of the patrols sorted for this shift and then I can tell you what you need to know, okay?"

I was equal parts nervous and excited, but I just nodded and concealed my feelings behind a calm expression. If nothing else, my time as First Lady had taught me how to give the impression of confidence even when I felt unsure.

Sharra motioned for Gabe and Len to join us at the map. Ever the gentlemen, they grunted to acknowledge my presence before giving their attention to Sharra. She assigned them a patrol section by outlining an area on the east side of downtown with her index finger. It was mostly blue and edged with red areas on the outer boundaries, so it was controlled by the Liberty pack but bordered by stretches of wild territory that were dangerous to enter.

Gabe and Len grunted again to acknowledge Sharra's instructions and headed out the door. Len gave me a short nod as he passed. Gabe didn't bother.

"Friendly," I commented after they'd cleared the door.

Sharra chuckled. "They're men of few words. They'll warm up a little when they get to know you. Still won't say a lot though."

"So they're off to patrol that section … What does that involve exactly? What do we do when we're on patrol?"

"Basically, just walk the beat," Sharra told me. She motioned me over to the table and we sat down with Marcii. "We have our territory pretty well cleared of dangers, but it doesn't stay that way for long unless we keep an eye on things. So you'll take a mag-lev bike to get to the patrol area and then walk the blocks of your patrol looking for anything out of place."

"Keep an eye out for dangerous animals," Marcii told me. "That's pretty much anything big with sharp teeth or claws. You want to avoid confrontation but report anything you see to the hunters when you get back from patrol. They'll track it and bring back the meat if it's something we can eat."

Nathan entered the room and threw me a friendly wink as he walked to the map wall. Marcii waited with me as Sharra excused herself to assign him a solo patrol along the eastern edge of pack territory. He waved at us and headed out the door less than five minutes after walking in.

Sharra came back to lean on the table as she finished my orientation to guard duty. "You'll also run into people out there. Mostly Lurkers and Vultures. Lurkers target people and are willing to cosh someone on the head and take everything from them, right down to the clothes on their backs and the shoes on their feet.

"Vultures scavenge places looking for trade goods, which is what we do ourselves, but it's our territory so that's allowed. Vultures are sneaking into someone else's territory and trying to find anything of value. Both of them should be escorted out of our borders immediately.

"That's the basics," she said. "The rest is pretty much on-the-job training."

I nodded, anxious to get out on my first patrol and see things for myself. "Who am I partnering with?" I asked, careful to keep my voice casual, concealing my nervousness at the thought of going out with a stranger.

Sharra made a face. "That's the bad news," she said. "I'm going to have to send you out with Mateo."

I couldn't quite conceal my dismay. Marcii patted me on the shoulder with a heavy hand. "Don't worry, I've got your back," she said. "We wouldn't send you out with Mateo alone. We're gonna make it a three-person patrol today."

"Sorry," Sharra told me. "Mateo's section has to be patrolled, but his usual partner is on medical and this patrol really needs two people. Marcii's willing to take an extra shift, but she doesn't know that area well enough to take you on patrol without Mateo. This was the compromise we came up with."

"I can take the patrol with Mateo myself if you don't want to be around him," Marcii told me. "You'd just have to wait for another day to start working patrols."

I set my jaw. I wasn't going to let Mateo make me wimp out of my very first assigned shift. Marcii had more muscles than Mateo and I combined; if my fighting skills and her muscles couldn't keep me safe, nothing would.

"Thanks taking the extra shift, Marcii. Having you along will make it a lot easier to put up with Mateo for a few hours."

Sharra lowered her voice, "Marcii filled me in on the crap Mateo pulled before you joined the pack. I don't want you to think that we're ignoring you or don't believe you, but it's complicated. You can probably guess that you're not the only one to complain about Mateo."

"Then why—" I started to ask, but Sharra cut me off.

"But there have never been any witnesses to back up a complaint. And at the same time, a lot of women in the pack see Mateo as handsome and charming and are lining up to be his girlfriend. Basically, the pack council ends up letting it slide in order to keep a skilled guard in the pack."

"So as long as no one sees you do it, anything goes?"

Sharra blew out a frustrated breath. "It's not quite that bad, but yeah, kind of. I'm not saying it's the right way to handle it. If Lucas or I had the final say, Mateo would already be gone, but we're just part of the council. Even as the leader, Lucas just has one vote. We're stuck with it until we can bring the rest of the council around."

"So believe me when I say that I really don't want to send you with Mateo. If I could send you with anyone else, I would. I hate it, but least I know you can take care of yourself."

"Obviously I don't like it, but I get it," I told Sharra. "Especially with Marcii there, too. I just won't turn my back on him."

I did understand the position she was in. The pack council felt that losing a guard put the pack at risk and was more important to them than the risk he might pose to individual pack members. As my life in politics had taught me again and again, sometimes you had to suck it up and work with an asshole. Since I couldn't change the pack dynamics overnight, I would deal with it.

We looked up as the door to the guard room banged open, and Mateo swaggered into the room. A sneer twisted his full lips as he looked me up and down, his brown eyes cold. "So I am on babysitting duty, I hear?" he said to Sharra, turning his back on me. "We really must need new recruits if we are using children now. There are better uses for my time than taking this one on a field trip. Find someone else for this nonsense."

Sharra and Marcii weren't the type to try and fight my battles for me, so they stayed silent to see how I handled the situation. I rolled my eyes and sighed. "Marvi, I get to patrol with the resident comedian. But that particular bit is pretty tired. I mean, calling me a child just because I'm short? That's far from original. Just keep your jokes to yourself and your hands to yourself and let's get this over with."

We glared at each other until he jerked his head in agreement and turned to Sharra. "My usual patrol?" he bit out.

"Yes." For my benefit, she touched the map to outline an area at the south end of Liberty territory. It was bound by Wolf pack on the west, but the southern and eastern borders were wild territory. The section also had a large center area highlighted in red.

"This is your section tonight," Sharra told me. "This western edge bumps up against Big Eddie's patch, so you might see some of their guards, but otherwise it's usually pretty quiet.

"You're most likely to run into problems around this center section. Mateo knows the area, so he'll make sure you avoid wandering into the red territory."

She stared hard at Mateo until he nodded in acknowledgement.

"What's in the red zone?" I asked.

"No one knows," Marcii moaned in a spooky voice. Mateo scowled at her for clowning around, but I appreciated her attempt to lighten the mood in the room.

"The last two teams to go exploring in that section never returned," Mateo told me. "They simply disappeared. And another man is in medical now. He has been unconscious since his patrol partner discovered him lying just inside the red zone last week. Perhaps you think this will be a fun adventure? That you will go out there and play at being the tough girl? This is dangerous business, little princess, not a game. You must be ready for the real world if you think to come with me because I do not have time to come to your rescue when things get frightening."

It was hard, but I kept my voice low and controlled instead of shouting at him as I would have liked. "You think I don't know danger?" I asked. "I've battled mech warriors and won. I've escaped Shadows and turned a rival pack leader into puppy chow. I may be new to this city, but believe me, I am not a stranger to the real world. I know danger, and I can handle myself. I don't want or need you coming to my rescue."

I took a step forward and jabbed him in the chest with my index finger. "Condescend to me like that again, and you'll be the one needing a rescue, Mateo. And. Don't. Call. Me. Princess."

The last few words came through gritted teeth, each accompanied by another jab to the chest with my index finger. He glared down at me, his eyes furious but unsure of his next move. Finally, he nodded once and spun away to stride to the door.

"Come," he barked. "We will be late to our patrol."

He was almost out the door before Sharra called him back and reminded him to take weapons. Marcii picked up her own weapons and handed me a long, wooden staff and a stunner. I took a deep breath to fortify myself and set out for my first patrol with Mateo leading the way but Marcii watching my back.

CHAPTER TWENTY-SEVEN

We fell in a few steps behind Mateo, and our little group left the building and walked around the corner to the fenced-in parking lot holding the pack's mag-lev bikes. About a dozen bikes sat in full sunlight to soak up the solar energy and charge the engines.

A guard at the entrance to the parking lot noted our names before allowing us to enter and pick out bikes to use. I found my favorite; the bike I had inadvertently borrowed for my first few months in the city. I saw Marcii slip her staff into a loop on the back of the bike, so I found a matching loop hooked to my bike and used it to secure my own staff.

Climbing aboard the bike, I started the motor and followed Mateo onto Broadway, which was the main road cleared through this section of the city. There was no fun speeding and swooping through the streets on this trip. Instead, we worked our way south until we reached a huge traffic roundabout. Much of the area had been cleared and the debris piled around the edges of the circle. Roads and mag-lev rails entered the traffic circle from at least a dozen directions. Elevated ramps rose from the southern edges of the circle, each ramp snaking up to one of the many entrances on the ten or so levels of a gray concrete building. A sign still stood atop the structure identifying it as "Civic Center Station: Bus, Rail, and Train Depot."

Though the end of the building closest to us looked intact, the far end had taken plenty of damage. It crumbled away to a pile of shattered concrete about halfway down the length of the structure. The remains of a few ramps connected to nothing showed that the other end of the building had once looked similar to the side we now approached.

Mateo drove around the traffic circle until he reached a ramp marked with a number six tiled into the roadway. We made a sharp right turn to take the rail for ramp six, then zipped up a steep incline as the elevated road curved gracefully right and then slightly left before entering a tunnel in the side of the station. The tunnel was dark, lit only by the headlights of our bikes as we followed the rail deeper into the abandoned station. We came to a platform that looked like it had probably served as a boarding area back when this was used as a transportation center. Below the platform was an open area. In the light from our headlights, I could see two mag-lev bikes parked there.

Still giving us the silent treatment, Mateo stopped his bike at the platform and dismounted. Marcii rolled her eyes at his sulking but didn't say anything. I didn't break the tense silence either, preferring not to antagonize him any further. At least not yet—we had hours left in our patrol, so we'd have plenty of chances to continue snarking at each other.

Mateo rolled his bike beneath the platform to park it next to the two bikes already sitting there. He removed the ignition stick and stuffed it in a pocket, grabbed his staff, and headed for the stairs leading to the top of the platform.

Copying his actions, Marcii and I followed him across the platform and through a set of open glass doors into the main station. It was a little brighter here as faint light filtered through the dust and grime coating the skylights at the top of the open atrium in the center of the big building. The atrium was filled with overgrown plants. Vines climbed the walls to curl around the safety rails rimming each floor overlooking the empty lobby. It was a curiously tropical effect for a city so well known for its snow. I supposed the skylights had created a greenhouse-like environment to allow the plants to thrive.

"These are normal vines, right?" I asked Marcii. "None of the man-eating versions?"

Marcii's laugh echoed in the cavernous building. Whatever furnishings or other items the transport center had once held, it had all been scavenged and hauled away long ago so there was nothing to soak up the sound before it bounced off the concrete walls and floors.

"As far as I know, these are all normal plants. People come and go through here pretty often, and no one has noticed creeper vines looking for lunch."

That was a relief, though the whole area was still creepy with only the sullen light of the atrium to illuminate the hallway. Without the bright lights that had once blazed overhead, innocent doorways became gaping patches of darkness leading to unknown perils. The only sound was our own footsteps echoing through the concrete passageway, but I couldn't stop straining to hear something else. The building looked empty, but my nerves couldn't be convinced that we were alone in the darkness.

It was a relief to round a corner and see sunlight beaming in, even if the reason the sunlight could enter was because the end of the building had been ripped away and the floor we were walking on dropped abruptly into open air. My steps quickened a little as I followed Mateo toward the sunlit area. Unfortunately, he turned again before we reached the cheerful light and headed down a set of stairs. The stairway was the darkest section yet. I could barely make out Mateo's back as he hurried down the stairs ahead of me. I did my best to keep up as I made my way blindly down the steps. If it hadn't been for Marcii's reassuring presence behind me, I'm not sure I could have made myself step into that black stairwell.

Finally, another patch of light beckoned and led us into an open, grassy area outside the building. The late-morning sun on my face felt amazing as it melted away the tension brought by the spooky trip through the transport center. I enjoyed the feel of the grass beneath my feet as well even as we walked toward our next challenge.

That challenge was a massive wall of rubble higher than my head and stretching out for at least a hundred yards in either direction. It appeared to be made up of the remains of several large buildings and completely blocked all paths through to the other side. A beam of light bounced off something bright in the wreckage, and I turned to look closer. About half of an enormous rounded dome protruded from the debris, portions of it still speckled with delicate gold leaf gleaming in the bright morning sunlight. I remembered that dome from pictures taken before the war. Denver's historic capitol building, dating clear back to the 1800s, had been an impressive architectural gem. Now it was reduced to sad ruins.

Mateo headed for the wall and started up, using his staff to help him climb and balance. Following in his footsteps, I picked my way through the rubble. It was a hard climb, requiring us to scramble across shifting piles of loose bricks, scale chunks of concrete the size of boulders, and weave through forests of rebar and support beams still thrusting into the air. I was panting when I reached the top, but I was only moments behind Mateo, and he was breathing hard, too. Marcii had kept pace with me easily and seemed unfazed by the climb.

I took a moment to scan the view from the top of the wall. From this vantage point, I could tell that it was, in fact, a wall. It looked like heavy machinery had been used to push the debris together to form a long barricade, but there was no way to know what they had been defending against. Mech warriors, maybe, or even human soldiers back in those days. Whatever its purpose, it must not have been enough in the end since the destruction was comparable on both sides of the barrier.

The streaming sunlight was so bright that the scene had a faintly unworldly air. The light painted the crumbling streets and buildings in glowing gold and turned the dust in the air to dancing bits of brilliance. Nothing moved in the streets below, not even a bird call disturbed the total silence. It was terribly sad to think that these empty streets had once been a lively city full of people. Now, there was hardly an intact building to be seen for a long way on either side of the wall. Piles of destroyed masonry and the skeletal frameworks that were the only remains of elaborate building complexes were all that remained in this area. On the north side of the barrier, rubble had been pushed to the sides in order to clear streets. Not all of them, but at least enough to provide paths through the destruction.

The south side had not been cleared, though I could see faint trails through the wreckage. Rusting cars, broken buildings, and twisted rail tracks were only some of the debris clogging the alleys and roadways. From all appearances, no one had set foot there since the bombs fell. I knew that was not true since the pack guards were regular visitors. But it was so deserted that the very landscape seemed incompatible with life. I wasn't sure where or how we were supposed to patrol this section, but it was obvious that you couldn't take a bike through this section of town—not even using rollers instead of rails.

"Still think you're ready for this?" Mateo asked with a sneer.

His voice was loud after such complete silence, and I jumped, startled. He snickered spitefully, pleased with himself for surprising me. He didn't wait for me to answer, just turned and started down the south side of the massive pile.

His attitude was annoying, but I dismissed it. I was determined to prove myself to Marcii on this first patrol, but I didn't care what Mateo thought. We followed Mateo and worked our way down a faint path through the mounded refuse. It was less strenuous than the climb up had been, but as I hung by my hands from a slab of concrete hanging over a mound of sand and gravel, I knew that the trip back up would be hell.

I let go and dropped the last few feet to land with a thump on the shifting sand. I wobbled for a minute but caught my balance. The look on Mateo's face revealed his disappointment that I had managed without stumbling. I gave him a sweet smile, just to annoy him, and bent to pick up my staff from where I had let it fall before I dropped from the outcrop.

Familiar with the path, Mateo set a quick pace through the last section of the wreckage and soon disappeared from sight. Marcii and I moved more slowly as we picked our way along the faint path left by previous guards. Marcii could have moved faster, since she could step right over large obstacles that I had to scramble over or walk around, but she held herself to my speed.

By the time we emerged from the trail at the bottom of the wall, Mateo had already hailed a pair of guards who were waiting for us. I joined them in time to hear Mateo grumbling, "...little princess who wants to play at being a guard. I can only think that Sharra has been ... persuaded ... to allow this because the two have a special relationship."

I strolled up to the three men and didn't say a word to the misogynist ass. I just punched him in the left arm, which could have been a playful gesture, but I deliberately hit him halfway down the back of the arm where the triceps muscle ends. A large nerve crossed the bone right there and if it was hit just right, a person could cause pain without causing damage. I hit Mateo hard enough to make the muscle cramp and spasm. He yelped and clutched his arm while glaring at me with equal parts offense and astonishment.

"I told you not to call me 'princess,'" I reminded him. "Next time I'll really make it hurt."

"Bitch!" he spat at me, shaking out his arm. "Are you trying to cripple me before I go out on patrol? What if I need to fight?"

"Oh, don't be a baby," I responded, my voice vicious. "Are you such a wuss that a little knuckle punch is going to put you out of commission? Shake it off."

Marcii laughed until Mateo growled and raised his hand. She lurched forward to intervene. The guards we were replacing started to move as well, but I didn't need any of them to come to my rescue. I shot my own hand up and grabbed Mateo's wrist, digging my thumb into the pressure points there. He yelped again and yanked his hand away.

"I've told you before, I'm well-trained. Don't let my size mislead you. You don't want to take me on." I looked him straight in the eye and waited for him to back down. After a long moment, he looked away from me and took a step back.

"Bitch," he said again. "Fighting with you is not worth my time." He turned his back on me to talk to the other guards, who had been watching with interest. "What is the report?" he barked.

The two men were carefully neutral as they responded, telling us that their patrol had been quiet. They had seen nothing more than a few cats slinking around, but no sign of a pack, so the cats didn't seem to be a threat. They wished us good luck with our patrol and headed for the wall.

Mateo strode away and I followed with Marcii. "Fill me in," I asked her. "Why are we worried about cats?"

"We're not talking about kitty cats," Marcii said seriously, "Or even big, but civilized cats, like your Roomie. These are packs of predators with seriously sharp teeth and claws. Most of the cats in these packs are more than twenty pounds of muscle and mean as spit. So picture a dozen or more cats at least as big as Roomie.

"They'll work together as a group to bring down their prey. I've seen a pack of cats take down an antelope. They're cats, so they can come at you from any direction and they're flexible and agile enough that it's hard to get a solid hit on them.

"They don't give up, either," Marcii added. "The cats will just keep coming as long as there's one still moving. They'll just scatter and regroup—probably now angry and targeting you. So yes, we want to avoid the cats."

"Got it," I agreed, shaken at the idea of swarming attack cats. "It's a good thing Roomie didn't come along on patrol. I can just picture him deciding to pick a fight."

Marcii snorted. "That one would probably win the fight and take over the pack. Then he'd bring them all back to base and expect you to spoil the whole bunch of them."

I snickered at the mental image of Roomie holding court over a pack of ferals as they lounged around my room. "Again, I'm glad Roomie isn't here."

A hissed command to, "Be quiet!" floated back to us and Marcii and I exchanged annoyed looks but stopped talking. As much as I hated taking orders from Mateo, I knew that advertising our presence by chatting our way through the streets was not the best idea.

I decided the best course was just to keep my mouth shut and follow Mateo through this patrol so I could get a feel for my guard duties. His competence didn't seem to be an issue, just his nasty personality and inability to take no for an answer. I would learn what I could from him and go back to staying out of his way.

We walked through the streets, frequently detouring to go around piles of rubble blocking our path. I used my staff to help me climb up and over some of the obstacles as we worked our way west. I only knew we were headed west because I could see the Rocky Mountains looming in front of us. It was hard to keep my sense of direction with the convoluted route required to make our way through the streets, but I knew that Denver had mountains only to the west. As long I could spot the mountain range, I would be able to get my bearings.

I tried to watch for the markers Sharra had indicated on the map to show us our assigned patrol area, but it was difficult to find anything like street signs anymore and buildings looked different in person than they did on Sharra's map. Instead, I settled for committing our route to memory, so I could retrace our path if I was assigned to this patrol again. I kept my attention on my surroundings, basically ignoring Mateo except to follow him through the streets. I saw no signs of anything out of the ordinary. There were no people, no animals, and no threats of any kind. From the markings on the map back in the guard room, it seemed that this part of our territory was mostly used for hunting and was still being scavenged for useful goods.

We continued west until we came to a wide street that had been mostly cleared of wreckage. An intact street sign hung from a pole above the street and marked the road as Speer Boulevard. According to the map, that was the western border of Liberty territory. That must be why the street had been cleared, to make the boundary more obvious. Mateo stopped in the center of the street and simply stood there, staff held loosely in his right hand, and his left hand visibly open and empty. Since he was still refusing to speak to me, and I was not going to beg for an explanation, I had no idea what he was doing. Marcii and I leaned against a building to rest.

He ignored us and stared into the distance, obviously waiting for something. We stood there in silence for what felt like hours. I used the time to thoroughly inspect the area and commit the details to memory. I was careful to keep my eyes moving, never letting them fix in one spot for too long, since I knew staring that way would make my brain miss small changes in the environment that indicated someone was moving toward us. Apparently, no one had ever taught Mateo that lesson because his gaze was focused on a single point just above the horizon.

I had no idea what was going through his mind as he stared into space, but he didn't react when I caught sight of someone moving through the streets to the west and coming toward us. I nudged Marcii and murmured, "Incoming."

Mateo was the one who jumped this time, startled by the sound of my voice. He glared at me, but I wasn't going to apologize. He should have been paying attention. I turned my own attention to the man walking toward us along Speer. To my surprise, I recognized the slender, dark haired man.

"Rivers," I exclaimed. "Hey!" I raised my hand to wave at him in greeting.

He smiled and raised his hand in return. "Little Bit," he responded. "Looks like you're all joined up with a pack—you found Sharra?"

"Yes," I assured him. "Apparently, if Mateo had just been honest in the first place, I could have found her much earlier."

I didn't turn to watch my jibe hit home, but I could almost feel Mateo's angry glare scorching the side of my face. I really needed to stop needling him if we were going to make it through this patrol without killing each other, but I couldn't seem to help myself. I despised his creepy face and his sulky voice and everything else about him, and the snarky comments just leapt to my lips. Marcii only encouraged me by laughing every time.

I forced myself to stop baiting Mateo—for the moment—and focused on Rivers. "How have you been? I tried to come back and let you know I was okay, but you weren't there."

"Sorry," Rivers apologized. "We had some minor crises pop up, and I couldn't come meet you. I was going to head back down tomorrow to look for you. Now I guess I don't need to." He smiled at me, clearly relieved to see me settled safely with a pack of my own.

Mateo interrupted, obviously peeved with us for ignoring him. "Rivers," he said stiffly. "A bit out of your territory, aren't you?"

"I guess so. But I don't believe I'm required to clear it with you before I go visiting other packs." He glanced up and down the street as if to be certain of his position. "Speer is still neutral territory, as far as I'm aware. So since I'm not on Liberty territory, I'm not sure why you think you can question me here."

Mateo flushed at the rebuke. "Not questioning, just curious. I was expecting to see Jessie from Monarch pack. We usually bump into each other on patrol."

"I saw her a few minutes ago," Rivers replied. "She was already headed back to her base."

Mateo glared at me. "If we hadn't gotten off to such a late start for our patrol, we wouldn't have missed her."

I glared back. "If you hadn't decided to start our patrol by insulting me and Sharra, we wouldn't have been running late."

His glare deepened. I wasn't sure why meeting up with Jessie had been so important to him, but he was well and truly furious to have missed her. Seeing the curious looks from all of us, Mateo made an effort to pull himself together and hide his anger. He said nothing more, just turned on his heel and headed south along Speer.

Rivers stepped closer to me and leaned down to speak softly in my ear. His soft black hair fell forward to brush my cheek, and I shivered at the light stroke of his hand as he swept his hair back. I stared into his dark eyes rimmed by gorgeously thick, dark lashes. I was so busy gazing into his eyes that I almost missed his words.

"Watch your back, Little Bit. After what happened before, Mateo is not your friend. He'd be just as happy if you never came back from patrol."

"I'll be careful, Laughing Boy," I promised, leaning closer to breathe in his spicy, clean scent. Whatever soap they had found or made in Wolf pack smelled much better than what we had in Liberty.

"Good," he said with a sweet smile. This time when he touched my cheek, it was not an accidental brush. He used his index finger to trace a delicate line over the blue ink trailing down my cheek. "Take care of yourself, Pretty Poppy."

My life had not been sheltered up to this point. Traveling with my father, and later as the First Lady, I'd dealt with war, suffering, destruction, and the mostly bloodless carnage that was civilized politics since I was a tiny child. But I'd never had a lot of chances for one-on-one time with a boy. This was breathtaking new territory for me.

Marcii spoke up from her spot against the wall, breaking the intimate mood. "All right, no more time for flirting, my lovebirds. Our guide is leaving us behind." She gave Rivers a light shove to send him on his way. Of course, a light shove from Marcii had a lot of force behind it, and he staggered a few steps.

"I'll look after your Pretty Poppy for today," she told him. "And you can come see her at the base if you want time for lovey-dovey crap."

"I'll look after myself," I protested, my cheeks burning with embarrassment at Marcii's gruff teasing. I peeked at Rivers and added, "But yes, come by the base sometime."

He grinned at me and promised he would. I kept my mouth firmly closed so no embarrassing girly giggles could spill out as Marcii grabbed me by the elbow and pulled me away to follow Mateo.

CHAPTER TWENTY-EIGHT

Marcii and I followed Mateo down the diagonal street southeast until we came to another road still boasting a street sign. We turned off Speer to head east on the mostly cleared Eleventh Avenue. In this section, it was easier to see why the pack would want to claim the territory. There were dozens of high-rise apartment buildings in this neighborhood, many of them still partially intact. If the buildings were still being explored, there could be all sorts of useful things to scavenge.

I kept close watch for anything threatening as we continued east. Mateo conducted spot checks on some of the intact buildings by giving the doors a firm shake to ensure that they were still chained closed. Marcii and I moved to the other side of the street and started doing our own spot checks.

Eleventh Avenue came to an end at another wall of debris. Instead of climbing this one, Mateo turned north and then headed east again on the next street. Twelfth Avenue, I would assume. We continued our silent patrol, conducting spot checks on opposite sides of the street and watching for anything out of the ordinary. We followed the numbered avenues as much as possible to criss-cross the section several times as we worked our way north toward the wall and the transport station.

I wasn't certain where the wild territory shown on the map would be in real life, but I thought we must be getting close. Even the little animals we had seen scurrying through the streets had disappeared. I hadn't realized that I was hearing sounds from birds and other wildlife until all their noises stopped. Now, it was disturbingly quiet. I moved as soundlessly as possible as I walked toward a squat red-brick building. Whatever might be out there, I didn't think I wanted its attention.

I approached the door. I didn't have to tug on it; the door stood slightly ajar. It was obviously not locked up anymore.

"Mateo," I called. "This door is open."

He raised an eyebrow. He didn't do it nearly as well as Rivers had managed it. "Well then, I guess you'd better go inside and check it out. I'll wait for you here."

Marcii scoffed. "Brave man, sending the newbie in. Come on, Pops. We'll take care of this for him." She jerked the door open and stepped inside.

I sent Mateo a dirty look. I was quite sure that he would have tried the same thing even if I hadn't had Marcii as my backup. On the other hand, having Mateo as my backup was so unappealing that going in alone probably would have been better.

I followed Marcii into the building, listening intently for any sounds. All the windows here were covered and I couldn't see more than a foot or two in front of me. I swallowed hard, very aware of my racing heart and shaking hands. Anything could be hiding in the darkness.

I would have stepped right back outside, but I couldn't see Marcii anywhere. "Marcii," I called in a whisper. No response came.

As my eyes adjusted I could see the outlines of furniture still in place but there was no sign of Marcii. She was moving fast, I reassured myself. She's probably already half finished with the walkthrough. Any minute now she would pop back into the entry hall and haul me back outside.

But since I still couldn't see or hear her, I went looking. Based on the signs outside, this building had once been a small school. From the little bit I could see, the hallway was mostly empty with a bench or two placed along the walls. Open doors lined both sides of the wall, gaping pools of deeper dark opening off the main path. I tried looking inside a couple of classrooms, but it was too dark to make out anything.

I walked faster, anxious to find Marcii and get out of here. Maybe the door was ajar because someone had intended to move in but ended up disliking the dark rooms as much as I did.

At the end of the hallway something caught my eye—a tiny gleam of pale color against the wall where it should have been dark. I turned my steps to investigate and crouched down to look closer. It took me a minute to realize what I was looking at and when realization came, I shoved my hand hard against my mouth to hold back a whimper. The white gleam came from bones piled in a jumbled heap against the wall. Judging by the empty skull peering from the mound, the bones were human.

Even worse, behind the first heap of bones was another. And another. I wasn't sure how many there might be continuing back through that hallway. I wasn't going to find out either. Investigating this was not a job for one guard on her first patrol. I stumbled to my feet so I could turn and run for the exit. Suddenly, I heard a noise behind me. Not much, just a whisper of sound like a sliding footstep against the tiled floor. I whirled, trying to locate the source of the noise, but I could see nothing.

"Marcii?" I called. I admit it, my voice shook a little. Silence answered me. "Hello?" I called again.

A heartbeat later, strong arms wrapped around me from behind and yanked me off my feet. I immediately threw my head back as hard as I could manage. Because my assailant had lifted me, my head was in perfect position and I heard the distinctive crunch of cartilage as the back of my skull smashed his nose. He howled and dropped me as he staggered back clutching his face. I stopped my follow-up strike when I recognized his voice as he screamed. It was Mateo. Doubtless he thought it would be a funny prank to sneak up on me and terrorize me in the dark. I barely restrained myself from beating him bloody; I didn't want to spend that much time in this place.

"Bitch!" he shouted at me, his voice muffled by his hands cupped over his face. "Look at dis. You broke by dose!"

"You deserved it," I responded. "You are an ass with the emotional maturity of a ten-year-old." I stalked past him, determined to find Marcii and go back to base.

I was stomping down the hall when I heard another slither behind me. I spun around to confront Mateo, incensed that he would try to sneak up on me again. What I saw instead was the biggest freaking snake in existence sliding down the hallway toward me.

The snake's head was easily the size of a watermelon—a large watermelon. The snake's body was a couple of feet in diameter and patterned in dark green and black diamonds. Each individual scale was as large as the tip of my thumb. The snake's dead-white eyes were bigger than my clenched fist and when its tongue flickered out to taste the air, it was as thick as a rope. Though the snake's head was still about three feet behind me, the tongue almost touched my face.

The near brush of the snake's tongue snapped me out of my stupor, and I bolted down the hall. Mateo's footsteps suddenly pounded behind me as he ran up from the end of the hall, hurdled the snake, and brushed past me, disappearing through the door and slamming it closed behind him.

"Mateo!" I screamed. "Open the door. Marcii!"

I reached the end of the hall and frantically felt along the wall for the door but couldn't locate it in the pitch black. I could hear the dry slip and slide of the snake's scales as it undulated toward me. It wasn't in a hurry. It knew I had nowhere left to run. I stared back into the darkness, trying desperately to get a glimpse of the snake. Finally, I saw its outline. It had almost reached me. If I took time to find the exit door, it would have me.

The snake slid along the right side of the hallway, so I jumped left, running with all my might for one of those open classroom doors. The snake realized I was trying to escape and moved to stop me. It struck with terrifying speed, and only sheer luck let me duck and dodge just in time. The snake's jaws closed on empty air as I dove through the first door I came to.

Jumping to my feet, I grabbed the edge of the door and slammed it shut as the snake struck at me again. The door swung closed but not quite fast enough. The snake's head was inside the room, pinned just behind the jaws by the heavy steel door. I thanked whatever city code had required classrooms to have reinforced fire doors as I braced myself against the door, pressing it closed with all my might.

The snake's head was just above mine, and I could see and feel its tongue lashing the air frantically as it tried to escape. I heard the snake's body thrashing against the tiles in the hallway. It was big and strong and really determined to move the door crushing its throat, but I was fueled by life-or-death adrenaline and had the assistance of pneumatic hinges attempting to do their job of closing the door.

I had the stunner in my pocket, but I was afraid to shift my grip on the door to grab it. I wasn't sure what a stunner would do to the monster snake anyway. Unable to think of anything else, I braced my feet against the floor and shoved back even harder. I heard a dull crack and felt the snake's thrashing slow. Slower. Slower.

When it finally stopped moving altogether, I still couldn't bring myself to open the door. I stayed there, door pinning the snake tight, for at least ten minutes before I dared to move. When I finally left the doorway, I did it in one huge leap to the other side of the room. I didn't want to be anywhere near that thing if it wasn't dead after all.

Without me bracing the door, the snake's weight pushed it open again. The head fell limply to the floor, striking the tile with a thud. I stared through the darkness, barely breathing. The snake seemed to be dead, but the thought of walking past the enormous thing to leave the room was nauseating. In the end, it was only the realization that the snake might not live here alone that got me moving.

I took a deep breath and bolted for the doorway. I raced past the snake at top speed and almost knocked myself unconscious when I crashed into the wall at the end of the hall. Gasping for breath, I ran frantic hands over the wall looking for the door. At last my hands touched the smooth metal bar of the door handle, and I wrenched it violently open, leapt through the door, and banged it closed again behind me. I leaned against the door shaking from head to toe.

Mateo was nowhere in sight. When I found him, I was going to skin him alive. Worse, I couldn't see any sign of Marcii either. Fighting back panic, I forced myself back inside the building for a lightning-fast search, but found nothing. Marcii had vanished.

Back in the street, I tried to figure out my next steps. Without knowing this territory, I was likely to just get myself in more trouble searching for Marcii. I needed to return to base and get help.

From here I could see the wall with the transport center rising behind it. They were only a few blocks north, and it was tempting to just cut through the streets and head directly for safety on the other side of the wall. But I didn't know exactly where the dangerous wild territory began—and the presence of the giant snake argued that I was probably pretty close. I didn't want to risk finding myself in the middle of something even worse than what I had just encountered.

I would have to retrace my steps. It would take longer, but at least I would be on streets I'd already walked without incident. I followed the path back to Speer and from there found my way back to the wall where we'd rendezvoused with the previous patrol. Feeling a hundred throbbing aches by now, I painfully worked my way over the wall. I felt a huge rush of relief when I dropped to the ground on the far side. I still had to get through the transport center, but that creepy dimness seemed minor now in comparison to the dark and snaky school.

I trudged up the stairs. My mind was racing with fear over Marcii's disappearance and lingering adrenaline from fighting the snake, but my body was so exhausted that I couldn't move any faster.

I was really dragging by the time I got to the sixth level and wondered if there was a good reason for parking this high instead of in a nice ground-level spot. I wanted nothing more than to go back to base and turn the search and rescue effort over to experienced guards. And then I was signing up for a domestic rotation. Scrubbing toilets couldn't be worse than this.

I had almost reached the platform where we'd parked the bikes when a figure stepped out of the shadows. It was Mateo. Deep inside I was equal parts scared and furious, but I was so tired that the emotions barely registered.

I leaned against the wall for support and waited to see what he would do. I would fight if I had to, but I dearly hoped I could get out of this with words. My exhaustion put me at a major disadvantage.

"Get out of the way, Mateo," I said wearily.

"I cannot believe you made it back," he said, astonished. "That snake was big enough to snap you in two."

"Well, you would know," I said acidly, finding some of my anger. "After all, you did jump right over it in your rush to abandon me in that building."

He was looking at me very oddly, and it made me uneasy. I slipped my hand along my side, feeling for the stunner in my hip pocket. It wasn't there. I'd lost it somewhere during my altercation with the snake. I didn't remember dropping my staff either, but I didn't have it in my hands, so it was also somewhere back in the streets.

I shook my head, trying to clear the fuzzy cobwebs of fatigue and tried again.

"Let's get back home," I told Mateo. "We need to send a team looking for Marcii."

"Back home ... so you can brag to everyone that you broke my nose? And share stories of my cowardice? I do not like that idea."

I talked fast now. Whatever Mateo had in mind was definitely not going to be good for me. "Hey, I don't need any credit for taking down the snake. It was all you, okay? You investigated the open door while I waited outside. You fought the snake and killed it. The snake broke your nose. No one else ever needs to hear anything different.

"The important thing is that we need to send help for Marcii. You're the expert in this territory, so they'll need you to lead the way. You'll be a hero when you find her."

He looked at me for a long, long moment as he considered my words. He gave me a charming smile, and I relaxed just a little. My efforts to mollify him were working.

"You know," he said, "there is a saying for moments like these. 'Two can keep a secret but only if one of them is dead.'"

I was sore and tired and my reaction time was slower than usual, which is why I didn't manage to dodge his lunge. He had me around the throat pressing me back against the atrium railing as he choked me. I clawed at his hands, carving deep scratches in his skin, but he didn't even notice.

I aimed a jab at his throat, punching him just below the Adam's apple. He gagged and his hands loosened for a moment in reflex, but I hadn't been able to put enough force behind the blow. He recovered before I could break loose and tightened his grip on my throat.

He shoved me harder against the rail. Bent backward and hanging into open space above the atrium as I was, I couldn't get any leverage. I desperately hooked my heels into the lower part of the railing, trying to anchor myself so I could fight back effectively.

Mateo laughed at my efforts and squeezed harder. I wasn't sure whether I would die first from choking or from being pushed off a six-story drop, but one or the other seemed inevitable.

My vision was shading to black around the edges, and I hated that the last thing I would see was Mateo's maniacally grinning face. I wasn't going out alone though. I prepared to kick loose from the rail and take Mateo over with me.

In the back of my foggy brain, I heard shouting but didn't register its significance. All I knew was that I was about to go over the edge into the mysterious growth of the atrium, and then suddenly Mateo and I were both flying through the air. But we were flying away from the atrium, not into it. Even as I tried to puzzle out this mystery, Mateo was ripped roughly away from me. I kept sliding across the slick floor until I crashed into the wall. My body struck first, meaning my head didn't hit the wall quite as hard as it could have. Ouch, I thought. Third time today.

I lay there, dazed, not understanding what was happening as I watched a tangle of shadows dancing in front of me. Pretty, I thought vaguely, gazing at the shifting patterns of dark shadow on a background of lighter shadow. It was several long seconds before my head and vision cleared enough to realize that I was watching a vicious fight taking place in the dim corridor.

Mateo had pulled a knife from somewhere, and he was using it to hold Lucas and Sharra at bay. He snarled and lunged for Sharra, but it was a feint. And as Lucas moved to block him, Mateo swept the knife backward and sliced it across Lucas' stomach. Lucas had moved back just enough that the stroke didn't gut him, but a thin line of dripping red was visible through the cut in his tee. It didn't seem to slow him down. His movements were as sure and fluid as ever.

Lucas lunged forward in a classic football tackle and knocked Mateo to the floor. That should have ended it. Lucas was at least three hundred pounds of solid muscle, but Mateo was crazy. And in a fight, crazy gives you a lot of strength.

Mateo managed to work his knife hand free and would have plunged the blade into Lucas' broad back if Sharra had not stepped in at that moment with a sharp and accurate kick to Mateo's wrist. The knife flew free and skittered across the floor until it slid off the edge into the atrium.

Mateo finally stopped struggling and lay still on the floor. Cautiously, Lucas levered himself to his feet, always keeping a big hand wrapped around Mateo's shirt collar to be sure he didn't decide to bolt.

"What the hell, Mateo?" Lucas rumbled. "Have you completely snapped? I'd ask what happened on patrol, but between the report we got from the guards you relieved and the conversation we heard before you tried to choke Poppy and throw her off the edge, I think we've got the gist. Where's Marcii?"

I struggled to sit up, and Sharra ran to help me. Mateo spit contemptuously at Lucas' feet and jerk himself free of the other man's hold.

"I am done," he announced. "You and your pussyfoot leadership team are constantly 'gathering information' as an excuse not to take action. You are a group of spineless cowards. I will join Jessie and the Monarch pack, and you will see what a revolutionary group is supposed to be."

Mateo stormed away, and Lucas let him go. Mateo disappeared around the corner and we listened to his footsteps descending the stairs until the echoes disappeared.

Lucas came to check on me then. He crouched down in front of me and took my head in his two big hands, running his fingers through my hair to feel the lumps. He tilted my head back so he could look into my eyes.

"Your eyes are so pretty," I rasped. I blamed my confession on my probable concussion. "Even darker than your skin but with such a nice sparkle."

Sharra stifled a laugh, and Lucas smiled down at me in amusement. "Thank you, Poppy. You have very nice eyes, too. Even if they are a little unfocused just now. You should probably try not to talk too much. Your throat must be very sore."

"It is," I agreed in astonishment. "How did you know?"

His lips quirked again and he informed me, "You have a lovely ring of bruises forming all around your neck. Your sore throat will probably get worse before it gets better. Your sore head, too."

I nodded solemnly, then clutched at my head as the movement caused violent pain to shatter through my skull. I moaned and tried not to throw up, but at least the pain cleared my head again. I closed my eyes in humiliation and vowed to myself that I would not say another word until I had my head on straight again.

Sharra laughed outright this time. "You just said that out loud," she informed me.

I groaned again and sealed my lips shut. Lucas got to his feet, reaching down and scooping me into his arms as though I weighed nothing.

"Probably best not to have you walking, especially in the dark. And definitely no riding a bike. You'll have to ride with me, and we'll send someone back for the extra bikes." He carried me down the platform stairs and placed me on the back of his bike.

Sharra helped me put on a helmet as Lucas mounted in front of me and pulled my arms around his waist. He sucked a sharp breath as my hands scraped over the cut on his abdomen, and reached back to shift my arms just a bit lower. I clutched him tightly and leaned into his strong back. My head was swimming, and I was worried about falling off the bike.

Lucas was a cautious driver with none of the theatrics Sharra and I were fond of. I wasn't sure whether that was his usual style or if he was being careful on my behalf. Either way, I felt safe as I rested my aching head against his back. He smelled good in that musky way that men smell after hard labor. I was breathing the scent in deeply, trying to analyze the attraction when I realized that we had come to a halt back in the bike lot.

Sharra was already off her bike and calling for guards and hunters to head back to the wall and go looking for Marcii. Lucas sat still, patiently waiting for me to let go of him so he could dismount.

"Are you ... smelling me?" Lucas asked, amusement clear in his voice.

I cleared my throat and sat up straight as I pulled my arms from around his waist. "Certainly not," I responded primly. "I don't know what you're talking about."

He just chuckled and climbed off the bike, careful not to jostle me. He scooped me into his arms again and smiled down at me.

"Helluva first patrol, Red."

"You should see the other guy," I told him with a loopy grin.

"Oh, I will," he assured me. "As soon as we get you settled, I'm going out there with the hunters to take a look at that snake of yours."

"Not my snake," I slurred. I waved one hand magnanimously. "It's all yours. You can have it." I was staring into his eyes again. They really were so pretty. And right now, they were looking at me like I was the only person in the world. It was a heady feeling, especially on top of a concussion.

And then, as if I weren't already confused enough by the events of the day, Lucas leaned down and brushed a kiss lightly across my lips.

"You need to take better care of yourself, Poppy. You just got here. I don't want to lose you already."

CHAPTER TWENTY-NINE

I woke up in Medical. The big conference room was set up as an infirmary with half a dozen twin beds lined up against the wall. The bed next to mine was the only other one with an occupant.

"Marcii!" I exclaimed in relief. Or tried to, anyway, since all that emerged from my throat was a rasping croak. I touched my throat and felt hot, swollen skin.

The noise I'd managed was enough to alert Marcii, and she rolled her head gingerly to look at me. "Yep," the woman confirmed. "Your poor throat looks awful. I bet it feels even worse."

I nodded, then clutched at my head as the motion made my pounding skull throb even harder.

"We've got matching concussions," Marcii informed me with a weak grin. "Move slow and careful."

I tried to force my voice to work and was rewarded with nothing more than a few squeaks. Coupled with my questioning expression, it was enough.

"You want to know what happened to me?" she asked. I gave her a tiny nod, then closed my eyes again as even that small movement made my head swim.

"Well, from what I remember, I headed up to the second floor in that school and literally ran into that freaking snake at the top of the stairs. I bounced off its snout and fell backwards down the stairs—knocked myself out somewhere along the way.

"Next thing I remember was waking up at the bottom of the stairs and remembering my last view of that freakin' snake slithering down the stairs. Now I figure you must have distracted it or the freakin' snake would have made a meal of me. At the time, I didn't even remember you existed. I just bailed out the first window I saw and hauled ass."

She shuddered and I heard her mutter, "Freakin' snake," again under her breath. Either her injury or her traumatic encounter with the snake was really getting to her. Her vocabulary was usually much more extensive—and profane.

"Anyway," she finished, "my head was all messed up and I ended up just kinda wandering around until a rescue team found me and brought me home. You were already here by then, so … that's it, I guess. Thanks for distracting the freakin' snake so he didn't eat me."

Not bothering to open my eyes, I gave her a weak thumbs-up in acknowledgement. I cracked one eye when I heard footsteps approach and saw a dark-haired, heavyset woman hurrying to the beds

"Doc will be glad to hear that you're finally awake," she said. "How are you feeling?"

I made a so-so motion with my hand and she tutted. "Poor lamb—lambs. You're both so banged up. Doc will be here soon, and she'll get you set up with some pain meds to help." She rubbed my shoulder with a comforting hand as she introduced herself.

"I'm Deb," she told me. "I'm one of the nurses here in Medical. Doc Jaq—that's short for Jaqueline—will be by soon. She's been in to check on you a few times already, but you've been pretty out of it for almost twenty-four hours. We were starting to get a little worried, I can tell you."

Deb's kind eyes and reassuring touch went a long way toward making me feel better. She fussed with my pillows to help me sit up more comfortably and straightened the light blanket over my legs. I felt my eyes well up a little at her tender care. It had been so long since anyone had fussed over me so affectionately that it made me think of the mother I had never really known and the father who had adored me. The ache of missing him flared to life again, and I felt too rotten to push it away like I usually did. Deb saw the tears starting in my eyes and pulled me into a warm hug, her bosom like a soft pillow.

She pulled away when new footsteps announced the arrival of the doctor, but the affectionate hug had me feeling better already. I had seen Doc Jaq from a distance at meals, but this was my first close contact. The short, stocky woman had white hair, white skin, and eyes of such a light gray that they seemed almost to disappear into the paleness of her face.

She didn't say a word, but her hands were gentle as she ran them over my head to feel my swollen bumps. She looked into my eyes, prodded the bruised skin on my neck, and pulled out a stethoscope to listen to my lungs. Finally, she nodded in satisfaction and stepped back.

"No sign of worse damage," she told us. "Just the concussion that we'd already presumed, so there's nothing to do but wait for the body to heal itself. I want you to stay here for another day or so until the headache has gone. We'll keep an eye on you and keep you supplied with meds to help the pain."

She turned to Deb and said, "Same instructions as for Marcii. She can have the strong stuff for three or four days depending on her pain levels, then ease her off to willowbark tea to keep the edge off things until the headaches stop." Deb nodded and stepped away to find the medicine, and Doc turned back to me.

"You're on bedrest for at least a couple of days and light duty for a week or two after that. Everyone recovers differently from a concussion, so just take it slow until I clear you. Behave yourself and rest."

Marcii and I each got pain tablets from Deb, and I felt better almost immediately. Marcii fell asleep again, but though I was lethargic and woozy, I felt too awake to sleep. Instead, I watched with interest as a slow but steady stream of patients visited Medical. A boy had sprained his ankle during a game of chase. A kitchen worker had a nasty slice across her left hand from a slip of the knife while chopping vegetables. And there were guards with animal bites, sores, and rashes from various plants, and a wide variety of bumps and scrapes acquired in the course of their patrols. About a dozen guards were sent out on each shift, and it seemed that almost all of them ended patrol with a visit to Medical.

I worried that I was making a bad first impression, meeting my fellow guards while lying in my hospital bed. I didn't want anyone to think I was weak and helpless. But I soon learned that Sharra had tried to avoid the spread of misinformation and had called all the guards together to tell them exactly what had happened. Since Mateo was widely acknowledged to be both a jerk and a tough son of a bitch, no one was too sorry to see him go, even if it did leave the pack short one guard.

Everyone seemed impressed that I had held my own with him in a fight, even though I privately burned with embarrassment that he had gotten the better of me. I swore to myself that I was going to train even harder as soon as I was allowed to get back to working out.

Lucas and Mac had already taken a hunting party out to the wild territory where we'd encountered the snake. Investigating the area hadn't been a high priority yet, but now that they knew what was in there, everyone wanted to be sure there were no more giant snakes looking for a meal. No one wanted the snakes to expand their territory.

The hunters had discovered the body of the snake I'd killed. They'd also found three more live snakes—none of them quite as large as the first—and a nest containing several eggs. The hunters had killed the monstrous snakes and smashed the eggs. They weren't ready to call the area cleared yet. That would take another week or two of checks to be sure no more snakes were lurking.

The hunting team had decided against bringing the snakes back for meat. Given the snakes' recent diet, it just didn't feel right. Instead, they removed the giant skins to bring back to base and buried the carcasses. They also brought back the head of the largest snake as a kind of macabre trophy. After seeing the size of that head and learning that I had killed it single-handedly, no one saw me as a weakling, despite my explanations that I had been very, very lucky.

I got to know a lot of different guards during my time in Medical and learned more about what I could expect from a typical patrol. They stopped by to see Marcii and stayed to get to know me. Roomie had assumed guard duty and made a spot for himself on the foot of my bed, and most guards brought a little treat for him. He seemed pretty pleased with himself.

Even Lucas stopped by to see me while I was laid up. To my disappointment, there were no heated looks and lingering touches this time. He stood at the side of the bed and inquired after my health with the stiff concern of a general for his soldier.

I watched him walk away, confused by the abrupt change in attitude. Had something changed while I was in Medical? Or maybe my bruised brain had just imagined the whole thing?

"That's Lucas for you," Marcii said with a sigh. "Every time he has the possibility of a relationship he overthinks it, runs hot and cold, and eventually ruins it before it can go anywhere."

"Relationship?" I sputtered, embarrassed. "No! I just … well, he … and Rivers. I'm interested in Rivers, remember?"

Marcii looked skeptical but let me slide. "Yeah, I suppose you and Rivers might make a go of things. Hard when you're in separate packs, but maybe you'd finally give him the incentive to bring his friends and join up with Liberty."

"There's no rule against socializing with other packs, then, right?"

"Nah, you're fine. Plenty of people have friends from other packs."

We were quiet for a few minutes before Marcii spoke again. "Listen, I have to ask. "Perfect Poppy," right?"

I groaned dramatically and covered my eyes with my arm. "I can't believe that stupid nickname has even followed me out here! Denver doesn't even get the news-holos. How does anyone know that name?"

Marcii laughed at my dramatics. "The techie types doing all the sneaky Resistance stuff upstairs can download some of the holos. They tell us what's going on in civilization."

"There's sneaky Resistance stuff going on upstairs?"

"Yeah," she said with a shrug. "It's not my thing. Lucas is in charge, and Sharra does some stuff. I don't really know. Or care. They get real pissy if you try to sneak up there and check it out, though."

I tucked that bit of information away with the other little pieces I had gathered since my arrival. I'd tried asking Sharra about the Resistance, but she would only tell me that I would have to wait. Membership in the Resistance was an invitation-only kind of thing.

Knowing I wouldn't get any more on that topic right now, I asked instead, "So does everyone know who I am?"

"Mmm, not everyone. Word's getting around though. This pack can't keep a secret. Which is probably why the Resistance-types don't tell the rest of us anything. We gossip too much. Just within the pack, though. It won't spread from here."

I hoped she was right. It would be disastrous if Cruz got word that I was out here. I was sure he'd send bombers to pulverize the city in order to be sure I was dead, never caring how many others were killed with me.

CHAPTER THIRTY

After being released from bedrest, Marcii, Roomie, and I spent our recovery time hanging out in the guardroom with Sharra. There I learned more about the various sections of our pack territory and our nearest neighbors. By the time Doc allowed me to return to normal activity I was a solid member of the team even with only one patrol under my belt.

After I was cleared for duty again, I quickly became accustomed to scrambling over walls of debris and strolling through spooky abandoned buildings while patrolling with various partners. I learned that we used the sixth floor of the transport center because lower levels were choked with jungle-like plants growing wild from the atrium. I learned to navigate the streets with ease, whether by bike or on foot. I learned to love my new home, the people I worked with, and the pack family we were protecting.

As guards we chased away dangerous animals and people who trespassed on our territory. We worked with the hunters to bring back wild game to feed the pack. We gathered information and passed messages as we met up with guards from other packs. We even helped a woman and a small girl, both with obvious bruising revealing they'd been badly beaten, when they showed up in Liberty territory looking for a safe place to go. They were given asylum and quickly absorbed into the pack.

In the deep of winter, the job became at once harder and easier. Howling blizzards confined us to base for days at a time while piles of snow fell on the city. Between storms we struggled through waist-high drifts to complete our patrols on foot, unable to use the mag-lev bikes when the tracks were buried in snow. But the thick snow also meant that people and animals left clear signs of their presence. It was easy to follow and find them.

I had never spent much time in the snow until this winter. It had always been an inconvenience to be avoided whenever possible. But now I discovered the peace of being alone in a silent, snow-covered landscape. The refreshing slap of cold hitting my cheeks as I left the warm base. The satisfaction of breaking trail through a deep snowdrift. And the exhilaration of sliding down a tall pile of snow on a makeshift sled.

I loved being a guard, and I didn't miss my life as First Lady. I tried not to think about my former life too much, and I was mostly successful. Instead, I focused on the here and now and on being content with my new situation. I still missed my father terribly every day, but I tried not to think about Cruz at all. I couldn't bear to dwell on his terrible betrayal and the fact that he had gotten away with it all. As much as I had thought about it, I hadn't been able to come up with a plan to bring him down.

I needed the Resistance, but they weren't ready to let me in yet. I still hadn't even seen the upper floors—not that I hadn't tried to sneak up there a couple of times. I pestered Lucas and Sharra for more information, but they only told me I would have to be patient until the rest of the decision-makers were ready to let me in. I was annoyed but resigned, so I concentrated on my new life for now.

I saw Rivers often. No matter what section of our territory I was assigned to patrol, he seemed able to find me within a day or two. He would casually stroll up to me and my partner and chat for a few minutes, flirting outrageously and blatantly. My partners found this amusing and generally found an excuse to leave us alone for a few minutes.

After all my time at political functions and events, I was adept at casual flirting and easily played that game. I greeted Rivers with a kiss on the cheek or left him with a quick hug, but since that's as far as my experience went, I was taken by surprise when he kissed me under a bright March moon.

We'd been flirtatiously exchanging messages as usual when my patrol partner Rick excused himself to find "the facilities." Rivers was cupping my hands inside his own to warm them against the midnight chill as Rick disappeared around the corner. Rivers watched him go, then used his grip on my hands to pull me close to his chest. I gazed up at him, the strong planes of his cheeks silvered by moonlight and shadows deepening the soft curves of his full lips. Quick puffs of frozen breath betrayed his quickened breathing as he leaned toward me and covered my lips with his own.

My heart pounded with excitement. Here it was, finally. My first real kiss. And from a handsome boy in romantic moonlight no less. I leaned into his chest and did my best to kiss him back. At this show of enthusiasm, Rivers dropped my hands and wrapped his arms around me, pressing me close to his taut body and deepened the kiss.

My heart was pounding, but oddly once the initial excitement at being kissed had ebbed, I was struggling to feel the passion I was sure I should be experiencing right now. It felt nice, but I didn't feel the tingling, melting, thrilling pleasure that I'd been led to expect.

Rivers realized that I wasn't responding quite as enthusiastically as he'd hoped and pulled away to search my eyes. I gave him a tremulous smile, and he leaned in to kiss me again. I tried to throw myself into it. I really did. Was kissing just this mildly enjoyable connection? Or was there something missing between us?

Rivers broke the kiss again and stroked my hair back from my forehead with gentle fingers.

"That was nice," I told him.

"Nice," he repeated, looking at me a little oddly.

"Yes," I said earnestly. "Really ... nice."

Rivers smiled at me and dropped his arms, taking a step back. "Very nice," he agreed. "Your partner's on his way back, Little Bit. You'd better get back to your patrol."

"Yep." I nodded, feeling awkward, and took a step toward him. But suddenly the casual kiss I dropped onto his cheek felt uncomfortable. I blushed and backed away, clearing my throat self-consciously. "Yep," I said again. "I'd better go." I didn't look back as I hurried away.

CHAPTER THIRTY-ONE

For the next week, I both dreaded and hoped to bump into Rivers on patrol but he was nowhere to be seen. I was so busy watching for him and worrying that I'd completely ruined our relationship that I wasn't paying enough attention to my surroundings. Luckily, my patrol partner was paying attention and managed to grab my arm and pull me to a halt as I was about to jump off a pile of bricks into an innocuous patch of greenery.

"Watch it!" Marcii snapped. "That's a Burning Bush."

"A Burning Bush?" I repeated, amused. "Of the Biblical variety?"

"No," she told me, "of the dangerous variety. The bushes give off some kind of flammable gas. A tiny spark is all it takes to light it up." She indicated our perch atop the crumbled bricks and added, "Even a couple of bricks knocking together or your boots skidding on the concrete can create enough of a spark to set it off."

Marcii backed cautiously away from the edge of the rubble, and I followed her. We circled around the pile and came at the bush from another angle. Marcii took me as close as she deemed safe so that I could get a good look at the bush. I committed the thick oval shape and greasy green look of the leaves to memory, so I could recognize the species again if I saw it on another patrol. Once Marcii pointed it out, I was also able to smell the faint, overly sweet floral scent of the gas.

When I indicated to Marcii that I had seen enough, we backed away until we could no longer smell the gas.

Marcii grinned at me, her white teeth flashing in the faded evening light. "Now comes the fun part," she told me, searching for something in her hip pack. "You don't want to let the gas build up too long, or when something finally sets it off, it could create a monster fire. So we make a point of burning off the accumulated gas any time we come across a Burning Bush."

Marcii pulled out a portable spark from her pack, which was a single-use firestarter. The spark was a tiny organo-plastic tube filled with a couple of different chemicals that were separated by a thin membrane. When you needed a flame, you simply twisted the tube to break the membrane and allow the chemicals to mix. In less than a minute, the chemical reaction would create a small, hot flame that lasted until the combustible material of the tube was consumed. That gave you enough time to light a candle or coax a larger flame to life with tinder and kindling for a cooking fire.

"Get ready to move," Marcii told me and gave the spark a firm twist.

I heard the faint crackle that meant the chemical reaction had begun as Marcii lobbed the little tube directly into the center of the Burning Bush. She immediately spun around and sprinted away. I was only a step behind her as we dashed down the block and ducked behind the rusting hulk of an old car for shelter.

Moments after we took cover, the bush ignited with a loud whump of burning air. A column of flame raced into the sky and lit the streets around us with wild orange light. I yelped in surprise at the mini-explosion, and Marcii laughed at me. She had a contagious, snorting laugh that suddenly struck me as hilarious. I whooped with laughter too, which only made her laugh harder. We laughed until tears ran down our cheeks, our stomachs hurt, and our knees were weak, forcing us to first lean against the car for support and then slide all the way down to sit on the ground.

By the time we managed to compose ourselves, the flames were dying down to something more like a campfire than a bonfire. Marcii and I crawled around to the other side of the car so we could lean against it and watch the dying blaze. We had to stick around until it had burned itself out, and we could stomp and bury the final embers. We made ourselves as comfortable as we could on the cold concrete. At least this section had been scoured clear by wind, so we weren't sitting in a snowdrift.

We sat in companionable quiet for a while. Marcii finally broke the silence. "I'm about to pry into your personal life here," she said. "Because you've been off your game this week. Whatever's going on with you and Pretty-Boy Rivers, you gotta keep your head straight when you're on patrol. You can't let yourself get distracted like this, or someone is gonna get hurt."

I was embarrassed to realize that my mental turmoil had been so evident and felt my cheeks flush with shame. "Sorry," I mumbled.

"S'okay," Marcii shrugged, not pressing for more.

I said nothing for a few minutes, then blurted, "I don't know what's wrong with me! Rivers is gorgeous. He's nice. And smart. And fun. And he seems to like me a lot. And I thought I liked him a lot. But then he kissed me and it was just … not … Cha, I don't know. It just wasn't what I thought it would be."

"Cha, of course it wasn't," Marcii responded.

"Of course?" I echoed. "Why 'of course'?"

"Because you're the type who's looking for love. And you're not in love with Rivers. He's a buddy, not a lover. For you, anyway. You have a great time flirting with him, but it's just a game, nothing deeper."

"That makes me sound awfully shallow," I protested. "I wasn't trying to play any games."

"No, you were just playing at love. You wanted it to be love, but the spark isn't there. That's the same thing I told Rivers when I saw him yesterday by the way. He's in the same boat you are of wanting it to be more … but it's just not."

I felt a huge weight lift off my shoulders at that little revelation. The worst part of this whole thing had been the idea of hurting Rivers with my confused feelings. "Really?" I breathed. "How did he react to that?"

"About the way you did," she said with a little laugh. "Annoyed at me at first and then relieved to realize he wasn't going to break your heart. I told him to lay low for a couple of days so you could both put it behind you and then move on like it never happened. That what you want?"

"Yes," I said fervently. "That's exactly right."

"I thought so," she said in satisfaction. She stood up and dusted off her pants, then held out a hand to help me to my feet. "Glad I could straighten the two of you out. I may be a big ol' busy-body, but at least it's for a good cause."

We stomped out the final sparks from the Burning Bush, and I was fascinated to see that the bush itself hadn't even been scorched by the conflagration. Marcii and I finished our patrol without further incident, and I climbed into bed with Roomie for the best night of sleep I'd had all week.

CHAPTER THIRTY-TWO

I shoved Len's shoulder. "Scoot over, you big lump. I can't even breathe, here."

I was surrounded by enormous people. Gabe and Len sat on either side of me and Marcii sat across from me at the small cafeteria table. Nathan wasn't as tall as the others, but since he was sitting on the end of the table instead of in a chair, he loomed over me as well. I was starting to feel claustrophobic.

Len obligingly moved his chair away to give me some elbow room. Almost immediately that space was filled by Lucas, who dragged a chair over and squeezed into the spot.

Having Lucas in that space made me feel breathless for a different reason. My heart thumped double-time as I felt his leg pressing against mine and inhaled his fresh, spicy scent.

Cut it out, I told myself. I'd been through this a number of times already. Every time I convinced myself that he was just watching out for me like he did for everyone in the pack, he would suddenly do something like this: sitting extra close at the table, stopping me in the hall to give me a sweet compliment, or dropping by my patrol just to see how I was doing.

Then he would leave, and the next time I saw him, he would be cool and distant with no sign of personal interest at all. It was making me crazy.

I shifted away, determined to keep my distance and hold my emotions in check. I wasn't going to get my hopes up again today just to have him withdraw and leave me hanging tomorrow.

Moving away had the opposite effect from what I intended. My action caught Lucas' attention, and he leaned in to talk to me.

"Are you on patrol tonight?" he asked.

"Yeah, I'm covering the Broadway stretch. That one's easy duty most nights. I'll probably even come back without any injuries," I joked.

"But Deb and Doc look forward to your daily visits to Medical," he teased. "They'll miss you if you don't go in."

I pulled a face at him. Maybe I did pick up a few more injuries than the other guards, but it was just because I was diligent about my patrols. If I needed to climb a wall or slide through some bushes to be sure that the area was safe, I would. That often resulted in minor injuries, so I was a frequent visitor in Medical.

"It would make a nice change to come back from patrol without any new bruises," I admitted.

Lucas brushed a loose strand of hair from my forehead. "Maybe I should tag along," he suggested. "I can watch your back tonight."

"That would be nice," I breathed. I swayed toward him, mesmerized by the tender expression in his dark eyes. A loud thump startled me out of my crush-induced trance and I jerked upright.

I turned my head to see Roomie strolling down the center of the table as if no one should have any complaints about a twenty-pound cat wandering through their meal. He sat down next to my plate and looked at me, then at Lucas, then back to me, and gave his head a hard shake before sneezing in my face. It could have been normal cat behavior—but I was somehow sure it was commentary on my plans for the evening. He didn't approve.

He was right, too. Hadn't I told Roomie just this morning that I was done with this game of back-and-forth romance? I patted Roomie in thanks for his reminder and turned back to Lucas. I would tell him I'd be fine patrolling on my own tonight. For once, I was going to be the one delivering a brush-off.

But I was too late. While I was wrapped up in a probably imaginary conversation with my cat, people had started coming over to grab "just a minute or two" with Lucas. It always amazed me how many people felt like they had to get Lucas to settle arguments, offer opinions, or give advice about things they should have been able to deal with on their own.

Lucas sighed and glanced at me. "Sorry, Pops. We'll have to hang out another time." He stood and walked away, leaving me with an absent pat on the top of my head. A head pat.

I suppressed a growl of frustration as I realized that Lucas had once again been the one to cool things off. I was still the brushee instead of the brusher.

Roomie shook his head again, disappointed in me, and helped himself to the rest of my dinner.

CHAPTER THIRTY-THREE

It was a cool April night, and I was slogging through ankle-deep mud on a solo patrol along our border with Rivers' pack. As the weather had warmed, the falling snow turned to rain and the standing snow to streams of brown water rushing through the canyons of collapsed masonry. The muddy runoff mixed with debris and refuse in the streets to create a thick sludge that grabbed at my boots and forced me to heave my feet free of the muck for every step.

The miserable trek fit my rotten mood as I obsessed over my relationship—or lack of one—with Lucas. I would have liked to have a love connection with Lucas, but I couldn't figure out what was going on in his head.

Sharra and Marcii insisted that he was interested, just inexperienced with relationships. He wasn't much older than me—only twenty-five—yet he'd had responsibility for the pack since his father had died nearly ten years ago. He'd been so focused on pack business that he'd never made time for a girlfriend.

I could understand that, having been in pretty much the same situation back in Goodland. So I had tried being patient, I had tried making the first move myself, and I had tried backing off to give him space to make a move; none of those strategies had worked.

I reached the end of the street and heaved myself out of the mud to clamber onto a half wall that would finally get me out of the filthy slurry clogging the street. I paused to scrape the worst of the mud from my boots with a stick and resolved—yet again—to forget about romance.

I was going to focus on the Resistance group operating out of the upper floors. I would figure out what they were doing and how I could use their help to go after Cruz. Whatever this group had been resisting up until now, I was going to give them another target.

Filled with righteous motivation and in a much better mood, I stuck to the higher ground and worked my way through crumbling piles of brick and drywall. I was out of the muck, but this route had its hazards, too.

This section of the city had been almost entirely destroyed during the war, so there was no cover from the near-constant spring rain. The moisture left the stones slippery, requiring me to watch every step and find handholds on the twisted rebar and support beams that still thrust into the air in many places.

As I was cautiously picking my way back down to street level from the tumbled remnants of the Coors Field baseball stadium, I saw Rivers walking in my direction. He raised a hand in a casual salute and leaned against a crooked lamppost to wait for me.

Since Marcii had set us straight, we had fallen back into our friendly flirtation. Now that we both knew it was just for fun, we could enjoy our friendship again without clouding it with other issues.

Since we always traded information and gossip, Rivers started the conversation by asking, "Anything interesting on patrol today?"

"Not really," I told him. "A few animals that I'll report back to the hunters but nothing dangerous." I nodded toward Coors Field. "It looks like someone camped out in the stadium for a day or two, but they seem to be gone now. You might want to keep an eye out for them."

Rivers nodded and shared his own news. "We've spotted big cat tracks near our western border, but we have hunting parties out looking for it. They'll either take it down or chase it back past the freeway."

"Thanks. I'll let the patrols know they should keep an eye out in case it slips our way."

We shared a few more bits of information, including the fact that Jessie had finally had it with Mateo and kicked him out of her pack. He was currently a loner. We speculated for a few minutes on what he might do next; we were all waiting for the other shoe to drop there. Not for the first time, I wished the packs had a way to lock up dangerous people instead of just kicking them loose to live packless. I had a feeling Mateo wasn't done with me; I'd have felt a lot safer if I knew he was behind bars.

I said my goodbyes to Rivers and set out to finish my patrol, my mind busily working through I stayed alert for danger. Working my way south for a few blocks, I reached the overgrown remnants of an old park. It had been left untouched since the city's abandonment and the greenery from the small park had taken over the streets for blocks in every direction. There was no way past without hiking through the park or making a long detour that would take me outside Liberty territory. The tall trees grew so closely together that even in early spring the branches wove a dense canopy overhead that offered a welcome break from the drizzling rain. Unfortunately, the cover also blocked the moonlight, leaving me in deep shadow. It was hard work wiggling my way through the thick undergrowth of weeds and bushes. At least I didn't have to worry that these plants were dangerous; a team had recently cleared this neighborhood of any threatening vegetation.

I paid careful attention to my surroundings while moving as quietly as I could. The plant-life might be safe, but the near-impenetrable forest that had taken over the crumbling city blocks was a perfect sanctuary for any number of intruders, both animal and human. I looked for any signs of trespassers under the trees and saw nothing out of place. A particularly thick tangle of vines and weeds covered the short brick wall that used to mark the boundaries of the park. The vines were covered in sharp thorns the size of my thumbnail, making it painful to climb over the wall. I usually opted to grab the low branch hanging over the wall from a tree growing outside the park. I could hoist myself onto the branch and work my way back to the trunk, then slide down to street level.

I had just reached the crook of the tree when I heard a small rustle in the bushes below me. I froze and looked for the source of the sound. Scanning the area around me, I listened closely, trying to hear the swishing branches again. Everything was silent. Even the insects had gone quiet. Without making a sound, I turned to prop my back against the tree trunk for added stability and pulled my legs up in front of me. I didn't want anything dangling down into the darkness when I didn't know what might be moving around below me. Hugging my legs with my arms, I waited for another sound or movement from the brush. Whatever it was, it wasn't making any noise now. I was going to have to wait it out.

From my position in the tree, I could see the moon again. The clouds had finally cleared, leaving a smooth, dark velvet sky studded with diamond-bright stars. Back in Goodland, the streets and buildings were brightly lit at all times. You couldn't see the sky through the glare of the lights. Now one of my favorite things about night patrols was the chance to see the bright sparks of the stars and the liquid glow of the moon.

I sat in the tree as the moon moved through the sky. One of my first lessons as a guard had been how to tell time by the moon or the sun, so I was able to estimate that I'd been in the tree for almost two hours. It was a long time, but both animals and people out here were canny. Whatever I had heard might be trying to wait me out as well. I reined in my impatience and sat still, waiting for the normal night sounds to resume and let me know the park was safe again. I didn't want to get down until I was very sure that nothing was out here with me.

I made myself stay put for another hour. My persistence paid off when I finally heard the cracking of branches underfoot. I watched the swaying greenery intently to see what or who emerged, and a moment later I saw a black, scaly snout break free of the bushes. I froze and held my breath as the Shadow's head swung back and forth, its red eyes scanning to try and spot me in the darkness.

The Shadow paced around my tree and sniffed around the wall for several minutes. But I had come across the wall on the branch, so no fresh scent trail led to my position in the tree. The Shadow continued searching for me for a bit longer, then seemed to give up. The Shadow gave one sharp bark, and suddenly an entire pack of Shadows melted out of the gloom around me, four adults and one small enough to be a puppy. I could see where the name Shadow came from because the animals had been invisible as shadows beneath the trees until they moved. The group milled around under the tree, exchanging growls and yips in a kind of conversation.

I shivered in fear. I had outrun a Shadow before but only because I'd had surprise on my side and had been able to provide a more convenient target for the Shadow to attack. I would have no chance against a pack of Shadows who were looking for me. I sat very still, barely breathing as I watched the animals trot back and forth beneath my branch. My muscles were knotted with anxiety by the time the lead dog finally raised its muzzle and gave another short bark. The Shadow loped away toward Park Avenue, and the rest of the pack followed. Within moments they had disappeared into the darkness of the park.

I was torn. Should I stay put to let them get further away or get out while I had an opportunity? If I left now, the dogs might still be close enough to hear me and give chase. But if I waited, there was always the chance that the Shadows would circle back without me noticing them until I hopped out of the tree and it was too late.

I hesitated for a few minutes before deciding to make a run for it. Unfolding myself from the branch, I hung from my hands to lower myself to the ground. I exploded into motion the moment my feet hit pavement and dashed down the street, dodging through trees, bushes, and fallen masonry until I reached the corner where I'd left my mag-lev bike at the beginning of my patrol. I jumped onto the bike without pause and was rolling down the street to click onto the rail before my butt even hit the seat. As soon as the bike reached the rail, I wrenched the throttle to full speed and raced away. I didn't breathe easy until I was a mile down the road with no sign of pursuit.

I was glad the streets were clear between the park and base because by the time I rolled my bike into the parking area the adrenaline rush had crashed, leaving me reeling with exhaustion. Though I'd spent much of the time crouched in a tree, I'd been constantly on alert with my muscles tensed and ready for action. I climbed off the bike and handed the ignition stick over to the guard watching the lot, then headed slowly for the base entrance. My muscles were leaden with fatigue, and I wanted nothing more than a fast shower to wash away the acrid sweat of fear and exertion and then to fall into bed for a long sleep.

Benny, the guard watching the hole in the wall that served as the front entrance, clapped me on the shoulder. "Glad to see you back," he told me. "People were starting to worry."

I abandoned my hopes for a quick shower before reporting in. If the guards currently on duty knew I was late, Sharra was sure to be waiting for me in the guard room and I'd better not delay any longer. I sighed and headed for the stairs instead of the showers. I eyed the long staircase with deep dislike before trudging up the steps to the second floor.

When I opened the door to the guard room, a couple of dozen faces turned my way. I could feel the tension draining from the room as I was recognized, and immediately people got up and started heading for the door now that they knew I was okay. Whenever someone was particularly late reporting in from patrol, all the guards who weren't on duty would gather in the guard room to wait it out. We were a close-knit group. Risking your lives together tended to have that effect. It happened often enough that someone came back badly injured or not at all, so when someone was missing, we all worried and hung out together until we knew what had happened.

I had waited here several times myself, but this was the first time since my ill-fated first patrol that I'd been the one they were waiting for. As my team members moved past me to head out the door, most gave me a friendly thump on the back or an acknowledging nod. Len ruffled my hair. Gabe gave me a fist bump that stung my knuckles, and Nathan dropped a brotherly kiss on the top of my head. Marcii simply stayed in her chair against the far wall, arms stubbornly crossed to indicate that she wouldn't be leaving until she heard the whole story.

Sharra and Lucas were standing near the map wall. They had probably been reviewing my assigned patrol route and trying to decide where to send teams to look for me. Sharra looked relieved to see me. Lucas just looked ticked off.

"Where have you been?" he rumbled. "We've been here for hours imagining the worst. We were just about to send people out searching for you because after this long, we figured you must be badly injured or dead. And here you come strolling in without a scratch on you. So help me, if you're late because you were off playing kissy-face with your buddy Rivers…" he trailed off, at a loss for words, but making up for the lack with a vicious glare.

I was tired and grubby and in no mood for this. His unreasonable anger ignited my own temper. "Sorry to disappoint you by returning uninjured, jerkwad," I said acidly. "Next time I get treed by a pack of freaking Shadows, I'll just go ahead and stroll through the middle of the group. 'Bite away,' I'll tell them. 'Lucas likes it better when I have an injury to show that I have a good reason for being late.'"

I turned away in righteous annoyance even as I saw the anger leave his face to be replaced by concern and regret. I refused to look at him and acknowledge the apology forming on his lips. Instead, I focused on Sharra and gave her my report. "Made my rounds down Nineteenth to Park and through the old apartments along there and saw nothing out of the ordinary. Saw Rivers briefly," I shot a venomous glare of my own in Lucas' direction, "by the old ballpark. He said his patrols have spotted signs of a big cat in the area, so you'll want to have people watch for that. He also said Mateo is no longer with Monarch pack; he's going loner. We should keep an eye out to be sure he doesn't try to settle in Liberty territory.

"Then I checked out Benedict Park and played a long game of chicken with a pack of Shadows. Four adults and a puppy. I stuck it out, and they eventually gave up and left. Then I hightailed it back to base. Sorry that I don't have any dramatic injuries to make it a better story."

I bit off the last sentence with barely contained anger. How dare Lucas accuse me of being derelict in my patrol duties? I had never done anything to earn such an accusation. I was a dedicated guard and always had the pack's best interests in mind.

Well, I had had enough. I was done with his shyness or uncertainty or whatever his issues were. I turned my back on him to talk only to Sharra and Marcii.

"The pack headed into Benedict Park; they were running toward Park Avenue. We should get word to the hunters that they need to go looking and spread the word to the other packs to be careful."

"I'm on it," Marcii said, getting to her feet. "I'll go tell Mac to get a hunting party together and get the word going out to the patrols."

"Thanks," Sharra told her. "Let everyone know that we're running no single patrols until we track down the pack. And spread the heads-up on Mateo."

Marcii nodded and slipped out the door.

I focused on Sharra now, studiously ignoring Lucas looming at my back. "That's it. I'm going to hit the showers and go to bed."

"Go for it," Sharra agreed. Being a good friend, she ignored Lucas as well as she gave me a quick hug. "Glad you made it back safely."

I headed for the door, determined to pay no heed to Lucas, but I could hear him following me out of the room. With every step I took, I thought about the injustice of his accusation, causing my anger to grow stronger and stronger. As I stepped into the hallway, my temper got away from me and I whirled back to face Lucas who was standing just behind me.

"And you! Just stay away from me until you're able to stop being such an ass. I am done with this nonsense, got it? You need to make up your mind. If you want me to be your girlfriend, then you treat me that way—and treat me right. And if you want to keep it all professional, then do that but don't you dare treat me any differently from any other guard. But I will not put up with you being sweet and flirty one day and ignoring me and being a jerk the next. Either way, make a choice, do you hear me?"

"Oh, I think we all heard you," drawled Nathan.

I looked past Lucas to see a group of guards loitering in the hallway, probably waiting to grill me for details about my late return. Without hesitating, I stomped over to the group of watching guards and buried my fist in Nathan's stomach—not hard enough to do damage, but with enough force to make my point. Nathan doubled over, gasping for air as I stalked away, leaving Lucas staring after me with his mouth gaping in astonishment.

CHAPTER THIRTY-FOUR

After a shower and a solid six hours of sleep, I sat on my bed contemplating my temper tantrum and wondering how long I could stay in my room and avoid the entire pack. A knock sounded at my door, and I ignored it, hoping whoever it was would assume I wasn't here and just go away.

Instead, the doorknob turned and Sharra walked in. Embarrassment tugged at my gut, and I might have sent her away if she hadn't come prepared with a platter bearing a huge sandwich and a pile of chunky cookies. My stomach rumbled, reminding me that I hadn't eaten since setting out on patrol nearly eighteen hours earlier. Sharra smiled at me and wiggled the platter invitingly.

"I have food," she sing-songed. "You know you want it."

"Oh fine," I grumbled. "Come in and shut the door."

Sharra bumped the door closed with her hip and set the food on the little desk by my window before dropping onto my bed. She made herself comfortable against the headboard while I tucked into the sandwich.

"So," she said with a wide grin. "That was fun."

I rolled my eyes at her, knowing exactly what she was referring to. "Sure," I agreed dryly. "Fun for all of you spectators. I'm not feeling the fun right now. I may never leave this room again."

Sharra laughed. "Oh, come on. It's not that bad. And he had it coming. He's been blowing hot and cold for months."

"Yeah, but I hadn't planned on having it out in such a public setting. I was tired and on edge and when he started throwing accusations at me, I just lost it."

"He was really worried about you," Sharra told me. "He'd been wearing a path in the carpet with his pacing while we waited for you. And then when you walked in looking like you'd only lost track of time … You know you have a total poker face. He couldn't tell how freaked you were."

"Glad to know I hid it from most people … even if I didn't manage to hide it from you."

"I know you too well," Sharra said smugly. She stole one of the cookies from my tray and bit into it. "So don't you want to know what he said after you left?" she mumbled with her mouth full.

My own mouth was full of sandwich, so I only waved at her to continue.

"Nothing," she told me. "Not a single word. He just stood there with this blank look on his face like he had no idea what he was supposed to do next." She shook her head. "The man is so smart when it comes to governing our little group here and keeping everything running smoothly, but he's just as clueless as any other guy when it comes to relationships. It's just sad."

I sighed. "I know we've gone through this over and over again, but really, it seems likely that he hasn't made a move—or responded to any of mine—because he's just not that interested."

"And as I tell you every time we've discussed this, he doesn't act like a man who isn't interested. He acts like a man who doesn't want to be interested for some reason. But he's definitely into you."

"You know what, I'm not going to obsess over it anymore. I am not going to sit here and fixate on what he said and what it meant. I'm just putting the whole thing out of my mind and moving on."

"Mmm-hmmm. Good luck with that."

I moaned and put my head down on the desktop. "I'm a mess," I mumbled. "I'm swearing off men completely."

My pity party was interrupted by another knock on the door. "It's Lucas," a deep voice called.

Sharra jumped up from the bed with a wicked grin. "Marvi. Come find me later and let me know where you stand with that whole swearing off men thing. If you decide to stick with it, I know a couple of nice girls I can set you up with."

She dodged as I threw the last cookie at her and even managed to snatch the flying snack from the air before opening the door to Lucas. She avoided talking to him by stuffing the cookie into her mouth and disappeared down the hall as he stepped inside. I didn't bother to get up. He didn't wait for an invitation but strolled across the room to lean against the wall next to the bed. I felt awkward sitting while he was standing, so I got to my feet as well. We stood in awkward silence for a couple of minutes before he spoke.

"You're right," he said abruptly. "I have been blowing hot and cold."

I nodded. "So the question is, why?"

He rubbed a big hand across the back of his neck. "Cha, I don't even know. I'm just not good at this kind of thing. You know, emotions and stuff. I don't know what I'm doing. I'm twenty-five years old, and I've never been in any kind of a real relationship. So the first time I fall for a girl I go for the freaking First Lady? You're so far out of my league that it's ridiculous.

I get distracted from pack business because I'm thinking you, and then I get mad at myself for neglecting my responsibilities. So I avoid you for a while until I can't stand it anymore.

And then tonight, when I thought you were late because you were hanging out with Rivers…" He stopped abruptly, his cheeks darkening with embarrassment at his own rambling. He folded his arms defensively across his wide chest.

I stepped forward and placed one hand on his crossed arms. I looked up into his eyes and called forth every bit of courage I could muster. "I've never been in a relationship either," I told him. "The thing with Rivers, it's nothing. We're just friends. But I'd like to try a relationship … with you."

I stood on tiptoe, stretching as tall as I could to reach Lucas' lips with my own. His arms immediately closed around me and he kissed me back, his lips gentle against mine. And this time the kiss was everything I thought a kiss should be.

CHAPTER THIRTY-FIVE

My life in Liberty pack continued largely unchanged by my new relationship with Lucas. Since romance was new to both of us, we were taking things slowly and carefully. The rest of the pack took it in stride. We both got our share of teasing, especially from the guards, but nothing we couldn't handle. I continued working as a guard, and Lucas was always busy with his responsibilities as pack leader, but we spent as much time together as we could outside of our pack duties.

Marcii, Sharra, Lucas, and I liked to hang out in the guard room in the evenings. Marcii and I usually stretched out on the couches while Lucas and Sharra worked on paperwork or schedules at the table.

Roomie had become almost domesticated these days. Though he was still fierce and threatening to those he didn't know, once you made his list of approved humans, he was willing to sit with you and be petted. He acted as if he was doing you a favor by permitting such affection, but sometimes he forgot his dignity enough to purr loudly. Marcii was one of his favorite humans, and he generally divided his time between her lap and mine.

Tonight, Lucas was caught up on his tasks, so he sat at the other end of my couch. I promptly plopped my feet in his lap, angling for a foot rub. I was just back from a long patrol, and my feet were sore. Lucas obliged, massaging my feet with his large, strong hands. The firm pressure of his thumbs rubbing my aching insteps felt heavenly, and I hated to take the risk of ending it, but I had promised myself that tonight I was going to have an important conversation with Lucas.

Lucas and I were the only ones in the guardroom at the moment. Even Roomie was elsewhere. I took a deep breath to brace myself and jumped in.

"So I've been here almost a year now. I'm Sharra's best friend and I'm your girlfriend. I guard and protect the pack every single day. Have I finally earned enough trust that you can let me in on the Resistance?"

His hands stilled and he said nothing.

"Come on, I don't even know what you're resisting! I mean, you've built amazing things with the resources at hand, but why? Why stay here in the rough instead of finding a city you like? There are all kinds of social programs that would help you get settled into a new city so you wouldn't have to live in a bombed out, abandoned hotel."

"Sure," Lucas drawled. "All kinds of social programs would be more than glad to help us out. Just as long as we're willing to turn over control of our entire lives to the government."

"That's just conspiracy theorist nonsense," I responded firmly. "The government isn't 'running' anyone's life! The government exists to take care of and protect the populace, and for some reason you lot twist that to make the government into some kind of evil overlord. It's ridiculous."

"So the government doesn't decide what your career should be, then?"

"No! Not the way you're making it sound. I mean, you take aptitude and psychological tests during high school that provide a list of good careers, but that's just help ensure that everyone find a job they enjoy."

"Hmmm. Very benign," he agreed. "What if you don't want to follow any of your 'suggested' career tracks?"

"Well...," I fumbled a little because I didn't know the answer. "Well, I've never heard of that particular situation. The testing is very thorough so that people get a choice of areas that they will be interested in and suited for. But—if that were to happen—I assume it would be handled with some re-testing since apparently the results were faulty."

He nodded, obviously unconvinced, and moved on to his next point. "What about the way the government decides who you can marry?"

"Well that's just taking things out of context again. It's just a public health issue to test your DNA samples when you apply for a marriage license. That way you'll know if either of you carries any damaged genes that could affect future children. Even if your DNA was incompatible you could still get married."

"So there's no such thing as a marriage match list?" he asked.

"Well, yes, there is. But that's not telling you who you have to marry. It's just a convenience. Some people prefer to know up front that a relationship is compatible in that way. It's just to simplify dating, that's all. But again, no one has to marry someone from the match list."

"Only if you want to be able to have children," Lucas pointed out. "Don't you think it's more than a little intrusive that you have get a license to have children?"

"Do you know how many children were starving, abandoned, neglected, and abused before the war?" I asked passionately. "Because I do, and the numbers are appalling. Yes, you have to have a license before you have a child. That's to be sure that parents are financially and emotionally prepared to raise a child. A child should never have to suffer because their parents did not have the money or the knowledge to care for a child.

"No one enters into parenthood on a whim anymore, or has a baby by accident, or as an attempt to cement a crumbling relationship. Children are a precious responsibility, and the reason for licensing is so parents understand that."

Lucas mulled that over. "You just might convince me on that one, Poppy. You make some interesting arguments."

"You see?" I asked earnestly. "All this government control nonsense is just taking the facts out of context and not understanding the rationale behind them."

"Mmm-hmm. I have just one more question, and it's one that I think will be dear to your politically-minded heart. How do you feel about free elections?"

"Obviously you already know how I feel about this. Free elections are central to a successful democracy. That's why my father pushed to eliminate the electoral college model in favor of the current 'every vote counts' model."

"And if the populace only thinks that their votes count?" Sharra asked. She walked into the room and closed the door before dropping into the chair across from the couch.

I narrowed my eyes. "Don't beat around the bush. You've mentioned this before, so I know a little about your suspicions. Now I want to know exactly what you think is happening with the elections. What are you saying?"

"I'm saying that Lucas' group has monitored the last several general elections, and every vote disappears. The data servers that collect the online votes aren't connected to anything else. They don't even store the voting data. It just drops into a big black hole in cyberspace. The election results that are announced have nothing to do with any votes that are cast."

The room went utterly silent. Not a single word came to my mind, let alone my mouth. I just sat there, unable to process this massive betrayal of the entire democratic philosophy.

As the silence stretched uncomfortably long, Sharra offered, "If it helps, the data they intercepted shows that your father would have won his elections anyway. They didn't need to fake those results."

My voice was hoarse as I asked, "Did he know? Did my father know how the voting worked?"

"I'm sorry, Poppy," Sharra said gently. "It really looks like he did know."

My whole body felt cold and numb. This had to be a mistake. My father would never be a part of something like this. I was sure of it. But now that the seed of doubt had been planted, I needed to know for myself. Raising my head, I met Lucas' eyes.

"I need to see the proof," I said.

He looked sympathetic and nodded. "I'll take you."

CHAPTER THIRTY-SIX

Lucas and I climbed a lot of stairs. I lost track of how many flights, mostly because I wasn't paying attention. Eventually, we left the stairs through a rusty gray fire door and entered another corridor with many rooms branching away. We walked down the hall until we reached a room with a faded plaque marked 1723. Lucas turned the knob and ushered me inside a darkened cave of a room, lit only by the computer monitors lining tables around the wall.

Curiosity broke through my emotionless shock. "Where are you getting the electricity for the computers? Solaris-Web doesn't produce enough power to run computers."

"We scavenged undamaged solar panels from various places around the city and set them up on the highest intact floor so they could catch the light. Once we wired the panels into the existing electrical system, we were able to get enough power to run the machines. We don't have a lot of panels though, so we pretty much save the electricity for running the computers. We get our Internet access the same way. A scavenged satellite receiver tied into the existing systems lets us siphon a cyber-signal from some official sources," Lucas explained while he sat at the computer nearest the window and began sliding his big fingers through the holo interface to access the files he was looking for.

After a moment, he stood and motioned for me to take his place. "This is all the data we've compiled on the elections," he told me. "Voting data we retrieved, comparisons of that data to the announced results, texts and mails that we intercepted, that sort of thing. I'll give you some time to look through it and come back to check on you in a while. Don't leave here without me, please. The higher floors of the building have some dangerous areas. I wouldn't want you to wander into them."

He looked at the two men sitting at other computers in the room as he added the last part, and we all understood that they were under orders to keep me from leaving the room. Whatever. I didn't care about that right now. I turned my back on Lucas and opened the first file. I needed to see this proof with my own eyes.

During the long night I spent sifting through the data I'd been given, I vaguely noticed that Lucas returned to check on me occasionally. It didn't interrupt my reading though. I wanted to review every byte in these files.

The sun was beginning to show through the large windows across the room when Lucas came to check on me again and stood beside me, waiting for my attention. I was staring silently at the display, deep in thought. There was a lot of proof that everything Sharra and Lucas had told me was true. While I wanted to declare that it was all faked, it just didn't add up that way. There were hundreds of communications going back more than five years.

If someone had wanted to create false evidence, just a few incriminating documents would have done the job. And wouldn't phony evidence point more directly at the accused? Instead, I'd had to read through bytes and bytes of data, sifting subtle clues from the words and subtext to realize what was going on. The writers of the various texts and emails had gone to some lengths to hide their own identities and there were no names mentioned in their correspondence.

Again, it seemed that false evidence would include names in order to better point the finger at someone.

Finally, there was the fact that no outsider could have known all of these players well enough to flawlessly mimic the tone and style of each of these writers. When they went to such lengths to hide their identities, they could never have known that someday I would be reading the messages. I knew these people. I recognized habitual turns of phrase and patterns of speech.

As my father's trusted assistant, I read his mails and messages every day. I messaged back and forth with people almost constantly either as myself or on behalf of my father. I had corresponded with every one of these anonymous writers.

From what I saw in the e-trails, Cruz was actually just a figurehead. He obviously tried to give the impression that he was in charge, but the subtext of the messages made it clear that he was not the leader. The orders he received were phrased as suggestions, but Cruz caved every time even when he seemed to be in disagreement.

It was interesting to see that those giving the orders were people I'd always considered to be involved but largely unimportant political supporters. They were wealthy and well-connected enough to be invited to all the right events, but I'd never seen them express a strong opinion on any specific issues or policies.

I touched one of the files on the display to open another message. This one was from Luis Gutierrez. He was a friend of my father, a frequent visitor to the White House, and the head of SolarSource Energy. SolarSource was currently the only solar energy company doing business in the NAA, and Luis had been making money hand-over-fist since the end of the war. As might be expected, he was rabidly against any attempt to diversify energy providers. I suspected that Luis got involved in all this to ensure that he kept a strangle-hold on the energy market and block any potential competition.

I opened another message and thought about Madelaine and Antoine Carlson. She was the scandalously young second wife for the Canadian real-estate magnate. Most people assumed Madelaine was just a trophy wife, but I had worked with her on a number of different charity projects. She was smart and manipulative and sneaky. The messages looked like Antoine was giving the orders, but I was sure that Madeline running things behind the scenes.

Raymond Nexen was next on the list. Somewhere in his eighties, he'd always struck me as a bit of a harmless old coot. It was hard to reconcile my picture of him as a slightly senile old man with the scathing tyrant revealed in his email. Still, I was familiar enough with his speech patterns and personal history to be certain it was him based on the content of the messages.

The final member of this shadow government was the most astonishing. I pulled up the last group of messages one more time. There was no doubt. The messages were written by Louisa, my eternally disapproving personal secretary.

Louisa had been a part of my life for as long as I could remember. When I was younger, she had efficiently arranged my schedule to include my schooling, hobbies, and the various personal appearances I was making even as a child. After my father asked me to take on the responsibilities of the First Lady, Louisa had smoothly stepped in to assist me.

She and I had never been friendly, but her calm competence had been a valuable asset. I had been genuinely relieved to see her in the background at Cruz's press conference and know that she had survived the attack.

I didn't know how Louisa had come to be a part of this group. She wasn't wealthy or well-connected like the others, but it was obvious that she was more than just a spy reporting back to them.

In many of the messages, she was more likely to give orders than to take them. In fact, Louisa was the first person to suggest removing President Walker. She made contact with Cruz to discuss the change in leadership. And worst of all, she was the one who arranged to have my father, the governors, and me in the library at precisely the right time for the invaders to find us. She specifically suggested that I be eliminated along with my father so they could "make a clean start."

It was another harsh blow, but I forced myself to shrug it off. At this point, I had been through too many shocks to be staggered by the betrayal of someone who had never truly been my friend.

Indeed, from the venomous tone in a few of her texts, she had disliked me intensely. It was a testament to her acting skills that I had seen only benign disapproval in her attitude.

Lucas cleared his throat to remind me of his presence and then lowered himself to sit back on his heels beside my chair, elbows resting on his thighs and hands hanging loosely between his knees. With him crouched so low and me seated in the chair, our heads were at the same height. He looked at me, eyes questioning and waited silently for me to speak.

"I found these files particularly interesting," I told him quietly, not yet meeting his eyes.

I used my index finger to circle a group of icons I had moved to the center of the display. He looked closely at the file names as the selected icons glowed.

"Yes," he said. "I thought those would be the most significant right now."

Finally, I looked at him. I knew my face was wet with tears and didn't care. "He was a good man," I told Lucas, silently begging him to believe me. "He thought he was doing what he had to do to hold everything together. He never intended for things to go so far down this road. He was good."

"He was," Lucas agreed. "From the conversations, you can see that he was pushing back hard against totalitarian measures. He said that what made sense in a time of war and unrest was no longer viable in a time of freedom."

"He wanted to go back to honest elections," I said, my voice ragged. "He still believed in the things he taught me. He just took a few wrong turns."

Lucas nodded.

"He was trying to turn around," I pointed out. "He kept telling them that changes had to be made. That he was willing to tell the nation everything if that's what had to be done." I circled another group of files and set them aglow. "That appears to be when they decided to kill him."

Lucas nodded again, his eyes steady on mine. "It looks like they approached Cruz about eighteen months ago and spent some time convincing him to go along with their plan."

"Cha," I muttered in disgust. "He didn't need any convincing. You can read it in the subtext of the messages. He was on board from the beginning; he just wanted them to woo him."

Lucas glanced down at his hands, unsure of what he should say. The other two men in the room continued to desperately pretend they were invisible. It was obvious they wished to be anywhere but here and equally obvious that they thought drawing attention to themselves by leaving would make things even more awkward. Not in the mood to be charitable, I didn't bother letting them off the hook by telling them to leave.

"You knew this was going down. I presume that's why Sharra believed me so readily when I told her my sad little story?"

"She didn't recognize you at first," Lucas rumbled. "Not when she was helping you escape from the alley. She didn't know it was you until you told her your name. When you told her what had happened, she knew it had to be true. It fit with all the bits and pieces we had gathered. You've read the files. You know we didn't have enough details to predict what, where, and when. We only knew that something was in the works.

That's the whole reason Sharra went to Goodland. She was going to nose around a little and pass the information we did have to a contact in the city." A large sigh escaped his lips. "We thought Walker was someone we could work with. We were trying to find a way to approach him. I'm sorry we didn't learn enough to save him."

His remorse seemed genuine. I had seen for myself that they had only pieces of information. I gave a short nod acknowledging his condolences and moved on before I could tear up again. "How did you get all these bytes?" I asked him.

"We have some excellent hackers," he told me, jerking his chin to indicate the two guys hunched at their computers. "Anything in an electronic form leaves traces even when you think it's been deleted. These guys are good enough to find the traces and put them back together."

"Not as good as Cruz though," one of them commented. "That man has some marvi skills with the e. We haven't been able to revive any of his docs."

"It was probably never e to begin with," I said absently, flipping through the files I'd been working with to find the ones I wanted. "Cruz knows very well that anything e can never

273

really disappear. When he's worried about security, he writes it down with a pen and paper and then uses a courier to send handwritten notes instead of messaging an e version."

The hackers stared at me, astonished. The second man asked, "He uses a pen and paper? Cha, where do you even find those anymore?"

"He was able to arm an entire strike force with weapons that were supposed to have been destroyed decades ago," I pointed out. "I don't imagine some stationery would be much of a challenge. I get the impression that he tried to get his compatriots to avoid e communications as well, but they thought he was being paranoid."

Lucas chuckled and stood. "Guess he knew what he was talking about," he said. "Gentlemen, that could give you a new line to tug. Check out courier deliveries from Cruz that correspond with communications he received."

The hackers nodded and immediately turned back to the computers, their hands flying through the air as they started looking through the web for new information. Lucas pulled a spare chair over to my terminal and sat. He gestured at the files I had open on the display. "I assume there's something you want to tell me about these files?"

"Do you know all the players here?" I asked. "Because I do."

I could see the excitement kindle in his dark eyes though he tried to conceal it with a calm expression. "It would be helpful if you could confirm our ideas," he agreed. "Who did you recognize?"

"Everyone. I recognize everyone. And now that I have this information, I know how to take them down. So, what do you think? Want to overthrow the government with me?"

Continue the story in:

INTO LIGHT (Shadow and Light book 2)

ABOUT THE AUTHOR

After writing stories in her head for the last 30+ years, Tara finally decided to take a stab at writing them down to share them with others.

Tara has a husband, 4 kids, and 4 cats to care for along with a full-time job, so finding time to write is the biggest challenge. Since her most productive hours are from 12-5 a.m. anyway, Tara often gives up sleep for the sake of a good story.